GUILTY UNTIL PROVEN INNOCENT

Robert Archibald

Cactus Mystery Press
An imprint of Blue Fortune Enterprises, LLC

For information contact :
Blue Fortune Enterprises, LLC
Cactus Mystery Press
P.O. Box 554
Yorktown, VA 23690
http://blue-fortune.com

Book and Cover design by Wesley Miller, WAMCreate, wamcreate.co

ISBN: 978-1-948979-39-9

First Edition: July 2020

Dedication

This book is about strong smart women. I would like to dedicate it to one of the strongest, smartest women I know, my wife, Nancy.

Fiction by Robert Archibald

Guilty Until Proven Innocent
Roundabout Revenge

Reviews for Roundabout Revenge

Archibald's plot line is incredible and well developed with unforeseen twists and turns. His characters are carefully molded and become very real as the plot thickens... This is not a book to easily put down. It is a good read. Enjoy!
Wilford Kale, *Virginia Gazette*

I loved *Roundabout Revenge.* Author Robert Archibald is a retired college professor whose writing demonstrates that he is a scholar not only in his professional field of study, but also in his observations on society. In this engrossing novel, he sheds light on why law and justice are sometimes at odds with each other. There also are wonderful discussions among the characters about sports, diversity in schools and society, and about how conservatives and liberals have come to hold their beliefs. I look forward to the sequel.
- CW Stacks, *Amazon review*

Fascinating plot, thoughtfully developed. Looking forward to what story twists his next book will bring. - Fred Cason, *Amazon Review*

Acknowledgements

Guilty Until Proven Innocent is a work of fiction. Any resemblance between the characters in this book and anyone I have known or met is a complete coincidence.

This book benefited from the efforts of several individuals who read drafts and gave me helpful comments. I would like to especially thank Kirk Lovenberry and Sudie Watkins who read and commented on the entire draft. Also, the book benefited from the efforts of the members of my writer's group: Sharon Dillon, Cindy Freeman, Elizabeth Lee, Barbara McLennan, Christian Pascale, Dave Pistorese, Patti Procipi, Peter Stipe, and Susan Williamson. None of these people should be blamed for anything. They should be praised for helping.

I would like to especially thank Narielle Living for an extensive edit that improved the book immensely.

Finally, everything I do benefits from the help of my wife, Nancy.

Chapter One

AT ELEVEN P.M., PHIL PHILEMON and Ralph Williams collected the camera they'd installed the night before. Back in their hotel room, they were pleased with the clear picture of the front of the brownstone housing the Smith, Banbridge, and Sites law firm.

"Can you fast forward to check for a night watchman?" Phil asked.

"We didn't use a motion-activated camera because of the traffic. I'll have to do it manually."

Ralph stopped fast forwarding when a security firm's car pulled up.

"Back it up to when he gets there," Phil said.

"Okay, okay, I'm on it. There's not much light on the street. I almost didn't spot the car."

"Sorry, I don't know why I'm so nervous. We haven't actually done anything yet."

The security guy got out of his car and typed a code into the keypad next to the door to gain entry into the building. They saw his flashlight passing by windows. Finally, he left.

"He got there at one-thirty and left by one-fifty. Let's check, he might come back," Ralph said as he switched to fast forward. The security guard didn't show again, so Ralph didn't slow the video until people started arriving for work.

When Ralph saw the first person approaching the building, he switched to slow motion. After watching the guy enter, they both shook their heads in disappointment.

"He's very security conscious," Phil said. "He cupped his hands around the keypad. There's no way to tell what he typed."

"Yeah, we'll have to hope everyone isn't as careful."

After three more disappointments, the fifth person came with a bundle under one arm, so she wasn't able to mask what she entered.

"Bingo, I got it. Three, seven, three, four," Ralph said.

"Yes, I got the same. Rewind it, I want to be absolutely sure."

"Okay, let's look at her again. Also, we had better hope we get another shot. While I know it's unlikely, there might be different codes for different people."

There were only two other employees of Smith, Bainbridge, and Sites who were sloppy about their use of the keypad. Phil and Ralph got three, seven, three, four each time.

"We have what we need." Phil walked away from the computer screen. "What do you want to do in Milwaukee? We've got most of tomorrow to kill."

"I investigated the web. I'm most interested in the Harley Davidson Museum. What about you?"

"I want to check out the Frank Lloyd Wright houses. There's a whole block of houses he designed called the Burnham Block. They give tours."

"Houses don't do it for me. So, I guess we'll go our separate ways."

"All right, after breakfast tomorrow we'll split up."

The next morning, Phil gazed at himself in the mirror before breakfast. What he saw didn't entirely please him. He still had clear blue eyes, but at 60, he sagged in places. Also, he didn't like his hair. Balding or graying were in a race, and he didn't like the in-between. At least he'd been able to keep his weight down, so at a fraction under six feet he was thin. He shook his head. He remembered his mother saying, "Getting old isn't for sissies."

He got to the hotel's breakfast before Ralph, so he sat down and waited. He waved at Ralph when he saw him at the entrance. He took a good look at his friend as he walked toward the table. Clearly, living with Beth had improved Ralph's appearance. They'd been exercising. As a result, Ralph had shed ten or fifteen pounds he didn't need. Ralph measured only five nine, and Phil had always thought of him as pudgy. Not true anymore. Also, it appeared Beth had changed his wardrobe and his hair. He had new clothes and a new haircut. His sandy-colored hair appeared neater than Phil remembered. Phil recognized he'd be considered the dowdy one of the pair. It didn't make him feel good.

After breakfast, they went their separate ways to explore. Phil got back to the hotel at 4:00. He'd enjoyed the Frank Lloyd Wright houses. After lunch at a nice sandwich shop, he'd wandered around the city. Having grown up in a small town, he always found cities fascinating. When he returned, he took an hour-long nap. He wanted to be well rested for the night's events.

At 11:30 that night, Phil and Ralph approached Smith, Banbridge, and Sites. They had a collapsible ladder in a carrying case. The case looked like a regular suitcase, not like a ladder. Ralph punched the code in the keypad, and they entered. They took the stairs to the third floor. While the building had some years on it, the interior had been upgraded with lots of glass and chrome.

"Samuel Turbridge, right?" Ralph asked.

"Yep, he's the one."

They entered the first room in Turbridge's suite. "The secretary sits here," Phil said. "And his office is through the door."

Ralph turned on the flashlight on his phone and searched the ceiling briefly. "Get the ladder; I see where we can plant the first camera."

Phil took the ladder out of its case, unfolded it, and handed it to Ralph. Ralph then put the ladder below the sprinkler in the middle of the ceiling. He climbed the ladder and mounted the tiny camera in the sprinkler. "It fits," Ralph explained. "Using the camera with sound recordings makes it tight. We're safe. People never notice sprinklers. They're part of the background."

"I hope you're right. Even in the dark, I can see the camera."

"You know it's there. I'm going to mount the other camera in the same place in the inner office. Why don't you go check the street?"

Phil headed back toward the stairwell. The window looked onto the street below, where Phil spotted the security guard's car parked in front. The guard had just entered the code on the keypad. Phil ran back to Ralph. "The security guard's about to come in the building," he whispered.

"I'm done. There's no way we can get out of here. We'll have to find a place to hide."

"Where? We can't hide in one of the offices."

"I think there's a janitor's closet at the end of the main hall," Ralph said. "I sure hope we both fit."

They moved quickly and tried to be quiet. The flashlight on Ralph's phone showed barely enough room for them and their ladder in the closet. They squeezed in and closed the door. Darkness descended. The only thing audible was their breathing. It sounded incredibly loud. They listened carefully, trying to hear when the security guard passed their location. They couldn't hear anything.

After what seemed like a long time, Ralph turned on his phone to check the time. Only ten minutes had passed. He turned off the phone quickly. After another eternity, Ralph checked again. This time they'd been in the closet for twenty-five minutes. Last night, the guard had taken twenty minutes to do his rounds. To be safe, Ralph decided they'd better wait another ten minutes. Finally, after another check of his phone, Ralph whispered, "It's been almost thirty-five minutes. Let's be quiet. I think the security dude's out of here."

Phil tiptoed to the stairwell and looked out the window. No car. He gave Ralph a thumb's up and heaved a big sigh of relief. Phil was drenched in sweat, and his legs were about to cramp. He'd only been standing still in the closet, but his legs felt as if he'd been climbing stairs.

"Too close for comfort," Ralph said as they went down the stairs.

"Yes. There is no telling when the guy would come. Last night he came at 1:30. He probably doesn't come at the same time every night."

"I guess you're right. We got lucky. It's a good thing you checked when you did."

"Let's get out of here," Phil said as they reached the ground floor.

The next morning, they packed and took a bus to the airport. Ralph took the flight to Pittsburgh, and Phil rented a car. Phil had a week to kill, and he didn't want to hang around Milwaukee. He headed north along the lake, stopping often to gaze at the beaches.

After a leisurely drive, he checked into a motel in Green Bay. Later in the afternoon, he drove by Lambeau Field, the home of the Green Bay Packers. Phil liked knowing that lots of the townspeople owned shares in the team. After Green Bay, he continued north to Michigan, the Upper Peninsula. He stayed in Marquette. The upper Midwest had lots of farms. Phil wondered how the farmers made a go of it with such a short growing season. Apparently, they did. By the end of the week, he was back in Milwaukee.

He repeated the same work he and Ralph had done. The outside camera showed him the law firm hadn't changed the code. Nervously, he entered the building at 11:00. Everything went smoothly. The cameras came down with no trouble. Phil didn't think they had been tampered with in any way. As he returned to his hotel, the security firm's car arrived at the building when he was only a block away. He'd been incredibly lucky again.

Chapter Two

THE NEXT MORNING ON THE plane home, Phil wondered what he'd gotten into. The last year had been a whirlwind. It started with his wife's death as the result of a car accident. She'd been run into by Jake McMahan, a local lout who'd been drunk at the time of the accident.

At the hearing, the judge accepted Jake's guilty plea for leaving the scene of the accident. When Jake wasn't charged with drunken driving and vehicular manslaughter, Phil exploded. He got up and caused a commotion by shouting threats at Jake. Ralph and another friend, Jeremy Terrell, dragged him out of the courtroom.

Later, in a meeting with the district attorney, Phil and his friends learned the more serious charges had to be dropped. After the accident, the police had found Jake at his house and gave him a breathalyzer test, which showed an alcohol level well above the legal maximum. Since he was in his house, and they didn't have a warrant, the evidence wasn't admissible. There were no witnesses, so the more serious charges had to be dropped.

Phil remembered living in a fog after the courtroom fiasco. He couldn't get past how wrong it had all been. If Jake hadn't committed a minor crime, leaving the scene, the breathalyzer test would have been done at the accident site, and the evidence would have been admissible. Or if the officer had arrested him and done the test in his police cruiser, or back at the station, the results could have been used in court. Jake committed a minor crime and as a result got away with more serious crimes. The district attorney called it police misconduct. Phil didn't buy it. Police misconduct was different. The policeman didn't harass anyone with an unnecessary search. Still, the evidence wasn't admissible because of what Phil considered a trivial technicality.

Phil got mad all over again. He'd known he wanted to get back at Jake, yet he'd be in big trouble if he tried. In a very loud voice, he'd threatened Jake in open court. Everyone heard it. If anything happened to Jake, Phil would be the obvious suspect. After moping around for weeks, he finally figured out a plan. He'd get his revenge. It would be indirect, but he couldn't do any better.

Phil enlisted his friend Ralph, who ran a local computer store, as a helper. They took revenge on other guilty people who'd gotten off on technicalities. They were very careful to put up surveillance cameras to find ways of administering the poison Phil had obtained on a trip to Central America. The poison caused partial paralysis. Phil liked this punishment for his chosen victims, all of whom had committed murder. They poisoned five people who lived in different parts of the country.

To bring the revenge back to Jake, Phil emailed a crime reporter at the *New York Times*. The email, simply signed "V," had the web addresses for the original stories about his victims getting off on technicalities and stories about the poisonings. There were nine urls; one of the poisonings didn't get reported to a paper. The *Times* reporter put it all together and wrote a big, front-page story.

Multi-state crime is unusual, and the story about V created an internet sensation. Lots of people praised the vigilante. Others disagreed. One of the fans created a website for people to nominate V's next victim. Ralph nominated Jake, and he came in second in the national balloting. Phil and Ralph were thrilled, and because Ralph shared Facebook friends with Jake, they learned Jake hadn't been thrilled at all. He seemed really pissed off and a little anxious.

Phil knew it wasn't real revenge; still, he felt good about Jake being upset. And he continued to slowly heal. The poisonings had given him a project, a focus. He'd probably never fully recover from Mary Jane's death. Still, he showed himself he was able to function.

Then came the shock. Phil and Ralph thought they'd gotten away with everything completely. They hadn't. Sherry Ahearn, Phil's sort of girlfriend, and Beth Watson, Ralph's for-sure girlfriend, figured out they were V.

To Phil's relief, Sherry and Beth didn't turn them in. No, instead they had another project for them. This led to him coming back from Milwaukee with two cameras. The women were eager to download the videos.

Chapter Three

THE DAY AFTER PHIL'S RETURN from Milwaukee, Sherry went to Beth and Ralph's apartment on her lunch break from the library. Beth had the day off, and she'd been editing the videos. They gathered around the computer. The first shot showed about ten seconds of Rochelle Martin sitting at her desk. She served as the receptionist/secretary for Sam Turbridge.

"She's pretty," Sherry said. "I like the way she's fixed her hair."

"Yeah, it's cute," added Beth. "Do you think I could fix mine that way?"

"Maybe it would frame your face a little better. Not that there's anything wrong with your hair now."

Beth restarted the video. The second shot showed Sam's office behind Rochelle's desk.

"I wanted to show the layout and the view from both cameras," Beth said. "We got Turbridge's name on the door, and Rochelle's nameplate is clear. Also, there's a great big clock on the wall in her office."

"The pictures are very clear."

The video then showed Rochelle responding to a call from her boss. She went into his office. The video switched to the camera in the second office. Sam handed a piece of paper to Rochelle and moved around his desk, so he stood beside her. Sherry and Beth heard him saying, "I've made a few corrections on this letter." After he finished pointing out the corrections, his right hand reached around and stroked Rochelle's butt.

"Please don't!" Rochelle said as she turned and wriggled away from him.

The next part of the video showed Rochelle at her desk typing on her computer.

"Look at the clock," Beth said. "It's five-thirty. They're getting ready to quit."

Sam left his office with a briefcase in his hand. He put the briefcase down and leaned over Rochelle. After a few moments, he reached around and grabbed her breast. Rochelle reacted instantly by slapping his hand away. She turned on him angrily. Sam backed up, grabbed his briefcase, and walked out the door with a smile on his face.

"Perfect, Beth," Sherry said. "You've done a wonderful editing job. What a jerk. He acts like he can paw her any time he wants."

"Thanks, and yes, he's a jerk. I put six other videos of him doing similar things in a separate file. I selected these two because they were the best shots. A few of the others are good, too. It's horrible there are so many. The cameras were only there a week."

"I don't know how she can stand to work with him."

"Her postings explained it. It's a good job with a reasonable salary. She's afraid she wouldn't be able to get as good a job if she quits. She's afraid a sexual harassment complaint would backfire. It would be her word against his. She doesn't have any witnesses."

"She does now," Sherry said.

"Yeah, she sure does. Let's explain the rest of the process to the guys at dinner. We're going to Phil's, right?"

"Yes, he's a little nervous about it. I'm not interested in him for his cooking. I'm sure he can put something edible on the table."

After Sherry left, Beth recognized how pleased she'd been that Sherry liked the video. She shouldn't be so happy about it. Sherry is a friend. Still, Beth found herself a little in awe of Sherry. Despite being older, she was gorgeous. She had beautiful, long brown hair, a great figure, flawless skin, and deep dimples when she smiled. Women like Sherry intimidated Beth. She knew she didn't look bad herself, particularly since she'd lost weight, but she wasn't in Sherry's league. She still had to get rid of five pounds and, while her skin had cleared, it didn't glow like Sherry's. She liked her long black hair. Maybe a cut like Rochelle's might be an improvement.

Beth remembered when she'd first met Sherry. Sherry suspected Phil and Ralph might be behind the V business, and she wanted a listing of when Ralph had been away. Entries in Beth's diary helped Sherry make her case. Then came the big meeting where Sherry confronted the men. It all seemed like a long time ago. Now they had this new project.

The team, the INHSSSA Group, contained an odd mix. There were two age groups represented. Phil, a college professor, had taken early retirement. Beth had been a good friend of Phil's wife, Mary Jane. They were both nurses. It had been tragic when she'd been killed. Phil had to be in his early 60s; Beth wasn't sure. He provided the funding for the group. He'd been the beneficiary of a large life insurance policy Mary Jane's parents had taken out. Sherry, the gorgeous librarian, was a little younger than Phil. Phil and Sherry were a couple, or at least she thought they were.

She and Ralph were the younger set. Ralph and Phil had a long-standing friendship. Phil had been one of Ralph's professors. If Beth understood the story right, Phil had been a big help in getting Ralph through Lackey College. Ralph, a thirty-two-year-old computer expert, ran a store in town. He repaired computers and sold used ones. She worried she had the least solid connection. Beth had lots of reasons to be committed to what they were trying to do. *Maybe I've only been included because Ralph and I are living together.* Also, she was the youngest member, only thirty. She and Ralph had only been dating for about six months before they moved in together. She felt like they were solid. Working together in the group helped.

She liked contributing to the team. *It's not just editing the video.* In a way, she'd made it all possible. Finding the women to help required hacking the chat room website. She and Ralph had been able to do the job. Ralph, the computer expert, couldn't have done it without her. In fact, she had taken the lead.

As part of the process, she'd had to tell Ralph about her old boyfriend,

Billy. Billy had taught her a lot about computers and hacking. Much to her relief, Ralph had taken it well. He said he didn't care about old boyfriends. He's the current one. She hoped he really meant it. Anyway, Ralph had been amazed at how much she knew. *Actually, to be honest, the chat room's security wasn't very good.*

Chapter Four

AS SHE SAT BEHIND THE reference desk in the library after returning from Beth's, Sherry wondered if their plan would work. It had been her idea. She had to stop herself from tapping her pencil. This project, based on ideas swirling around in her head for years, had only been fully thought out a month ago.

People had always complemented Sherry on her looks. It had been a curse as much as a blessing. When she was twelve, an uncle had touched her inappropriately. She'd been afraid to tell her parents, so she went out of her way to avoid the guy. Luckily, there weren't many family gatherings. She thought she'd gotten out of trouble by marrying Joel. Joel had been a popular high school senior, and she'd been thrilled when he asked her out in her sophomore year. She'd fought with her parents, who didn't like Joel. Marrying him a month after high-school graduation had been a colossal mistake.

Joel had been a skirt chaser. While she knew it, she thought she'd be enough for him. She soon realized her mistake. Joel tried to run her life, even to the extent of letting his friends have their way with her. She was mortified when one of his friends started fondling her with Joel in the room. She ran out and never came back. The whole thing made her wonder if she'd been at fault. Then again, how could he ever imagine she'd put up with it?

Because of her disastrous early marriage, in college Sherry found herself older than the other students. Wary of men, she fought off the few advances she'd received. Dropping her defenses in New York City where she got her first job, she'd fallen for William Burris, her boss. While she knew she shouldn't mix business and dating, she wasn't able to stop. Just when she thought everything was going to work out, she'd caught Bill making love to his secretary.

Things got worse. Sherry had a terrible time getting another job. Apparently, Bill blackballed her with many of the firms she applied to. To get another shot at the job market, she decided to earn an MBA. During her second semester, one of her professors hit on her. She went to the Dean. Nothing happened. The professor denied the whole thing. It came down to her word against his.

Sherry dropped out and had a rough time with interviews. At one of the interviews, the guy propositioned her. Enraged, she went to his boss. It became a replay of the interaction with the Dean. The guy denied it. Again, her word against his and nothing happened. Finally, she did get a job, a miserable one. The bosses were all men. They constantly leered at her and made suggestive comments. She gritted her teeth and saved her money.

After two years she quit and went back to school for an MA in library science. To avoid attention from men, in library school she'd decided to adopt a dowdy look. She wore loose clothes, let her hair go, and stopped wearing makeup. It worked. She no longer had trouble with men. At the time she thought she had been clever. Later, she recognized it as a cop-out.

That was when the idea for this project started to germinate. She'd gone through the sexual harassment procedures twice. Both times she'd gotten no satisfaction. It came down to a he-said-she-said situation, and nothing happened. And she didn't always get sympathy from her women colleagues. One of them even told her to lighten up, saying, "Boys will be boys, you know." Sherry had been furious at the time. While she knew her situation wasn't unusual, she didn't have the faintest idea how to overcome the problem.

The Me-Too movement interested her. It showed the possibility of justice if lots of women accused a high-profile person. Even in those situations, the men denied everything. Too often their defense succeeded. Most sexual harassment happened in private. The guys knew they would be cooked if there were witnesses, so they did what they did when they were alone with the woman. And they usually succeeded. If accused, they claimed the woman lied, or exaggerated, or had been a willing partner.

When she moved back to Lackey to be with her elderly mother, she ran into one of her old professors, Phil. His wife had recently been killed in a horrible car accident. She and Phil got along, and, truth be told, were slowly, ever so slowly, getting close. Then she found out Phil was V. At first, Sherry didn't know how to react. As she thought about confronting Phil, it came to her. Phil and Ralph had used surveillance cameras to figure out how to poison their victims, exactly what she needed.

Also, Beth and Ralph's computer expertise had been incredibly valuable. More than anything else, Sherry felt good about doing something, or at least trying. In the past, she'd been running from her problems. Now she'd started to fight back. It excited her to be finally taking action.

Chapter Five

WHEN SHERRY ARRIVED AT PHIL'S house, the other three were eating pizza and salad in the dining room. She apologized for being late. She explained the stupid head librarian didn't know how to control a meeting. "Librarians are awful," she said. "Our meetings cycle around all the time. If I were running the meetings, I'd cut off discussion when people started repeating themselves."

After the meal, they moved to the living room. Sherry and Beth sat on the couch and the guys pulled up chairs. Then Ralph and Phil went to fiddle with the TV. Ralph showed Phil how to display the video on his new flat-screen TV.

When they finished, Beth exclaimed, "It's way better on the big TV."

"Yeah, even enlarged, the videos from those small cameras are clear. The offices were well lit," explained Ralph.

After they'd viewed the videos twice, Phil spoke. "These are great. We've clearly got the goods on this guy. Now let's go over the next steps. Even though we talked about it before, I'm still a little hazy on the details."

"From our end, most of it happens on the internet. We won't need any more breaking and entering," Sherry said. "I've composed the email to send to Rochelle. Essentially, it says we know she's being harassed at work, and we want her to lodge a formal complaint. Her complaint should accuse Turbridge of unwanted touching."

"Don't we give her the video evidence? Her complaint would be a slam-dunk with what I saw," Phil said.

"No," Sherry answered. "We want her to go through the procedure to see how her bosses respond. If it goes like most of these cases, nothing happens. Turbridge'll deny everything, and it'll come down to her word against his. We'll tell her we have a backup. That's where the video comes in."

"I still don't get it." Ralph leaned back in his chair. "Why go through the procedure? We've got him dead to rights."

Sherry explained patiently, "What we want to do is show how poor the procedures typically are. You can't get the procedures changed if you ignore them. Look, sexual harassment is about unwanted behavior, and the victim is the only one who knows what's unwanted. If the accused claims she consented, like in many rape cases, it's her word against his. In lots of those situations, the man gets off. Basically, the default is the guy isn't punished."

"It's exactly what happened in my case," Beth interjected. "The hospital said it was his word against mine, so he got off. While it's innocent until proven guilty for him, everyone treated me like the guilty party. We want to show how those procedures aren't satisfactory."

"How will we communicate with Rochelle?" Ralph asked. "We don't want her emailing us. It would be too easy to trace."

"Yes, we've got a plan," Beth answered. "I found her on the *Female Friends* chat room where women unload about problems at work. Then you and I hacked the system to find her email address."

"Yes."

"We're going to email her from an untraceable site, and she's going to be instructed to respond to us in the chat room. We'll have her address her message to the I. N. H. S. S. S. A. Group."

"I still don't like having an acronym no one can pronounce," Ralph muttered.

"Quiet," Beth said. "We've all heard you on the subject, and it stands out because it's unpronounceable."

"I've got an idea." Sherry stood and began pacing. "When we talk about it, let's add an i and drop an s. Then it becomes the In Hissa Group. We can pronounce it."

"I like it. It will be easier for us to talk," Beth said.

"We'll still use the initials when we correspond with the women. Right?" Ralph asked.

"Yes."

"Let's get back to next steps. Is your first email going to tell her about the video?" Phil asked.

"Yes, it has to," Sherry said as she sat back down. "Rochelle has to be confident we have her covered. She should go into the complaint procedure knowing she's going to eventually win. Otherwise, I'm not sure she'd be willing to put herself through it."

"This email you've composed is going to be fairly long," Ralph said. "I'm worried. It's going to be difficult to make it all clear to Rochelle. The whole thing is a little convoluted. We have her go through the complaint procedure aware she is likely to lose. Then, and only then, we send the video. With the video, she can appeal, and she'll be sure to win."

"And what do we do if her complaint is upheld?" Phil said. "What do we do if they decide to sweep it under the table? Say they switch her to another lawyer and don't punish Turbridge?"

"It might happen," Sherry answered. "I bet it's unlikely. But if they do, I guess we'll have to reconsider our strategy. My best guess at this point is to send the video to the law firm's managing partner. No matter what happens to Rochelle, Turbridge shouldn't go away unpunished."

"I still feel it's gutsy to start off with a law firm," Phil commented.

"We talked about that before, and I understand your concern," Sherry said. "There's no getting around it. What you and Ralph did in Milwaukee would be called breaking and entering. We're already law breakers. And taking the videos is invasion of privacy—doubling down on the law breaking. Lawyers are all about upholding the law. Nevertheless, if she worked in another kind of business, that firm would get a lawyer. It doesn't matter."

"If we follow through all the way, it gets worse," Beth added. "Here's the set up. If Rochelle loses her case, she shows them the video. Suppose they still don't do anything? We're going to have her tell them the video's going live on their website in three days, if she doesn't get satisfaction. Suppose they still dig in their heels. When we follow through, it'd be hacking, another crime. There's no way around it; we're breaking laws. I thought we all understood."

"Yes, we do," Ralph said. "And for that reason, we have to be stealthy. Setting up and retrieving the cameras is the most dangerous part. Otherwise, we should be okay. The communication plan is good. I hope Rochelle and the others follow directions."

"Too many of my students weren't very good at following directions," Phil commented.

"All we can do is try," Sherry said. "It's our first attempt. If we need to adjust anything, we can do it on the next one."

"Okay. Ralph will send the email tonight," Beth said.

Chapter Six

WHEN RALPH AND BETH RETURNED to their apartment after sending the email, Ralph asked, "What you said about your experience? I didn't know you had trouble with sexual harassment."

"It's not the kind of thing you talk to boyfriends about, but I guess I should tell you."

"The way you talked about it tonight told me it's still bothering you."

"I guess it is."

"When Sherry explained this project to us, she explained her motivation clearly. She'd had a lot of trouble with men in her past, and she hadn't gotten any satisfaction when she'd lodged sexual harassment complaints. The men denied any wrongdoing. It came down to he-said-she said, and the men got off. I thought you were joining the team because of me. I had no knowledge about anything you'd gone through. Can you tell me about it?"

"Let's grab a beer and sit on the couch. It's a bit of a long story."

Ralph went to the refrigerator and took out two beers. Beth liked low-calorie beer. He thought it too weak. He opened their beers and headed for the couch.

Beth seemed a little nervous. "I got my first job at a big hospital in Pittsburgh. From the very start one of the doctors, Doctor Burns, took too much interest in me. He kept asking me to go out with him after our shifts. He was married. Heck, I'd even met his wife. I turned him down flat. Actually, he was in his fifties. I found the whole thing creepy. He didn't get the message. He wouldn't stop. He continued to pester me for dates. When he started grabbing me inappropriately, I finally lodged a sexual harassment complaint at the hospital. It didn't work. The hospital personnel people told me they didn't find any evidence to back my complaint. My experience resembled Sherry's."

Ralph put his arm around Beth. "It must have been frustrating. I guess he only made advances when you were alone."

"Yeah, it was always just the two of us, and as much as I tried, I couldn't avoid those situations."

"Sure, nurses and doctors have to work close together at times."

"Right, but that's not the worst of it. Things changed after the sexual harassment complaint. People started treating me differently. Doctor Burns had lots of friends on the staff, and they all turned against me. It depressed me. I found it completely unfair, yet I couldn't do anything about it. It was so wrong. Burns had misbehaved, yet I got punished."

Ralph hugged Beth, whose eyes were tearing. "It's all right. It's in the past."

"Even now when I think about it, it still bothers me. And I guess I didn't handle it well. I started eating too much. Food provided comfort. I broke up with my boyfriend, Billy. He didn't show any sympathy at all. Finally, after I put on close to thirty pounds, I decided I had to make a complete life change."

"So, you moved to Lackey?"

"I wanted to get out of the city. I applied to a bunch of small-town hospitals, and Lackey responded first. Nursing jobs are fairly easy to get. And the hospital here is a good one. After I moved, I put myself on a diet, but I had trouble sticking to it. I guess I'd still been upset about what had happened. Luckily, my work went well. The people in Lackey are nice. As I told you before, I got along with Phil's wife Mary Jane right away. I even told her about why I left the hospital in Pittsburg, but I didn't tell anyone else.

"Finally, I started to come out of my shell and got more serious about my diet. Meeting you gave me an impetus to change. I really liked our exercise group. Dieting together really helps."

"I always wondered why you wound up here. I never really thought about it too hard. I figured I had good luck. Now I'm torn. Part of me is glad you had trouble at the Pittsburg hospital, but that's not right. I shouldn't think that way."

Beth responded. "I never thought about it like that. So, you're saying we'd have never met if I hadn't had my problems?"

"Yeah."

"I understand. Nevertheless, I'd have been happier if we'd have met some other way."

Ralph gave Beth a kiss. "Whatever, now we have each other."

"And it's great," Beth said. "Now you've got the full story, I guess you can understand why I'm so eager to be part of the project along with you and Phil and Sherry."

"You bet. It makes a lot of sense."

Beth glanced at her phone. "Look at what time it is. We'd better get to bed," she said as she pulled Ralph off the couch.

"You don't have to ask twice."

Chapter Seven

THAT SAME EVENING IN MILWAUKEE, Rochelle Martin got home at 6:15 and fixed dinner. Her roommate Elizabeth had a late shift at the restaurant, so she had the apartment to herself. After dinner, she logged into the chat room. She had to unload about the constant harassment by her boss Sam. While she didn't like to complain all the time, she kept her feelings bottled up at work. The chat room gave her a chance to vent.

After spending an hour in the chat room, she didn't feel much better. She knew she wasn't alone. Lots of women had horrible bosses. Knowing others had similar problems didn't change her situation. Still, it helped a little. She switched to her email. She didn't get much email worth her time. Stores always wanted your email address. Giving it to them generated lots of useless messages she deleted in a hurry. Rochelle stopped at the email from INHSSSA. She didn't have the faintest idea what or who they were. Curious, she opened it.

Dear Rochelle Martin,

You don't know who we are, but we know quite a bit about you. Most importantly, we are aware your boss, Samuel Turbridge, treats you terribly. We would like to help you with this situation.

Last week we installed video cameras in your office, and we

captured several shots of Mr. Turbridge pawing you. We will provide you a copy of this video if you need it.

Here is how we would like to proceed. To start, we would like you to file a formal sexual harassment complaint. In your case, go to Mrs. Higgins to start the process. Be open with her and describe the kinds of things Mr. Turbridge does. We have clear video evidence of unwanted touching, but our video only covers one week. Tell her everything you've had to put up with.

Let the process play out. We understand this will be difficult. It is important to see if Smith, Banbridge, and Sites will do the right thing. There are two options. First, they may find in your favor. Maybe they will change your work assignment. Maybe they will sanction Mr. Turbridge. We don't know. In that case, you will have to tell us whether you are satisfied with the outcome. Second, and this is more likely, they will do nothing. Mr. Turbridge will say he didn't do anything, or you were asking for it. Essentially it becomes a he-said-she-said situation. This is where the video comes in. If they don't believe what you are saying, tell us. In that case, we will provide you the video. Go back to Mrs. Higgins and show her the video. Tell her it will go live on the firm's website in three days if they don't reverse their decision.

Please do not show anyone this email or at any time divulge where you got the video. We can only help you and other people like you if we remain anonymous.

We understand we are asking a great deal of you, but we are confident you will get justice in the end. For all this to work, we have to be able to communicate. We will be in contact with you via email. There is no way you can respond to our emails. When you want to communicate with us, post a message on the *Female Friends* chat room. Messages to us should start with "INHSSSA". To start out, tell us when you have filed your complaint. We will respond. Also, if you have questions, feel free to ask. We will not respond to questions like: Who are you? Where are you? Why are you doing this?

All we can say is we have been in situations like yours, and we needed a powerful friend.

We are the powerful friend you need.

INHSSSA Group

Rochelle didn't know how to react. She read the email again slowly. She'd had friends who'd made sexual harassment complaints, and it almost always turned out to have been a mistake. Most people at their workplaces, particularly the men, blamed the victim. As a result, the one filing the sexual harassment complaint had to spend a lot of time defending herself. These people were asking her to take a big risk. *What if it's a hoax?*

She decided to set up communication with these people. She logged on to the chat room. She typed INHSSSA and then, 'What does INHSSSA stand for?' She thought for a moment, then the next step came to her. Before she embarked on what these people wanted her to do, she had to have this video. The more she thought about it, the more she wanted to take a look at the video. She typed, "I'm not doing anything until I have the video. Sorry." She wondered if the "sorry" sounded weak. In the end, she left it and posted the chat.

Chapter Eight

THE NEXT EVENING, BETH CALLED the others for a meeting. When they all gathered, she showed them Rochelle's post.

"It's reasonable," Phil said. "We're asking her to take a big risk, and she doesn't have the faintest idea who we are."

"I agree," Sherry added. "If I were in her shoes, I'd want verification. There are lots of weird people on the internet."

The others nodded.

Then Ralph spoke. "I've got her home address from a previous search. The video can go on a thumb drive. I guess we'd better take a trip. We don't want the postmark to lead back to us. Also, do we send the short version or the longer one or both?"

"Let's send both," Beth suggested. "We can enclose a note explaining there are two videos and what's on them. I agree the postmark shouldn't lead back to us. Also, we need to be careful not to leave fingerprints on anything."

"Are fingerprints really a concern?" Sherry asked.

"Beth's right," Ralph answered. "We have to be extra careful. We have no idea how this will turn out. Remember, lawyers are involved. We don't want any chance we can be implicated. She only communicates with us through the chat room, which is a public forum, and that's good.

And we are using an untraceable email. Mailing the video is the only physical contact we'll ever have with her."

"Let's send her two thumb drives," Sherry said. "Then she has the option of handing one of them to her bosses without having to give her only copy."

"We'll retain a copy," Phil said.

"She'd be able to make another copy if she wanted one," Ralph said.

"We want to be extra nice to her," Sherry said. "Sending two copies will help her. Any help we give will make her like us more. Remember, we came completely out of the blue."

Phil looked at Sherry and Beth. "Okay, it's settled. You guys should answer Rochelle's email. Tell her what the acronym stands for and that the video is on the way. Ralph, you have thumb drives, don't you? When everything's ready, I'll drive to Cleveland to mail the package."

****

Three days later, Rochelle Martin received a small package in the mail. She opened it eagerly. The INHSSSA Group, whoever they were, sure seemed to follow through. They'd already answered her first question. INHSSSA stood for It's Not He Said She Said Anymore. Now they'd sent the video like she'd asked. The instructions were clear:

> The two thumb drives are identical. They both contain two videos. Video one is very short. It shows two encounters you had with Sam Turbridge. These are the two clearest pieces of evidence of unwanted touching. Video two contains every other instance of unwanted touching we picked up during the week. A few of the views on video two are not as clear as those on video one. Use either or both.
>
> We are sending two copies. Always keep one in a safe place. There is a chance you will have to give the other one to your employer.
>
> Please do not discuss the fact you have this video evidence when you make your first complaint. It should only be used if

the resolution of your complaint is unsatisfactory.

Rochelle put one of the thumb drives in her computer. The files were MPeg video files, easy for her to view. She viewed the first video. She didn't like the way she looked. She guessed it couldn't be helped. The INHSSSA people were right. The first video showed the problem clearly. Sam grabbed her twice, and her reaction made it clear she didn't want to be grabbed. Video two showed more of the same. She understood why they'd chosen the ones for the short video. The angles weren't as good in the second one, and things weren't as well focused. Still, Rochelle thought video two also worth showing. She also liked the time stamps on the videos.

Rochelle logged into the chat room. She wrote a short message to the INHSSSA group telling them she'd received the videos. She told them she planned to make her sexual harassment complaint the next day. Despite wondering what she'd gotten herself into, she was excited.

Chapter Nine

THE NEXT DAY ROCHELLE WENT into Mrs. Higgins' office. She'd called ahead to make an appointment. She'd always been a little intimidated by Mrs. Higgins, the law firm's administrator. She was quite a bit older than Rochelle and seemed incredibly business-like in their few encounters.

"What can I do for you, Rochelle?" Mrs. Higgins asked.

Rochelle gulped. "I need to file a sexual harassment complaint against Sam Turbridge. He's making my life miserable, and I want it to stop."

Mrs. Higgins paused to see if Rochelle had anything to add. "This is a very serious business. Are you sure you want to go through with it?"

"Yes."

"I'll need more specifics, and of course you'll have to file a written complaint. The procedures are in the employee handbook. You've read it, haven't you?"

Rochelle responded, "Yes, I've reviewed the handbook, and here is my written complaint." She handed a sheet of paper to Mrs. Higgins.

During an uncomfortable silence, Mrs. Higgins read what Rochelle had given her. She finally spoke. "This is serious. We can't have unwanted touching at this law firm. Are there any witnesses who can verify what you've written?"

Remembering about the video made Rochelle pause. The INHSSSA people had been clear. They told her not to say anything about the video yet. "No, our office suite is private, and almost all of it happens there. He's careful. I've complained to a few of the other secretaries. I guess that wouldn't count."

"No, hearsay evidence won't count. Still, as I've said, this is serious. I'll have to talk to the managing partner, Mr. Sites. I'm sure we'll start an investigation quickly. Also, I have to warn you, we'll be talking to Mr. Turbridge. We have to hear his response to these allegations."

"I expected it. Actually, being aware he's being investigated might get him to stop. I sure hope so," Rochelle said.

Rochelle went back to her desk and finished the day. She wanted to avoid Sam. It turned out to be easy because he had a court appearance on his calendar for the afternoon. She liked his court days. She knew there'd be a real dust up when Sam learned about her charges and wasn't looking forward to it. Nevertheless, having the video in her back pocket gave her confidence. She'd never have made the complaint without it.

In the evening, she posted to the INHSSSA group telling them she'd started the complaint process.

Chapter Ten

PHIL WENT TO HIS LUNCH group as he did every Wednesday he was in town. The group had been meeting for close to fifteen years. Out of the seven of them, six had Lackey College backgrounds. Phil had been, and Jeremy Terrell was, a historian. Bert Holman taught physics. Bob Latham taught mathematics. William Lin chaired the economics department, and George Nathan taught political science. The final member, the only woman, Sally Joins, the editor of the local newspaper, didn't have a college connection. They met in the back room of Andy's restaurant. They did so on purpose to avoid the TV monitors in the main room, which were always tuned to right-wing news they didn't like.

After they'd finished eating, Jeremy said, "I have an announcement."

"Okay, what is it?" asked Bert. "You have our attention."

"Rachel is getting married. We learned about the whole thing this weekend. The wedding is going to be here in October."

"Is this the guy she's been dating for the last year?" George asked. "Don't I remember you saying you liked him. What's his name?"

"Yes, Alan Wiggins. They met when Rachel took the job in Pittsburgh. He's been to visit several times. And you're right; we like him. He's got a good job. He works for one of those consulting firms. It's clear they're very much in love. Linda and I are thrilled."

"You'd better be sure the wedding doesn't put you into bankruptcy," William said. "While we helped with Jeff's wedding, most of it fell on the family of the bride. Weddings can be incredibly expensive."

"Linda and I talked about it, and we're going to give Rachel a limit, a figure we're willing to spend. If they're not on a budget, it might get out of hand."

"Sounds smart," Bert said. "It's incredible how much people spend on one day. Wouldn't the money be better spent on a down payment on a house or a car? At least something useful."

"Little girls spend quite a bit of time day dreaming about being a bride," George said. "My daughters do. I worry about how much they're going to expect us to spend."

Phil changed the subject. "I have a question for you, Jeremy."

"Go ahead."

"Did Alan come to you and ask for Rachel's hand in marriage?"

"Yes, as a matter of fact he did. He seemed to be a little nervous about it. I found it touching."

"Isn't that from the 'women are chattel' view of the world?" Phil asked. "Rachel's not your property. There's no dowry involved."

"Come on Phil, back off," Bert replied. "While it may be old fashioned, I don't see anything wrong with it. It's not like Jeremy is going to turn the guy down."

"I'm going to side with Phil on this," Sally inserted. "He's right. Asking the father for permission to marry the girl is offensive to women. Doesn't Rachel get a say in all this? And what about Linda? The guy should at least ask the parents, not only the father. No, scratch that. No one should be asked for permission. The couple, both of them, should announce they're getting married."

"What do you do when one set of parents objects to the marriage?" George asked.

"It happens," Bob said. "For example, marriages where there are two religions involved or when the parents don't like their daughter's choice."

"We've gone a little far afield from where I started," Phil said. "Parents don't own their daughters. We shouldn't perpetuate customs based on that idea. On occasion, parents don't like the prospective groom or bride.

It's a whole different problem."

"Not one we're going to solve at lunch," Bert said. "I'm going back to work."

"Hold on a minute, Bert," George said. "Margaret wanted to bounce something off you guys."

"Whoa, the college president wants our opinion. What is it?" Jeremy asked.

"You all know William Randolph, the big donor?" George asked.

They nodded.

"He wants to endow a lecture series and invite Senator David Katel as the first speaker. What's your opinion?"

Bert jumped in. "No! Absolutely no! We can't have a guy like Katel. Heck, even the right-wing TV network canceled his show. If they won't let him talk, we shouldn't."

"Yes. Still, he's been elected Senator from Montana," William said. "He's in Congress making laws. In addition, we don't want Margaret to be turning down donations. It would be good to have a well-funded lecture series around here. We should be able to get a better speaker next year."

"I don't know, William. Why did Katel lose his TV show? He lost it because he repeatedly flat-out lied. Nothing about his run for Senator changed anything. He doesn't tell the truth," Sally said.

"Sally's right, colleges should be about seeking truth," Bert said. "Katel doesn't seek the truth!"

George filled the silence following Bert's comment, "Margaret's view is we should let him speak. Lackey should show everyone we're a place where people can air different views. It's important. Too many places only hear from people they agree with. Also, we can make it a teachable moment by showing the students how to fact check a speech."

"Margaret only wants to be able to bring in the big donation," Bert said.

"Partly, but her other two points are reasonable," Bob said. "We wonder why the country is so split. Isn't this part of it? If we never listen to the other side, we'll stay split forever."

"I agree," Phil said. "Margaret's view is sensible. It'll be important to make it clear that we aren't endorsing Katel's remarks. We're simply providing a forum. We should come across as willing to countenance controversy."

"Should I tell Margaret that while the lunch group is not unanimous, it is generally supportive of going ahead?" George asked.

Be sure to emphasize the lack of unanimity." Bert stood and threw some money on the table.

Chapter Eleven

IN THE EVENING, PHIL RETURNED to Andy's for a late dinner with the In Hissa group. Sherry and Beth had seen Rochelle's post earlier, and they filled in the men. The restaurant started to thin out when they congregated, so they had no fellow diners close by. Still, they kept their voices down.

"Now we wait," Phil said. "How long will the process take?"

"I have no idea," Sherry answered. "When I made a sexual harassment charge against the professor who hit on me in grad school, it took a long time, at least three weeks. A big university has lots of layers of bureaucracy. I'm sure the layers slowed it down."

"My experience with the hospital turned out to be a little quicker. It should be similar in this case," Beth said. "Rochelle works at a fairly small law firm. And it's a charge of unwanted touching. I bet they take it more seriously than something like complaints about language."

"I sure hope so. I don't like waiting," Phil said. "What can we do in the meantime?"

The waitress interrupted the conversation. After she left, Sherry said, "Let's move on to the next case. Everything is going according to plan on this one. I see no reason for us to wait before we start another one. If we find out it isn't working out, we can stop the process. If everything continues as we expect, we can keep moving on to the next case."

"Fair enough," Ralph said. "Who's next?"

Beth spoke up. "Sherry and I have talked about it, and we are going to suggest Barbara Fairchild from Salt Lake City."

"What's her story?" Ralph asked.

Sherry folded her arms on the table. "She works in a big box store, and she has trouble with her boss, Tom Kelly. She gets breaks twice a day. Tom has scheduled her breaks so she's the only one in the break room. He's also told all the employees they're required to go to the break room. He says he doesn't want them wandering around the store. While Barbara takes long trips to the bathroom, she can't avoid the break room entirely. Almost every time she's there, Tom comes in. He's propositioned her several times. Actually, he's a lot like Sam Turbridge. He gropes her when he gets a chance."

"So, the camera should go in the break room," Phil said.

"Yeah. We hope it isn't too hard," Sherry commented.

"It should be easy," Ralph said. "While one person could do it, two would be better. One to plant the camera and the other to stand guard to deflect anyone who might be headed for the break room."

"I don't understand the need for the second person," Beth said. "I bet there aren't any breaks scheduled for the early morning."

"Hush honey, I'm angling for us to take a trip out West together," Ralph said. "I agree. The morning should be clear. Still, it's better to be safe than sorry."

"Oh, I get it," responded Beth, a bit embarrassed.

Phil and Sherry exchanged a glance and a smile at the young couple's expense. "Yes, better safe than sorry," Phil said. "Ralph and Beth should go to Salt Lake. Beth, check your schedule at the hospital to determine when you can get a few days off. And Sherry and I can go to retrieve the camera. We'll be there when the store is open. It'd be better if we don't have faces on the store cameras more than once."

"I hadn't considered store cameras," Beth said. "This'll be the first time I've done anything like this. Should I have a disguise?"

"Maybe you can put on tinted glasses and a rinse in your hair," Sherry said. "We don't need to do a lot. Still, it's fun to plan disguises. And it's good the women are going to be part of the operation. We've been behind the scenes with Rochelle."

****

A week later, Ralph and Beth walked into the big building supply store where Barbara Fairchild worked. They split up, and Beth walked by the cashiers. She spotted Barbara's name tag. She was young, in her early or mid-twenties, and attractive, slim with long blonde hair in a ponytail.

In the store, lots of builders seemed to be getting supplies for the day's job. They saw several guys in white painter's outfits. Ralph poked around the back of the big store until he found the break room.

At the appointed time, Ralph and Beth met by the dishwasher display. Ralph told Beth he'd found the break room, and they ambled toward it, being sure to stop at displays along the way. When they got close, Beth pretended to be interested in floor tiles, while Ralph slipped into the break room.

In the break room, Ralph spotted where he wanted the camera right away. A group of lockers lined the far wall. The lockers didn't go all the way to the ceiling. A bunch of random stuff covered the top of the lockers. Ralph used a chair and planted the camera on the top of the lockers. He hid it a little with an old newspaper. He got down, replaced the chair, and looked at his handy work. He could see the camera, of course, but then he knew what to look for. He didn't think anyone else would spot it. Finally, he took a picture with his phone. The picture would make it easier for Phil to find the camera.

Beth liked how quickly Ralph had planted the camera. No one came by, so she didn't have to do anything. Beth pointed Barbara out as she and Ralph left the store.

Ralph and Beth spent the next two days traveling around Salt Lake City. While they'd been living together for the past four months, they enjoyed checking into a hotel together. They found the city, ringed by mountains, spectacular. It wasn't anything like Pennsylvania, where they'd both grown up.

They were both struck by the dominance of the Mormon church. There were the impressive church buildings in the center of the city. The lack of bars surprised them more than anything else.

Chapter Twelve

WHEN THEY GOT BACK HOME, Beth called Sherry. After giving a brief report on their success in Salt Lake City, Beth asked if anything had happened with Rochelle Martin.

"There's one post on the chat room. Not directed at us," Sherry responded. "Rochelle said her boss seemed angry at her—probably because he's heard about the sexual harassment complaint. She'll probably be posting something for us soon."

"I guess all we can do is wait. It's the same with Barbara Fairchild. We have the camera in place. In a week you guys can pick it up. After we contact her, there's a lot of waiting. I'm not sure I like the waiting."

"Go to work like you normally would, Beth. There sure is a lot of waiting. It doesn't bother me. What bothers me is not being able to talk to anyone about it. You and Ralph live together, so you can talk about what we're doing. I live with my mother. I can't say a word. I'm not even going to tell her Phil and I are going to Salt Lake City together."

"I wondered," Beth said. "You two like each other a lot... what stage are you at?"

"It's complicated. His wife died a little over a year ago, and he's still dealing with it. Also, my history with men makes me leery of jumping into things. And as I said, I live with my mother. She's old fashioned. She wouldn't approve of my sleeping at Phil's."

"This trip might be a breakthrough?"

"I hope so. At least I want it to be. I'm not sure about Phil. Still, he's the one who suggested the two of us make the trip. I'm encouraged."

****

On Friday, Sherry picked Phil up at his house. Phil thought the man should be doing the driving. In this case, it wouldn't work. Shery didn't want her mother to know they were traveling together. He liked Sherry a lot, and she seemed to like him. Still, he felt a little unfaithful to his wife when he mulled over the idea of taking the next steps with Sherry. He knew Mary Jane would want him to find someone, but the whole thing unsettled him.

On the flight, Sherry looked at Phil, his head buried in a book. She wondered what would happen next. Phil had been one of her professors in undergrad. Since she started college so late, their ages weren't that far apart. Phil had been one of her favorite professors, and truth be told, she'd had a crush on him. Nothing had happened then because Phil had been very happily married.

Their current relationship started last year when Sherry had come back to Lackey College to work in the library. Phil's wife, Mary Jane, had died right before she'd arrived. They'd connected at sporting events and started to date; well, sort of date. Phil still had some grief associated with his wife's death, so it had all gone very slowly, which suited Sherry fine. She'd almost sworn off men. Then she and Phil started to click.

The plane landed smoothly, interrupting Sherry's musings. They grabbed their carry-ons and filed off the plane. When they got to the hotel in the rental car, Phil looked at Sherry and asked, "How many rooms?"

"One," she said. "It's okay, isn't it?"

"Yes."

When they found the room, Sherry broke the silence. "Was it too forward asking for one room?"

"Not at all," Phil said as he came next to her. "I think we've put this off long enough."

"Me too." Sherry leaned in and kissed him.

The kiss lasted a long time, and several others followed. While they fumbled with a few buttons along the way, they accomplished what they both wanted. Afterward, Phil looked at Sherry lying beside him, such a beautiful woman. He found the notion that she would be attracted to him amazing. He felt incredibly lucky and only slightly guilty.

The next morning, they arrived early at the store where Barbara Fairchild worked. Following Ralph's directions, Phil had no trouble finding the break room. Sherry went to the tile display where Beth had stood watch, and Phil headed toward the break room.

Ten feet from the break room, right before he had to commit to going down the short hallway leading to it, the door opened. Phil diverted quickly, hoping no one saw the maneuver. Two guys came out and disappeared into the store. Phil circled back, and this time made it into the break room. He took down the camera and left the room otherwise undisturbed. When he slipped out of the door, Sherry was talking to one of the salesmen. Phil walked by them and went down a nearby aisle. He waited in the aisle, feigning interest in the nuts and bolts in front of him. A few minutes later, Sherry met him.

They hugged, and Sherry said, "A salesman came by. He might have been going to the break room, so I flagged him down. I don't think he saw you come out. I got rid of him as soon as I could."

"Good job. It's the reason there are two of us on this trip."

"Is that the reason," Sherry said with a twinkle in her eye. "We still have the hotel room. We have time to go back and take a nap or whatever."

"Great idea. I vote for whatever," Phil said.

They went back to the hotel and didn't appear again until lunch. They spent the afternoon exploring Salt Lake City. Since Phil had grown up in Arizona, the wide-open vistas in Utah were not new to him. Sherry, a native Pennsylvanian, found the whole look and feel of the city very different. They had an early dinner and returned to the hotel. To get back at a reasonable hour, they took an early flight the next day. When they got to Lackey, Sherry told Phil she'd better get home to her mother. Phil said he understood, and they parted.

Chapter Thirteen

THE NEXT MORNING, PHIL TOOK the camera to Ralph at his computer repair/computer sales store. Phil worked part time at the store. He'd retired from his teaching job at Lackey College. He didn't need any money, so he didn't take any pay from Ralph. He liked working at the store. It gave him a chance to be around people.

"This should be easy to edit," Ralph said. "Barbara posted accounts in the chat room of the two run-ins she had with the jerk. I know the days I'm looking for. You mind the store while I go to the back to look at the video?"

After fifteen minutes Ralph called Phil back.

"I haven't looked at all of it by any means. I found the first encounter. Here, put on the headphones, the sound is an important part of the story."

Phil put on the headphones, and Ralph started the video. Barbara came into the break room and sat alone for a few seconds. Then a man joined her, presumably Tom Kelly. Barbara stiffened when he came in. Tom pulled a chair next to hers and put his arm around her. She tried unsuccessfully to remove his arm. Then Tom said, "Look Barbara, loosen up. You like me. I can't understand why you're resisting it. Let's go out."

"It's against store policy, Tom. You're my supervisor. We can't date," replied Barbara, still trying to remove his arm.

"Okay, if you won't go out with me, maybe you won't be working here much longer."

Barbara got out of her chair and turned on him. "You're saying you'd get me fired if I don't go out with you? Really?"

"Yeah, that's what I'm saying."

"You can't!"

"Oh yes I can." Tom got closer and put his arms around the startled Barbara and tried to kiss her. She turned her face away, wriggled out of his grasp, and tried to slap him. He caught her arm before the slap landed and laughed.

"Think about it," he said as he went out the door.

Ralph stopped the video there.

"Wow." Phil removed the headphones. "He's awful. Like she said in the chat room, he's threatening to fire her unless she goes out with him."

"It'll be interesting to see how it all plays out. Did you notice Barbara at the store when you were there? She may have quit or already been fired."

"No, we didn't see Barbara. Then again, we weren't looking. We were in and out really fast."

"Okay, fair enough. If you go out and monitor the store, I'll find the next time they're together in the break room. She called in sick for two days after what we saw. Eventually she had to come back to work. I should be able to find the next one, the one where he hit her."

A half hour later Ralph came out. "There is only the one other encounter. I caught Tom asking one of the other workers about Barbara calling in sick," Ralph said. "Then she had another woman with her in the break room the day she came back to work. Tom appeared really peeved when he finally had a chance to be alone with her. A big dustup followed. She told him she'd never go out with him, and he hit her. He avoided her face where the effects would show. He hit her on the upper arm, hard. I'm sure there's a bruise. Then he laughed and said she'd better change her mind fast or he'd fire her for sure."

"He hit her," Phil said. "We'd better move fast on this one."

"Yeah, I couldn't believe it. We heard about it on the chat site, still it bothered me. He hauled back and hit her hard."

"We're all meeting at your place right after the store closes, right?"

"No, Beth gets off at the hospital a half hour after I close, so 6:00 not 5:30."

"Good enough."

****

When they all got to Ralph and Beth's apartment, Ralph started the video on his computer. It only contained the two episodes. They all recoiled when Tom hit Barbara.

"That's outrageous!" Sherry said. "I want to nail this guy. He shouldn't be able to get away with this."

"I agree," Phil said. "He's awful. And we'd better move fast. He might have already fired her."

"Or maybe she quit," Beth said. "No job's worth the abuse she's taking."

"I hope she hasn't." said Sherry. "In any event, we should adjust the email we sent to Rochelle Martin and get it off to her tonight. My idea is to send her the videos and tell her to show them at the first meeting. She's in danger!"

****

The same evening in Salt Lake City, Barbara Fairchild got her three-year-old daughter, Julia, to bed with a minimum of fuss. She didn't like the stress of being a single mother. She sat back and wondered why she'd had such bad luck with men. First, Brad, her no-good husband, who'd abandoned her right before Julia's birth. Now she had to quit her job at the store before Tom Kelly fired her. *Why can't I find a sensible man?* she wondered.

She turned on her computer. Before quitting at the store, she'd better check job postings. Maybe she'd hang on at the store long enough to find another job. She didn't want to quit without having anything lined up. She was bound and determined not to move back in with her parents. *Still, what about recommendations?* She wasn't sure what kind of recommendation she would get from the store. Any new job would ask her to list her supervisor at her last job. The whole thing made her so mad. She started to get thoroughly depressed.

She checked her email, mostly junk. She saw one cheery email from her high school friend Charlotte. She'd told Charlotte about her problems with Tom Kelly, and Charlotte had been very supportive. Unfortunately, neither of them came up with an easy way out of the problem. Charlotte had urged her to go to Tom's boss. Barbara suspected it wouldn't work. She didn't have any proof of what Tom did. Now she had the bruise on her upper arm. Then again, the bruise might have happened lots of ways.

She paused when she came to the email from the INHSSSA group. She didn't have the faintest idea who they were. The first short paragraph startled her:

> You don't know who we are, but we know quite a bit about you. Most importantly we are aware your boss, Tom Kelly, treats you terribly. We would like to help you with this situation.

She read further. Then she read the whole thing again. These people, whoever they were, had put a camera in the break room. They had videos of Tom threatening to fire her if she wouldn't go out with him and hitting her after she refused. They wanted her to go to HR in corporate headquarters and lodge a sexual harassment complaint against Tom. They said she'd be getting two copies of the video, one to save and one to give to HR. Who were these people, and what did INHSSSA stand for? She couldn't even pronounce it.

Barbara closed her email and paced around her small apartment. She didn't want to go through the sexual harassment business. She'd heard stories about how it usually turned out. The proceeding became more about defending the woman making the complaint than about defending the man. She hadn't done anything to attract Tom Kelly's attention, but he'd try to paint it that way. He'd claim she came on to him. Thinking about it made her mad. Then she thought about the videos, if there were videos. They should show what a jerk he was. And he hit her—no one deserves to be hit. It all turned on the videos. He'd always managed to find ways for them to be alone in the break room. If the videos were as good as these people said, she'd have a great case. They'd fire Tom, and she'd keep her job.

She went back to her computer and logged on to the chat room. She followed the directions and made a simple post to see if INHSSSA followed through like they said they would. She said she'd received their email and asked what INHSSSA stood for.

****

Early the next morning, Beth found Barbara's post and sent a brief reply. Phil left in the morning for a quick trip to New York City to mail the package. There was still no news from Rochelle Martin in Milwaukee. Beth found the waiting difficult. She guessed sexual harassment complaints often took a long time.

Chapter Fourteen

THE WEDNESDAY AFTER HE RETURNED from New York City, Phil got to his lunch group early. He found Bert in a discussion with Andy Roberts, the restaurant owner. Andy tuned all the TVs to the channel the lunch group didn't like. Not surprisingly, he didn't share the lunch group's political views. He kept telling them they should eat in the main room, so they'd find out what the real people thought. Despite the differences, Andy got along with the group, and they often bantered back and forth.

"What are you two arguing about this time?" Phil asked as he approached.

"Immigration," Andy said. "Bert believes in open borders. We can't let in anyone who wants to come—we'd be swamped."

Bert replied, "I keep telling Andy it's not simple. We have to deal with the people who are already here and their kids. Lots of their kids are citizens. And we need to enforce our immigration system when we have a sensible system."

"A country is made up of citizens. We should kick noncitizens out," Andy said. "It's real simple."

"You two aren't going to agree on this one," Phil interrupted. "Here come the others. Come on Bert, let's go to the back room."

When they were seated, Bob asked, "Bert, what were you and Andy talking about?"

"Immigration. Andy wants to kick all noncitizens out. And he's for spending lots of money for border protection. He doesn't realize how complex the issue is."

"I agree," Jeremy said. "We've got a large number of illegal immigrants living in the country. Lots of them are couples, couples with children who were born here. Those children are citizens. If we kicked out all the noncitizens, we'd be breaking up those families. There's an irony there. The official immigration policy is based on reuniting families."

"You're right, Jeremy," Bert said. "Andy's proposal is inhumane. We have to give those living in the country a chance to become citizens."

"Yes, we'd all agree," William said. "Then it's more difficult. After we give those in the country a path to citizenship, what do we do? Andy's got a point. We can't have open borders. We'd be a magnet for people from poor countries who want to come here for economic reasons. It might be good for our economy to have more immigration, but not unlimited immigration."

"Don't we have programs to let people in on short-term work permits?" Sally asked.

"Yes, there are programs for temporary agricultural workers," George said. "I've heard they work well. They're small. Maybe they would work in other industries. It would be hard though. Farms need lots of seasonal workers for harvest. It's not the same in other industries."

"It's the basic approach to immigration we need to figure out," Phil said. "The current system mostly grants long-term visas for family unification or political asylum. I guess there are also long-term visas for foreign workers for jobs where there are no qualified U.S. workers."

"It's how I'm here," William said. "I'm not a citizen, so the econ department had to fill out a bunch of paperwork testifying I was the best person available. Basically, they had to say my qualifications surpassed those of any citizen on their list of applicants."

"Canada does it differently," Sally said. "They tilt their system toward immigrants with skills they need—more like William's case. Here, the people we bring in to unify families might not be the kind of people we need. And the same goes for those seeking political asylum. They might not be the kind of people we need."

Bob entered the discussion. "I want to get a word in. One's view on immigration is part of the split in the country. If you are poorly educated, you fear competition from immigrants. If you are well educated, maybe you should worry a little too. We all know the econ department is better because of William. And our math department has two Russians who are very sharp."

"Yes, and physics has a great guy from India," Bert said. "We're better off if we can attract the best and the brightest from everywhere in the world."

"It's a big political problem," George said. "The country is split on immigration. We can't pass an immigration bill in Congress. Bob has part of it. Low-wage workers fear immigrants. Law and order types like Andy emphasize the illegal part of illegal immigrant. They see granting them a path to citizenship as giving in to law breakers. They call it granting amnesty. It's a mess."

"What, again?" Jeremy said in mock shock. "A problem we can't solve at lunch. I for one have to get back."

"Wait," George said. "Margaret told me we're going ahead with the Katel lecture. It will be about a month from now. I need all of you to help calm everyone down."

"No fun being president of the faculty assembly, huh George," Bert said.

"You're right. At times it's not." With that, lunch ended.

Chapter Fifteen

IN MILWAUKEE THE NEXT MORNING, Rochelle Martin received a call to come to Mrs. Higgins' office. Rochelle had a rush job when the call came, so she made an appointment for two o'clock. She was very nervous when she finally got there. Mrs. Higgins offered her a chair and took a folder from her desk.

"We've investigated your complaint thoroughly," Mrs. Higgins said. "Basically, our investigation found no support for your claim. Mr. Turbridge categorically denies the charges. None of the other personnel we talked to had seen any behavior matching what you claimed. Sam Turbridge has been a lawyer at this firm for twelve years. He's a full partner. His record here is spotless. It comes down to his word against yours. I presented my findings to the managing partner, Mr. Sites, and we've decided to make a generous offer. We will move your assignment as soon as another secretarial position becomes available. You will not have to continue to work with Mr. Turbridge. We don't want employees working together who can't get along. We can't do anything more, and you're not to discuss this with anyone. Mr. Turbridge is aware of this offer. No one else is."

"You don't believe me. Is that it?" Rochelle asked. "You think Sam and I can't get along. It's more. He can't keep his hands off me."

"No, you're not right. We don't know who to believe. Frankly, we are trying to be nice to you. We don't have to offer a transfer."

"Is it because I'm younger than he is or because I'm a woman? Would Mr. Sites ever believe a woman? Or would he always side with the man?"

"Calm down, Rochelle. Consider things from our point of view. We're getting two contradictory accounts."

"I can't believe no one else is aware of what's going on. Did you interview his previous secretary?"

"Mr. Turbridge's previous secretary was Joe Mills, the only male who has ever held a secretarial position at the firm, so no, we didn't interview him. We didn't see a reason to."

"Will anything be in Sam's personnel file? I wouldn't want anyone else to go through what I've had to go through."

"No, it wouldn't. Especially when it is an unsubstantiated allegation."

Rochelle stewed for a while. "I get a transfer when a spot comes along. Will I take a pay cut if the position is at a lower rung on the pay scale?"

"I wouldn't believe so. You shouldn't have to. Honestly, I don't know."

Rochelle made up her mind. She stood. "This is not satisfactory. I'm being punished, and nothing is happening to Sam Turbridge. I want a meeting with you and Mr. Sites. I never got a chance to testify in this matter. Can we arrange a meeting?"

"I wanted to finish this today. Still, I guess you should have a chance to plead your case. Mr. Sites won't be happy about it. He'll only grant you fifteen minutes at the most. Let me call his secretary to see what I can arrange."

Mrs. Higgins placed the call. It wasn't easy to get on Site's schedule. They finally found fifteen minutes starting at 4:45 the next Monday.

As Rochelle got up to leave, Mrs. Higgins said, "I hope you're not holding out any hope for this meeting. It's not going to change anything. I only agreed to it because we don't like to see disgruntled employees. Mr. Sites is not one to change his mind."

Rochelle smiled. "We'll see." Actually, she felt good as she walked back to her office. She had an ace in the hole in this whole proceeding. She looked forward to the meeting.

Chapter Sixteen

BARBARA FAIRCHILD IN SALT LAKE City received a small package in the mail. She had to wait until Julia got settled to view the video. As the note said, the package contained two thumb drives. She put one of them in her computer. The first video showed her getting into the break room, and then Tom Kelly came in and sat beside her. She remembered the scene. Clearly, Tom threatened to fire her if she didn't go out with him. She was disgusted at how easily he blocked her attempted slap. The second scene showed the next encounter—the one where he hit her. She found it tough to watch.

After viewing the contents of the first thumb drive, she inserted the second. She found it to be identical. These INHSSSA people were efficient. They'd answered her one query right on time, and they'd come through with the videos they'd promised. Now, did she want to comply with their wishes? She considered her situation for a while. *I don't have much to lose.* If she went to corporate headquarters and put in a sexual harassment complaint, at worst she'd quit if they turned her down. She had decided to quit anyway. And maybe things would all work. Tom should not be able to get away with what he had done.

She went on the corporate website to find the requirements for making a sexual harassment claim. The instructions weren't clear at all; all they talked about was a grievance procedure. Barbara guessed the sexual harassment complaint had to be covered under the grievance policy. She sure had a grievance against Tom. Also, she figured there were probably other women who'd had troubles with Tom.

She wondered why she hadn't considered filing a grievance before. Actually, she knew why. Her mother and father had drilled into her to always find a way to get along. She'd followed their advice, but it didn't work, particularly with men. She'd tried to get along with Brad. Heck, she thought they were in love. Now Tom. At first, they had gotten along. Then he wanted to date. Though she didn't find him attractive at all, he didn't pick up any of the hints she'd made. He seemed oblivious. Now he'd become violent.

The next morning, Barbara called the HR department and made an appointment for 4:00. The person she talked to told her she'd call her boss and tell him Barbara needed to take off at 3:30. She liked not having to talk to Tom herself and managed to spend her entire break running a short errand at the far end of the store and hanging out in the bathroom. She didn't run into Tom until mid-afternoon when he came by her station.

"What are you doing in HR?" he asked.

"A couple of things about my files there aren't straight. No big deal," she replied. "We're allowed to take a trip to personnel on company time, aren't we?"

Tom looked a little peeved. "Yes."

Barbara found a parking space at the corporate headquarters. She'd never actually been there before. She applied for the job at the store, and an HR person had come to the store to help the new employees fill out all the paperwork. Barbara went in the front door and looked at the listings of the offices. She found HR on the third floor.

At the HR office, she gave the receptionist her name and said she had a 4:00 appointment. After a few minutes a man came out of an office. "Barbara Fairchild?"

"Yes."

"I'm Mr. Wolfe. Please come into my office."

Barbara followed Mr. Wolfe into his office. She was a little startled. She'd assumed a woman would be handling sexual harassment complaints. Then she realized she'd only said she had a grievance.

"What can I do for you?" Mr. Wolfe asked when they were both seated.

Barbara gulped. "I want to file a grievance; actually, a sexual harassment complaint. Am I in the right place?"

"Yes, I deal with all employee grievances, even this kind of complaint. Do you have anything in writing?"

"No, should I?"

"You don't have to. Eventually, we'll have to have a written record. Do you mind if I record this meeting? I find having a recording helps me make my reports."

Already nervous, Barbara didn't find this helpful. Clearly, he wanted to record the meeting. She had to let him, even if she didn't want to. She said, "Okay."

"So, who's involved, and what's going on? Use your own words; we'll put in the legal sounding words if this whole thing goes any further."

Barbara heaved a big sigh. "My boss, Tom Kelly. He's been asking me for dates, and he won't accept a no. Last week, he threatened to fire me if I didn't go out with him. He's arranged so no one else is on break the same time I am, and he comes in and hassles me."

"Hassles you? Only words or is there touching involved?"

"There's touching. And he's been violent with me. Here, let me show you." Barbara pulled back her sweater and showed Mr. Wolfe her upper arm. "This bruise is the result of the time he hit me last week."

"That looks like a serious bruise. You say he hit you there."

"Yeah, he's smart enough to know he can hit me where it wouldn't normally show."

"I'm very sorry you're having to go through this," Mr. Wolfe said. "I'll certainly write up what you've been telling me. In all honesty though, usually we need more than one person's account. Do you have any witnesses? Is there anyone else who's seen any of this?"

"No. Like I said, he schedules my breaks so I'm the only one in the break room. While there may be people who've seen him go in there when I'm there, they can't see anything. The door's always closed."

"Okay, I have enough to write up the case. Is there anything else you'd like to add?"

Barbara paused. Tom would deny everything. The whole case would come down to her word against his like the INHSSSA people warned her. This is where the videos came in. They told her to use the videos if she needed them, and she sure did. "I do have something else," she said. "I want to use your computer. Okay?"

"Why?" Mr. Wolfe asked as he watched Barbara extract a thumb drive from her purse.

"I have this thumb drive, and there's a video on it. I'll plug into the USB port on your computer."

When Mr. Wolfe didn't reach for the thumb drive Barbara offered, she took the initiative. "Here, let me show you," she said motioning for him to scoot over so she had room to put the thumb drive in the computer.

After a few seconds, Barbara had the video on Mr. Wolfe's computer. As the video started, she retreated to the other side of the desk. At first the sound was too low, so Barbara showed him how to increase the volume. Then she started the video again.

Mr. Wolfe watched the video clearly showing Tom trying to get a date and then threatening to fire her. The second scene, the one where he hit her, made Mr. Wolfe gasp.

When the video finished, Barbara filled the silence. "See, it's like I told you. These two encounters happened last week. Tom can't deny the evidence. He threatened me and he hit me."

"Calm down, Ms. Fairchild. I have a number of questions. First, you don't have the right to make videos of what goes on at your workplace."

"I didn't make the video," Barbara shot back.

"What? How'd you get the video?"

"I got an email from people who call themselves the I. N. H. S. S. S. A. Group. The acronym stands for 'it's not he said she said anymore.' They said they'd provide the video if I'd file a sexual harassment case against Tom. Here I am, and they sent me the video. I don't know who they are or why they're helping me. The video tells the story. What are you going to do?"

"This is most unusual. I've never been involved with anything like this. Still, making a video like this is illegal. Ms. Fairchild, these sexual harassment cases often result in court cases, and in court you can't use evidence obtained illegally."

A little taken aback, Barbara said, "There is no reason for this to go to court. The video's clear as day. He's a sexual harasser. There's evidence of unwanted touching, sexual blackmail, and violent behavior. Can't you admit that much?"

"Yes, of course."

"So, the way I see it, there's no way the company wants a person like Tom being a supervisor. Can't we find a way of getting rid of him without having to worry about courts and what's legal and illegal evidence? This seems crystal clear."

"Employees have rights," Mr. Wolfe said. "If we dismiss him for cause, he has the right to know why. And he has rights to appeal. He can have legal representation at the appeal hearing."

"Okay, let me tell you the rest of what the INHSSSA people told me. They said if Tom isn't fired, they would put this video on the company website. The company doesn't want the video there for the whole internet to see."

"You can't do that!" Mr. Wolfe exclaimed.

"I didn't say I would, I said they would. I don't control them. They're not me." Barbara was amazed she had the nerve to talk to Mr. Wolfe this way. His putting up barriers had annoyed her immensely.

"Okay, whatever. I'm going to have to bring my boss into this matter. Do you mind waiting? This is serious enough. I should be able to interrupt him right now. Please sit tight for a few minutes."

Barbara nodded, and Mr. Wolfe hurried out of the room. Barbara recognized she had perspired heavily. The whole proceeding had been nerve-wracking. Still, she felt satisfied with what she'd said. The videos were clear. There's no way she'd have been there without them. They showed Tom doing things he clearly shouldn't be doing.

After fifteen minutes, as Barbara began to become annoyed, Mr. Wolfe came back in the office followed by an older gentleman. Mr. Wolfe introduced him as Mr. Anderson, the head of HR for the corporation.

Mr. Anderson shook Barbara's hand. "Ms. Fairchild, we understand you're having trouble with your supervisor."

"Not just trouble," Barbara snapped. "Mr. Wolfe, let's show him the video? Things will move along quicker. Okay?"

"Please, let's all be calm," Mr. Anderson said. He talked in a manner Barbara found very condescending, as if he should be in charge. At that point, Barbara didn't need his superior attitude.

Barbara went to Mr. Wolfe's computer and turned on the video again. "Look at this."

No one said anything when the video finished, so Barbara filled the silence. "This is what I have to live with at work. Clearly sexual harassment. Can we all agree?"

Mr. Anderson finally ended the silence. "I don't know if I've ever seen anything like this. Yes, it is clearly sexual harassment. Kelly should be fired—fired today."

"Is this evidence we can use?" Mr. Wolfe asked.

"No, probably isn't, but we don't need the video to be legal evidence. We have Ms. Fairchild's testimony, and she showed you the bruise from the time he hit her. We can't have supervisors hitting employees. We can't have Kelly working for us. Not one day longer."

"Thank you," Barbara said.

"You're welcome," Mr. Anderson said. "I have a daughter who's a little older than you, and she's told me about bosses like Kelly. Frankly, I thought she was exaggerating. This video shows me different. I don't care if the video's legal evidence or not. It's clear."

He turned to Barbara. "Take tomorrow off. I'll send a notice to your store manager. We might need a day to remove Kelly. You can go back to work the day after tomorrow. You won't have to worry about Kelly. He'll be gone. Is there anything else we can do for you?"

The change shocked Barbara. "No, I don't think there's anything else. Thank you."

"No, thank you. We need to get rid of employees like Kelly," Mr. Anderson said. "He's a ticking time bomb. If you weren't his chosen target, he'd have probably been after another female employee. This corporation cannot have people like him working for us."

After Barbara walked out, the two men looked at each other, and Mr. Anderson said, "I worry about her."

"What do you mean?" Mr. Wolfe asked.

"When we fire Tom Kelly tomorrow, he's going to know she made a complaint. He knows she is in HR today. He's going to put two and two together, and it'll point to Barbara. He might well try to get back at her. He's already been violent."

"What can we do? If we tell him to stay away from Barbara, he'll know it's because of her for sure."

"I know. I think I'll get Barbara security for a week or so. There's no need to tell her. I'd feel better about everything if we know she'll be safe. We owe her that much."

Barbara was delighted when she got to her car. Everything had worked out. In the end, Mr. Anderson turned out to be incredibly nice. Still, if he'd had a son instead of a daughter, there's no telling how things might have turned out. Often events turned on little things. Today had been her day.

When she got home, she'd tell the INHSSSA people how things had worked out. As she drove off, she started composing her message.

Chapter Seventeen

BETH AND SHERRY SAW BARBARA'S post at about the same time. After Beth showed it to Ralph, she got a text about it from Sherry. Sherry said she'd call Phil to inform him. Beth and Ralph were excited.

"Wow, this happened in a hurry," Ralph said. "The other one is still going on as far as we can tell. Rochelle Martin is still waiting to see what's happened to her complaint."

"Yes, while she lost the first round, she still has her meeting with the big boss. This one should have gone faster. Rochelle hasn't shown anyone the video yet. We told Barbara to use it in her first meeting. She's in danger. Remember, he slugged her. While Rochelle is hassled, she's not in physical danger. We wanted Barbara to get fast action, and it worked."

"Yes, it worked," Ralph said. "Now we can celebrate. I sure like the idea of celebrating with you a lot more than high fiving Phil." He grinned.

"Will Sherry and Phil celebrate the same way?"

"I'm not sure. I hope so. They did take the trip to Salt Lake City together. Has she told you anything about how many rooms they got?"

"No, silly, we don't talk about that kind of thing."

"Don't girls talk about everything?"

****

Sherry reconsidered the idea of giving Phil the details on the phone. Instead, she called to tell him she had news for him. She'd see him in twenty minutes. She told her mother she had an errand to run and hurried to her car.

When Sherry got to Phil's house, he greeted her at the front door with a kiss. After they broke apart, he asked, "What's so important?"

"Barbara Fairchild just posted about her meeting with HR. Everything worked. It worked spectacularly. The store is going to fire Tom Kelly. They even told her not to go into work tomorrow while they get rid of him. The video did the trick. Like we all understood, it's hard to look at the video and not recognize what a jerk Kelly is."

"Congratulations, Sherry. You've had your first success. Does it feel good?"

"I don't know... yes, I guess it does. Why?"

"Well, when Ralph and I were doing the V business, poisoning the people, I always felt good about getting away with it. I felt good about everything working. I couldn't tell you whether I ever felt good about accomplishing my goal. I mean... I don't know what I mean. It was so removed from Jake McMahan. Aren't you doing this partly to get back at men who sexually harassed you? And aren't they pretty far removed from Tom Kelly in Salt Lake City?"

"Oh, I see what you mean," Sherry answered. "Yes, the guy in Salt Lake City is nowhere near the guys who bothered me. Still, I feel good. It's the first time I'm fighting back. I told you I became a librarian to avoid the aggressive men in the business world. It's complicated. Maybe deep down I felt cowardly. Now I'm not."

"I can see. We're never going to stop sexual harassment."

"Everyone has to contribute, and the more I thought about what you two did as V, the more I admired you for taking action. I wanted to do something, anything. Too much of my life, I've been running. I not sure how many of these cases we can do. To fully answer your first question, I'm more than happy. I'm thrilled! I'm taking action, and it's working."

"It's a good feeling, I'm sure. Where does it all stop? Ralph and I only had so much poison, so we had a natural stopping place."

"Good question," Sherry replied. "We're at the start. I'm not sure how many I want to do. I do know two is nowhere near enough."

"Okay. Do you have another person in mind?"

"Yeah, Beth and I have talked about it. The next one is more or less local. McKeesport, southeast of Pittsburgh. We can drive to plant the cameras. The girl is Dorothy McGuire, a second-grade teacher. Her school principal is harassing her. It's a little like the last one. He keeps asking her for dates. Actually, it's worse. He's married."

"We'll have to put the cameras in the school. Won't it be hard? Aren't schools very secure? Lots of them have surveillance cameras of their own."

"I'm sure you and Ralph can figure it out. You two know how to pick locks and avoid cameras, don't you?"

"We'll see. This one might be tougher. It's good McKeesport is close. We might have to make several trips."

"I've got to go, Phil. I told my mother I had to run an errand. I can't be out too late."

"Okay. While I understand, I don't have to like it."

Sherry laughed and gave him a big kiss. "No, you don't have to like it."

****

The next afternoon, Phil drove to McKeesport. He easily located the elementary school where Dorothy McGuire taught. As he suspected, it wasn't going to be easy to plant cameras inside the school. There were maybe thirty yards of lawn and then a big circular drive in front of the school. The sides of the school and its playground in back were ringed by a line of trees. There weren't any houses right next to it. He'd timed his arrival to coincide with the end of the school day. As a result, things were very crowded. School buses were loading, kids were walking away from the school, and cars were in line waiting for pickup. He stayed in the flow of traffic and drove away from the school.

On the drive to McKeesport, he'd puzzled over the difficulty of surveilling a grade school. He couldn't set himself up with binoculars to check out the building. At least not during school or when any kids were around. He'd be arrested as a pervert. And now he realized it had been stupid to get there when school had just finished, way too much activity. He decided to find a Starbucks while things calmed down at the school.

When he drove back by the school an hour and a half later, only a few cars were left in the parking lot. He turned into the circular drive in front of the school. He quickly photographed the front door. His camera had lots of megapixels, so the picture should enlarge well. He'd been quick and hoped he'd held the camera steady. He only took one picture and made his way out.

He would have to do the rest of his surveillance on foot. He went back to the shopping center closest to the school. After checking around, he put on his disguise, a wig and mustache. He didn't think he had to do a great job. He didn't expect to have to talk to anyone. He checked himself in the rearview mirror, and he looked okay.

He saw only two cars on his leisurely stroll to the school. He passed the school and ducked behind the trees on the far side. When he saw no activity surrounding the school and no cars were coming, he approached from the side. He didn't have to get too close, because he had confidence his camera would be good. After taking the picture, he hurried back to the trees. He figured pictures including the side door and the front door would be enough. These pictures would tell him if the school had any cameras. He stayed behind his tree to watch the last of the cars take off from the parking lot. He checked his watch. At 5:30, the last car—the principal, a teacher, a secretary or a janitor—drove away. He waited another hour to see if a police car came by to check the school. No one showed. He decided to stroll back to his car. The area was almost deserted, and he returned to his car without anyone getting a close look at him. Only a few cars had driven by during his walk.

Chapter Eighteen

IN MILWAUKEE ON MONDAY, ROCHELLE Martin checked her purse again. She had the thumb drive. She felt like she'd checked ten or twelve times already. *What did I think it would do, jump out of my purse?* She knocked on Mrs. Higgins' office door at 4:40 and was ushered in.

"Rochelle," Mrs. Higgins said. "It's good to be punctual with Mr. Sites. He is a very busy man. Don't sit down. Let's go."

They walked to the other end of the hallway to the corner office. Mr. Higgins introduced her to Mr. Sites' secretary, Joellen. Rochelle had seen her at meetings but didn't really know her. Rochelle sat down and looked around. Despite having the same arrangement as hers, with the secretary in an office in front of the lawyer's office, this space felt different. Everything was bigger. Joellen's office space exceeded Sam's, let alone hers. She wondered how big Mr. Sites' office would be.

After five minutes or so, during which Rochelle again reassured herself she had the thumb drive, someone walked out of Mr. Sites' office. Two minutes later, Joellen told them to go in.

The corner office was huge. Mr. Sites walked up to them as they entered. "Good to see you, Susan," he said to Mrs. Higgins. Then he turned to Rochelle. "You must be Ms. Martin?"

"Yes." Rochelle shook his outstretched hand.

"Here, let's sit around the conference table." Mr. Sites gestured toward a table on one side of the office. There might have been twelve chairs around the table. They went to one end. Mrs. Higgins sat on one side. Mr. Sites sat at the end, and he motioned for Rochelle to sit across from Mrs. Higgins.

After they'd taken their seats, Mr. Sites started the proceedings. "Ms. Martin, we did a thorough investigation of your very serious complaint. We found no evidence to corroborate your claims. Sam Turbridge is very offended to be accused. He categorically denied the charges. We didn't find anyone who witnessed the behavior in your complaint. In this kind of case, it is best to separate the two individuals involved, and we made a promise to transfer you when it becomes possible. Frankly, what more do you want from us?"

While nervous, Rochelle had prepared herself. "I want you to believe me," she replied.

Mr. Sites stared at her, then spoke. "I have your complaint and Mr. Turbridge's denial, and you want me to believe you and not him? Do I have it right?"

Mr. Sites was clearly annoyed. Things weren't going well. She needed the video. Rochelle wouldn't get anywhere without it. "I have evidence. It will show you I'm the one you should believe."

"What kind of evidence?" Mrs. Higgins asked.

"I want you to look at the videos on this." Rochelle held up the thumb drive.

"Wait, wait," Mr. Sites said. "You can't go around taking videos of people without their permission."

"I didn't take the videos," Rochelle responded.

"Then, how did you get them?"

"They were sent to me by people I don't know. They call themselves the I. N. H. S. S. S. A. Group."

"What?"

"It's an acronym. It stands for it's not he said she said anymore. It's not important where the videos came from. What's important is what they show. Can we get them on a computer? They're short. It won't take much time."

"I'm not sure I like this," Mr. Sites said.

Mrs. Higgins spoke up. "Thomas, if these videos show Ms. Martin has a good case, we need to see them. We can't have sexual harassment, not the kind she's talking about. She claimed unwanted touching. This isn't a secretary who objects to off-color jokes. We should see the videos."

"Okay. Okay."

The three of them trooped over to Mr. Sites' desk, and Mrs. Higgins loaded the thumb drive in his computer.

Rochelle explained, "There are two videos. The first one is short. It only shows two episodes. They're very clear. The other video covers an entire week; it shows more of the behavior I'm objecting to."

Mrs. Higgins played the first video. When it finished, the room went silent. Finally, Rochelle said, "You see I'm not making it up. It's like I said in my complaint. He paws me all the time."

Mr. Sites responded, "We'd better see the second video, Susan."

When the second video finished, Mr. Sites walked back to the table and the others followed. After they were seated, Mr. Sites spoke up. "We owe you an apology, Ms. Martin. You were clearly right; you're being sexually harassed. The videos are clear. Now we've got a big problem."

"A big problem? I don't understand," Rochelle said.

"This evidence isn't admissible. It can't have been obtained legally. As you're aware, this building is always locked. Visitors have to call security to get in. The only way these people, whoever they are, came into the building is by breaking and entering. It's illegal. The evidence would never stand up in court."

"This isn't a court," Rochelle said.

Mrs. Higgins spoke next. "Rochelle, these kinds of personnel issues often find their way into court. If we start proceedings to terminate Sam Turbridge, he has rights. He might sue us, and then we're in the courts."

"The video is as clear as it can be. He's guilty," Rochelle said, very annoyed.

"Calm down, Ms. Martin, we have to figure out what to do. Maybe we can come to an agreement with Sam," Mr. Sites said. "If he leaves of his own accord. If he quits, we don't fire him, the courts won't get involved. It's going to be tricky. We'd have to show him the videos, and he'd know they're not admissible in court."

"I'm not sure I like the outcome. If he quits, he walks away without being punished, right?"

"I'm sure he'll be punished," Mr. Sites said. "It'll be hard for him to find a job nearly as good as this one. Listen, Ms. Martin, this is all a shock to us. I haven't figured out quite what we'll do. First, I guess we'll confront Sam. Then we'll see how things proceed."

Mr. Sites glanced at the clock on the wall. "I'm sorry. This has all taken longer than I'd imagined. I'm late for my next engagement. I will be back in touch with both of you. I've got to figure out what to do."

With that, he grabbed his briefcase and hurried out.

Rochelle and Mrs. Higgins sat back in their chairs and watched him walk out of the room. After a few moments, Mrs. Higgins smiled and said, "You and your videos sure threw him for a loop. I not sure I've ever seen him so confused and flustered."

"I can't say I'm sorry."

"You've dropped a bomb on his desk. This firm abhors controversy. We're awfully conservative. A scandal is the last thing Mr. Sites wants on his watch. At the same time, he understands what you've been going through. He can't tolerate having unwanted touching or any other form of sexual harassment. And he wouldn't have me working for him if he did."

"So, we're not finished with this yet."

"No." Mrs. Higgins stood. "No, there'll be at least one more round before we're finished."

Chapter Nineteen

THE GROUP GATHERED IN THE back of Ralph's store to discuss their project. Sherry took the lead. "I guess you were right, Phil. The lawyers where Rochelle Martin works balked at using the video evidence."

"I still bet she'll get rid of her boss," Beth said.

"While we don't have the details yet, it looks like it'll happen. It's good Rochelle seems to be enjoying the whole thing. Her posts are upbeat. She knows she has them nervous. And you're right, Beth. No matter how it turns out, she won't have to work with Sam Turbridge much longer."

Ralph broke in. "Let's change the subject. It doesn't look like the security at the McKeesport school is very good. It'll be easy to pick the lock. And there don't appear to be any surveillance cameras. Are we ready to get started?"

"I don't see any reason to wait," Sherry answered. "Phil and I can drive to McKeesport this Friday afternoon. I have the afternoon off."

"It'll be good to have two of you. One can be the lookout," Ralph said.

****

In the evening in Salt Lake City, Barbara Fairchild put her daughter to bed. Things at work had been odd. Everyone wondered what had happened to Tom Kelly. Several people asked her if she knew anything. She'd claimed to have no idea. They'd pulled in a supervisor from one of the other stores to plug in temporarily. The woman seemed to be competent, and things were going smoothly for Barbara. She looked forward to going to work, since she didn't have to worry about being hassled by Tom.

As she got settled in front of her computer at the kitchen table, a loud crash came from Julia's room. Barbara ran back. Julia was screaming, so she dashed in and scooped her up. Julia's window was broken, and glass littered the room. Fortunately, Barbara had on her slippers. Shouts came from out front, so she returned to the living room and carefully looked out the front window. Barbara's apartment, on the second story, overlooked the front lawn and the parking lot. Two men wrestled on the lawn. *Is that Tom?*

Still carrying Julia, she returned to see what had broken the glass. A brick lay beside the crib. She'd missed it before in her panic to get Julia. Out Julia's broken window she saw the two men had separated, and one of them ran off. The other one seemed to be hurt. He held his bleeding head with one hand and a cell phone in his other.

A couple of her neighbors appeared to help the guy. After they got to him, he pointed to the broken window in Julia's room. A neighbor, John something or other, turned away from the group and headed into the building. A minute later, there was a knock on her door. Her neighbor, John, asked, "Are you okay?"

"Yes, I'm all right. Someone threw a brick through Julia's window."

"Yeah, I know. You'd better come down and talk to this guy out front."

"Why?"

"I'm not sure. He wanted to talk to you. He knows who threw the brick through your window."

"I've got to take Julia. She's still upset."

"No problem. And the police are on the way. I'm sure you're going to have to talk to them."

Barbara bundled Julia up and went outside.

A small crowd of neighbors had gathered. John led Barbara to the man she'd seen before. He now had an ice pack to his head. Another neighbor had apparently brought it. He asked, "Are you Barbara Fairchild?"

"Yes," Barbara said, somewhat startled.

"I've been watching your place for the last few nights, and I saw the guy throw the brick through your window. I stopped him from throwing another brick, but he got the better of me. He clobbered me with his brick and ran off. I got a good look at him. I know who he is."

"Tom Kelly?" Barbara asked.

"Yep."

The crowd turned as a police car with its lights flashing entered the parking lot and parked in front of them.

When the police got out, they walked to the man who'd been talking to Barbara.

"Josh," one of the police said, "What have you gotten yourself into now?"

"I had this short job for a friend. Bill Anderson wanted me to be sure Barbara wasn't hassled by her old boss. He'd been fired, and he might think Barbara caused it."

"So, what happened? How'd you get hit?"

"Well, sure enough, this guy, Tom Kelly, showed about fifteen minutes ago. I figured he was going to go to her apartment, so I got out of my car to stop him. Before I got close, he heaved a brick through her window."

"A brick?" asked one of the officers.

"Yes, we can see it later. Anyway, before he threw another brick, I tackled him. Unfortunately, things didn't go well. We wrestled on the ground for a bit. Then he got on top and crowned me with the brick and ran away. I called you guys, and these people came out and helped me."

"You okay? It looks like you've lost a lot of blood."

"I'll be all right. I might need stitches. Actually, he didn't hit me very hard. You know how head injuries bleed. It looks worse than it is."

The lead officer turned to Barbara. "Are you all right, ma'am?"

"I'm okay, and my daughter seems to have calmed down, too. The brick probably bounced off her crib. I guess you'll want to see it."

"Does she have blood on her pajamas?"

"What?" Barbara asked, panicked.

"There," the policeman said, pointing to a spot on Julia's upper arm.

"Oh my gosh. There's glass everywhere in her room—I guess she got cut." Then she turned Julia so she could talk to her. "Are you hurt, darling?"

Julia whimpered a little and said, "My arm."

An ambulance pulled up. The lead policeman motioned for Josh and Barbara to go to the ambulance.

One of the ER people pulled a little glass out of Julia's upper arm and put a BAND-AID on it. Then he inspected her carefully. They didn't find any other cuts. Barbara had taken off Julia's pajamas. The small bits of glass on them startled her. Apparently only one of them had actually injured Julia.

The medics bandaged Josh and checked him for a concussion. He checked out okay, so the policeman took charge again. "We'll have to take statements from both you and Josh," he said to Barbara.

Barbara turned to Josh. "I feel terrible. You're hurt, and I haven't even thanked you. You say Mr. Anderson had you guarding my apartment. I'm sure glad you were. Julia might have been hurt with the other brick, or it might've come through my living room window. Thank you so much!"

When things calmed down, the crowd dispersed, and Barbara, the police, and Josh went to her apartment. The police inspected the window and the brick. Barbara assured them she hadn't touched anything. They found nicks on a couple of the bars on the crib. Barbara had been right. The brick had bounced off the crib. The police put the brick into an evidence bag.

One of the policemen played with Julia while the other one took down the two statements. Barbara learned Josh Reilly was an off-duty policeman. He gave the police a picture of Tom Kelly he'd been given from the store's personnel file. He told the officers Tom had thrown the brick. He also had Tom's license plate number and address. The police called the information into headquarters. Barbara's statement was shorter. She said she thought one of the two people she'd seen wrestling in the front yard might have been Tom. She wasn't sure. Also, she said Tom had lost his supervisor job for harassing her. She felt silly for not recognizing he might come after her.

As the policemen were about to leave, they got a call on their radio.

Tom Kelly had been picked up at his home. They assured Barbara Tom wouldn't be on the loose for a long time. Josh's testimony and Tom's fingerprints on the brick would be enough to convict him. She probably wouldn't have to testify.

After the police left, Barbara called her parents. They said they'd be happy to have her and Julia stay with them until the window got fixed.

Chapter Twenty

THE NEXT AFTERNOON, PHIL PICKED Sherry up for the drive to McKeesport. After they'd left town, Phil asked, "How are you doing?"

"Fine, no sweat at work today. I like only working half days. Things are quiet at the library on Friday afternoons. It's sensible for one of us to take off."

"Good, I was asking—I guess repeating—a deeper question. How are you feeling about our project? It seems to be going well. Salt Lake City was a slam dunk, and Milwaukee is going okay too. Is this getting you what you wanted?"

"I've been wondering about it since you asked before. It's complicated. As you know, I experienced sexual harassment twice, and neither outcome satisfied me. It didn't seem useful to fight sexual harassment. We're helping these women have better outcomes. I like that. Still, It's frustrating working around the edges of such a big problem. I wish I believed our efforts would have a broader impact,"

"I thought it might be bothering you."

"I've been taking notes on everything we've done. Actually, it's an extension of my diary. And I've taken screen shots of the postings on the chat room. I have everything documented."

"You're keeping it all in a safe place, I hope." Phil wasn't able to keep the concern out of his voice.

"Yes, don't worry. It's on my laptop at home, which I keep locked in a drawer. My mom wouldn't know what to do with a laptop if she found it, so it's safe."

"Don't you two have a cleaning lady?"

"Yes, we do. Like I said, the drawer is locked. Everything's secure."

"Great, a good record of what we're doing might come in handy. Eventually we'll have a lot of evidence. Figuring out what to do with it is the problem."

Sherry sighed. "You're right. Still, it's down the road a way. Right now, we need to be sure we get these cameras planted tonight."

"I assume your black outfit is in the bag you brought."

"Yes, I feel like I'm preparing to be a cat burglar. I want to change the subject. Tell me what's got your Wednesday lunch group so riled up."

"I wouldn't say riled up. I guess we've had a few animated discussions lately."

"I saw Bert and Bob walking across campus early Wednesday afternoon, and it appeared they were in a heated discussion."

"You're right. You saw a continuation of a lunch discussion."

"What's the topic?"

"We were talking about guns. Bert's from Brooklyn, and he has very extreme views. Basically, he doesn't believe anyone should have a gun. He's not even sure the police should carry guns. On the other hand, Bob grew up in Ohio on a farm, and he and his family are hunters. He doesn't buy the NRA slippery slope arguments. While he's in favor of sensible gun control laws, he'd draw the line in a very different place than Bert."

"I thought you agreed more often than you apparently do."

"Again, you're right. We generally agree. On occasion, Bert can be a hot head. Guns clearly set him off. He keeps quoting statistics about how many accidents are caused by guns people bought for their own protection. He can't see why these statistics don't move people like Bob. The rest of us sit back and try to stay out of the way."

"Bert has a point. Lots of accidents, some tragic ones, are caused by guns people bought for protection. People think they are getting protection, and it backfires on them."

"No pun intended?"

"Oh, backfires, I get it. No—no pun intended."

"In my view the lunch group's analysis is actually good about the reason Bert's statistics don't have much effect on people. Here's the argument. It's like taking a plane versus crossing railroad tracks in your car. Statistics show crossing railroad tracks is actually more dangerous. It doesn't help much because people aren't moved by statistics. They are much more nervous on planes because they aren't in control. Having a gun for protection makes some people feel in control."

"Yeah, I see it. Even if statistically you are putting yourself and your loved ones in more jeopardy by having a gun, those statistics are about other, more foolish people. You're sure you'll be much more sensible with your gun."

"Right, but it doesn't add up. Those statistics result from lots of people like the person you're talking about. They make boneheaded mistakes," Phil concluded.

"I can see why the lunch conversation spilled out on to the walk back to campus," Sherry said. "There are interesting issues involved."

Phil and Sherry had a quick meal at a diner in McKeesport and parked their car at the shopping center Phil had used previously. When they got to the trees across from the school, Sherry whispered, "I'm nervous. I've never done anything like this."

"It's good to be nervous," replied Phil. "You wouldn't be normal if you weren't nervous. Put on the black top. This should be easy as long as I can make the lock picks work."

They checked the school for thirty minutes. While lights were on in the school, the parking lot was empty, and they didn't see any movement. Phil said, "Let's go," and they approached the side door quickly and quietly. Phil's lock picks worked very well, and they got inside easily. Sherry found a spot where she could see the approaches to the school and stood guard.

Phil bent over so he wouldn't be seen from the street and made his way to Miss McGuire's classroom. The school website had helped. Dorothy McGuire taught the second section of second grade, "the Tigers." A different set of picks allowed Phil to enter the room. He unfolded the ladder and mounted the camera in the sprinkler. He slanted the camera to point it at the teacher's desk. Next, he made his way to the principal's office. After making quick work of getting past the lock, he mounted the camera, again in the sprinkler, and made his escape. When he got to Sherry, he gave her hand a squeeze as they made their way out of the school. Back in the trees, Sherry started laughing.

"Why are you laughing? What's so funny?"

"I didn't know it would be this thrilling," Sherry replied as she gave Phil a big hug. "I was scared the whole time. It seemed like forever. I checked my watch. It only took five minutes. I loved seeing you coming down the hall. Everything worked?"

"Yes, everything worked. I can kinda see your reaction. There's a lot of suppressed energy when you get involved with things like this, and it's a big relief at the end. The nervous energy has to come out, and laughing is better than shouting. Let's get out of these black tops and back to the car. Remember, we're a couple out for an evening stroll."

On the way back, Sherry received a text message from Beth. They'd agreed to keep any text messages short and cryptic. No telling who might be able to figure out something from a string of text messages. The message only invited Sherry for coffee at Beth and Ralph's the next morning at 7:00, their code for an emergency meeting of the group. Sherry and Phil couldn't figure out what it could be, so they stopped trying to guess.

Chapter Twenty-One

THE NEXT MORNING THE GROUP assembled at 7:00, and Beth filled Phil and Sherry in on why they were meeting. Ralph regularly searched the internet for any mention of Sam Turbridge, Rochelle Martin, Barbara Fairchild, and Tom Kelly. Yesterday, he got a hit in the *Salt Lake City Tribune*. Tom Kelly showed up in the police blotter. He'd been arrested and charged with destruction of property and assault. There were no more details.

"This might be really important," Beth said.

With concern in his voice, Ralph said, "Yes, I hope Barbara's okay. Assault—you don't suppose he attacked her? I'd feel awful if she's hurt. It would be our fault all the way."

"I never thought about it," Sherry said. "Now I feel stupid. Tom had already been violent with her. Remember, he hit her. And he'd have to be pretty thick not to recognize she's the reason he lost his job. Ralph, you're right. It's our fault. If we hadn't stuck our noses in, this wouldn't have happened. Maybe it's a sign. Maybe we shouldn't be getting involved."

"Wait, wait, you two," Phil interrupted. "We don't have enough information to know what happened. Tom might have been upset and gotten into a fight in a bar."

"In Salt Lake City!" echoed the others.

"Okay, probably not a bar. Lots of other things could have happened. We don't even know Barbara's involved. We shouldn't jump to conclusions."

"Phil's right," Sherry said. "We need more information. I say we send Barbara an email asking her to post what she knows about Tom's arrest. It would let her know we're still here and want to help."

"If she's in the hospital, she won't be able to answer us," Beth said. "I have a real bad feeling about this whole mess. I don't know if I can take it. What do we do if Barbara doesn't get back to us in the chat room?"

Ralph put his arm around Beth. "Honey, like Phil said, Barbara might not be involved at all. It's never good to try to figure out things when you don't have sufficient information. It's too easy to imagine all kinds of horrible things. If push comes to shove, one of us can go out to Salt Lake City. Sherry's right, the first step is to email Barbara."

"All right, I'll try to calm down," Beth said reluctantly. "This whole thing makes me nervous. I didn't sleep much last night. And I guess we were a little naïve not to consider revenge. It makes sense. Tom might try to get back at Barbara."

"Beth's right," Sherry said. "We've got to think long and hard about the possibility of revenge. Fear of revenge is one of the reasons victims of sexual harassment often don't report it. It's not all the lack of witnesses leading to a he-said-she-said problem. There must be ways to thwart revenge. We might be able to get protective orders or police protection or something?"

"We're getting ahead of ourselves," Ralph said. "Then again, it's clear we haven't thought this through all the way. Right now, it's time for us to get to our jobs. There's not enough time to settle anything now."

"I'll write the email and keep it simple," Beth said. "We want to know if she's okay and does she know anything about Tom's arrest."

In the library, Sherry haunted the chat room every chance she got. Most of the traffic on the site happened in the evening, so she didn't expect to see anything. Still, she hoped Barbara would answer soon.

She was having second thoughts about their project. Violence against women is a common thing. Though she hadn't experienced anything herself, she knew several women who had. She'd been so focused on sexual harassment in the workplace she'd forgotten about violence. Now it seemed so clear. By directly taking on one problem, they may have made another one worse. She found it difficult to concentrate on her work. Finally, she called Phil and arranged to meet him during her lunch break.

When they got together at a picnic table in the Lackey woods, Phil let Sherry talk. She needed to. After she vented, Phil gave her a big hug. "I'm sorry you're so upset. You may be jumping the gun. We don't know if Tom Kelly's arrest has anything to do with Barbara. He only recently lost his job. Losing a job can cause a guy to do lots of crazy things."

"Phil, you're being a Pollyanna!" Sherry said. "Tom had to know Barbara was responsible for his firing. She goes to HR one day, and he's fired the next. Come on; it doesn't take a rocket scientist to make the connection."

"I guess you're right."

"You know I'm right."

"Okay, you're right. Still, we can't let the threat of violence stop us. If we did, we'd be giving in. There have to be things we can do to limit the possibility of violent revenge."

"What can we do?"

"We don't want to involve the police. Then again, maybe we should. It's possible to get protective orders."

"No, it's not going to work," Sherry said. "The way I understand it, there has to be a threat of violence or evidence of previous violence before you can get a protective order. You got any other ideas?"

"The whole thing is difficult because we want to remain anonymous." Phil paused. "I suppose we could hire a private detective to guard the women for a couple of weeks. We might be able to hire a private detective without revealing who we are."

"Wouldn't it be expensive?"

"I don't know. I've never hired one before. As you know, I've got quite a bit of money, and I'm willing to use it. At least we should find out how expensive it is. And we still need to find out exactly what happened with Tom Kelly."

"Actually, Phil, it won't matter. Even if Tom Kelly didn't attack Barbara, it's possible in other cases. We've been idiots not to anticipate the possibility. We'll have to deal with it no matter what we hear from Salt Lake City."

"I guess you're right. We can't ignore it. I'll keep thinking, and I'll find out how much it would cost to hire a private detective. I know it'll probably vary a lot. Still, it would be good to know the order of magnitude."

Sherry gave Phil a kiss. "It's a mess, but you've cheered me up. Private detectives might work. Still, I want to hear Barbara's not hurt. I don't know what I'd do if we caused her any harm, even indirectly. Not knowing isn't easy."

"I agree, all we can do is wait. The key is not to let your imagination go too far."

After lunch, Phil went to work at Ralph's store. At the start of Phil's stint, Ralph worked in the back room with a computer repair. The store was quiet when Ralph finished, so he motioned for Phil to come into the back room for a talk. The bell at the door would alert them if a customer entered.

"Beth was very upset last night. As she said, she didn't get much sleep, and our meeting this morning didn't calm her down much," Ralph said.

"Sherry's not in much better shape. I had lunch with her. We all feel a little stupid. How could all four of us not recognize we should worry about revenge? The feeling of stupidity is mixed with worry about Barbara and the recognition it would be our fault if she's hurt. There are a lot of emotions to deal with."

"So, Phil, why are you so calm?"

"Maybe I'm not. No, I guess I'm pretty calm. We can't undo what we've done, so it's not productive to worry about it. What we have to do is figure out how to avoid making any more mistakes. This morning you said we shouldn't let our imaginations go wild. We have to wait to see what happened in Salt Lake City. In the meantime, we have to figure out how we can adjust to deal with the possibility of revenge."

"Okay, how do we deal with the possibility of revenge?"

"Sherry and I talked about this. We might be able to hire private detectives to guard the women. Police protection won't be possible, but private detectives might work."

"How much would it cost? I guess it depends on where they live and on how long the women need the protection."

"I'm going to drive to Pittsburgh and talk to a private detective agency to see if they do this kind of thing and how it all works. A private detective in Salt Lake City or Milwaukee might charge different fees. If I ask, at least we'll have an idea. I'll also ask them if they have any idea how long we might need to provide protection. I bet most of the acts of revenge happen fairly quickly after the event."

"Sounds like a plan. It'll give you something to do. I guess the rest of us need to sit tight and worry about Barbara."

"You're right. I can't see anything the rest of you can do. I can't be here tomorrow. I'm going to go to Pittsburgh instead."

Chapter Twenty-Two

EARLY THE SAME AFTERNOON, ROCHELLE Martin in Milwaukee got a call from Mr. Site's secretary, Joellen. She wanted Rochelle to come to a meeting at Mr. Site's office in the afternoon at four. Rochelle said she'd be sure to be there. She had trouble concentrating on her work until three forty-five when she gave up entirely and went to the bathroom to check her appearance.

When Rochelle entered Mr. Site's office, she saw she was entering a meeting already in progress. As well as Mr. Sites, there were five of the firm's senior lawyers around the conference table. *This must be the management committee*, she thought. She saw Mrs. Higgins, too.

Mr. Sites got out of his chair and shook her hand. He introduced her to the group and asked her to take a seat beside him. Rochelle became even more nervous as several of the assembled lawyers stared at her.

Mr. Sites clearly controlled the meeting. "Rochelle," he said, "I haven't shown the committee the videos yet. I want them to know how you obtained them first. Would you tell us how you came to have them?"

"Well." Rochelle cleared her throat. "It started with an email from these people. They called themselves the I. N. H. S. S. S. A. group. I found out it stands for it's not he said she said anymore. Anyway, the email said they would provide me a video if I would file a sexual harassment complaint.

I told them I wouldn't do it unless they showed me the videos first. So, they sent it to me."

"And Rochelle," Mr. Sites said, "you don't have any idea where these people are from or who they are."

"No, I don't."

One of the other lawyers broke in. "How did these people get your name? How did they know anything?"

"I've been wondering," replied Rochelle. "And they must have known about me and my problems with Mr. Turbridge because I complain about it a lot on an internet chat room."

"Aren't chat rooms supposed to be anonymous?" asked another lawyer.

"Yes, I thought they were. Still, it's the only way I know they would have gotten the information."

"You don't complain to your friends about Sam?"

"Well, yes, I guess I do. I don't think any of them would have acted like these people. Maybe one of them is behind it, but it's unlikely."

Mr. Sites took control again. "The critical thing is—Rochelle did not set up the cameras. An outside group did it. Now let's look at the video."

"One more thing," broke in one of the other lawyers. "Ms. Martin, do you have copies of the emails from these people?"

"Yes, I do. I didn't erase them. Do you want them? I don't have them with me. I can bring them tomorrow."

"We might need them," replied the lawyer who'd asked the question.

Joellen came in, dimmed the lights, and started the computer. The video showed on a white board at one end of the conference table.

Rochelle had seen the video before, so she watched the faces of the men around the table. They were clearly paying attention, and several of them reacted when they saw Sam Turbridge pawing her on the screen. A few of them sneaked looks at her during the video. Mr. Sites showed both videos. When the videos stopped, and the lights came back on, Mr. Sites took over again.

"There you have it. The evidence couldn't be clearer. Ms. Martin is being sexually harassed by Sam Turbridge. It's not inappropriate language. It's unwanted touching, lots of unwanted touching."

"How many days are covered by the videos?" asked one of the lawyers.

Mr. Sites gestured to Rochelle, so she spoke up. "The video cameras were only there for a week. The two videos together show every episode of unwanted touching during the week."

"You say it's unwanted touching. How can we be sure it's unwanted?"

"For God's sake, Morty," jumped in Mr. Sites. "You can see how she flinches every time he touches her and slaps his hand away when she can. It's clear as day. And we have the sexual harassment complaint you've all read." He paused and looked around the room. "Are there any more questions for Ms. Martin?"

Several of the lawyers shook their heads. Finally, Mr. Sites said, "On behalf of the entire firm, I want to apologize to you, Ms. Martin. We had no idea this kind of behavior happened in our offices. We can't have it, and we won't have it. You can leave now. The committee and I will figure out what to do. We are going to give you a week's paid vacation starting tomorrow. When you return, Sam Turbridge will no longer be employed at Smith, Bainbridge and Sites. We can discuss your assignment when you return."

Rochelle walked out of the room in a daze. It had happened in such a hurry. She wanted to shout.

When Rochelle got home, she went to her computer and posted to INHSSSA in the chat room. She gave a brief description of the meeting and its outcome. She told them she couldn't thank them enough. Everything had worked out wonderfully.

Chapter Twenty-Three

THE NEXT MORNING, THE GROUP had another meeting at Beth and Ralph's. Sherry and Beth were monitoring the chat room, so they reported about Rochelle's post. "It looks like we have a complete success there. They gave her a week's paid leave to give them time to figure how to get rid of Sam Turbridge. It seems real smart," Beth said.

"Doesn't it leave us with the same problem we have in Salt Lake City? Don't we have to worry about revenge?" Phil asked.

"Yes, I suppose we still have to worry about revenge. In this case, it's a lawyer involved. You'd think he'd have enough sense not to make his problem bigger," Sherry said.

"He's a guy," Phil responded. "While I hate to say it, guys can be stupid. He's going to be incredibly angry. He's losing a good job. I don't know how much money he makes. Lawyers can make a whole lot."

"Phil's right," Beth said. "We have to do something to deal with possible revenge."

"I agree. What did you learn at the private detective agency, Phil?" Sherry asked.

"I've got their brochures, if you want more details. Actually, it's fairly straightforward. The detective I talked to thought it would be sufficient to post a guard for a week or ten days. Most of the possible revenge is from hot heads, and even they cool down after a while. It will be expensive, so I don't know if we want to do it in every case."

Ralph said, "We should take advantage of the fact the law firm gave Rochelle a week paid leave. Wouldn't it be good to suggest to her she should take a vacation? If she got out of Milwaukee, the possibility of Sam taking any kind of revenge would be vastly diminished."

"We can't be sure she'll go," Beth replied.

"You're right, Beth. Still, it's worth a try," Sherry said. "She might be very interested in a short trip. We should be up front with her about our reasons for the suggestion. We should do it right away."

"And maybe we should hire a private detective if she doesn't take us up on the idea," Beth added.

Sherry moved the meeting along. "Okay. We have a plan for Rochelle. I'll write the email. We still haven't heard a thing from Barbara. It's not like her to be silent. She's been good about responding the other times we've been in touch. She got right back to us with the news about Tom being fired."

"I know," Ralph said. "And it's easy to imagine all kinds of horrible things in Barbara's case. Tom was arrested for assault. We should try to keep calm. It's hard to know how to interpret silence and better not to try. Let's go to work and try not to dwell on it."

"Ralph's right," Sherry said. "I'll go with the men to the store so I can send the untraceable email from there. I can't use my machine at the library."

In the evening they saw a post from Rochelle telling them she'd decided to take a short vacation to Madison to see friends there.

Two agonizing days later, they finally found a post from Barbara. She assured them there were no problems. She'd had to go to her parent's house while the guys replaced the window, and the room was thoroughly cleaned. Her parents didn't have an internet connection, so she hadn't seen their email and couldn't respond sooner.

Beth emailed her asking about Tom and the assault charges. Barbara responded that the little piece of glass that had hit Julia resulted in the assault charge, and the broken glass had added destruction of property. It was nothing to be worried about. Julia proudly wore her BAND AID.

The next evening the group gathered for a congratulatory dinner at the Mexican restaurant in Henderson, a half hour from Lackey.

When they were seated, Sherry started. "Things have settled down. Barbara is in good shape, and Rochelle's on vacation. These two cases are pretty much finished. We have cameras to get in McKeesport in a few days. Otherwise, we don't have anything going. Beth and I want to pitch another case. Why don't you do the honors, Beth."

"Okay. What about New York City guys? One of the most compelling posts on the chat room is from Cindy Newsome who recently got promoted to a new job at a movie production company in New York City. Apparently, her new boss, the company vice president, is terrible. First of all, he wants her to change her wardrobe. He wants short skirts and high heels. In addition, he brushes up against her way too much. She's afraid it'll get worse. She's clearly upset."

"Should we get right on it?" Phil asked.

Sherry responded, "You should. Cindy is headed for trouble."

"I guess we can leave the cameras in the school in McKeesport for a while longer," Phil said. "Ralph, are you good for a quick trip to the Big Apple?"

"I've only been there once. It should be fun. Maybe, after we get the cameras installed, we can go see some sites. Jim can handle the store for a couple of days."

"This one is likely to be tough, guys," Sherry said. "Buildings in New York typically have lots of security. At the places I worked, visitors had to get passes from the front desk, and the elevators wouldn't work unless you had a card."

Chapter Twenty-Four

ON THE PLANE FROM PITTSBURGH to New York, Phil and Ralph reviewed pictures of Cindy Newsome's workplace. It appeared to cover most of the fifteenth floor of a medium-sized building in Manhattan. "I sure hope we can figure out a way to use an elevator," Ralph said.

"If we get past the security, I'll be willing to take the stairs," Phil said. "Sherry's right. The security at these buildings is likely to be tight. And there are likely to be lots of surveillance cameras around for us to avoid."

"Our plane lands early enough for us to scope the place out. You're right. This might be real tough."

Phil and Ralph gave the airport taxi driver an address a block away from where Cindy Newsome worked. They made it to the correct address at 3:30. "Wow, it's like being in a canyon," Ralph said.

"Yes, the buildings are all tall, and we're down here on the canyon floor." Phil and Ralph walked toward Cindy's building on the corner of the next block.

They paused by the front door to check out the entrance. "Let's move along quickly," Ralph said. "See the camera? I suspect we're right in its field of vision."

"Okay."

Phil and Ralph hurried out of the camera's range and then slowed their pace. Phil spoke next. "I'll change my disguise and then go back and check out the security arrangements." He looked up. "There's a coffee shop across the street. I can change in their restroom." In the restroom, he changed from his white beard to the mustache and black wig.

Fifteen minutes later, returning from his recon mission, Phil slipped into the booth in the coffee shop where Ralph nursed his coffee. "It's bad. There's a guard posted right inside the door. They have to call to the person you're meeting. If the person vouches for you, the guards take your ID and make a badge for you. The badge works in the elevator."

"Wow, you found that out fairly fast."

"I got lucky. There were two people in front of me waiting, so I figured out the process. After I'd seen enough, I acted sort of hurried, checked my watch, and left. Also, I made sure I didn't let the cameras inside get a good look at me."

"So, you figure we came to New York for nothing?" Ralph asked.
Phil shook his head.

"Okay, how do we get into the building?"

"I had a student who graduated maybe ten or eleven years ago, Sam Ellis. He told me an interesting story at homecoming a couple of years ago. He works in a big building in Houston. His boss is a real stickler about them leaving on time. There were instances when Sam needed to work extra hours, and he didn't want his boss to know. The building was like this one, with strict security. People had to register when they came and went. Sam found if he drove his car into the underground garage, he was able to bypass the security by using the stairs. Cindy's building has underground parking."

"So, we're supposed to dodge a car going out or coming into the parking garage to gain entrance and then walk up fifteen stories?"

"You catch on quick, Ralph my boy. That's exactly the plan. I can't see any other way to do it."

"I guess you're right. We'd better find our hotel, so we can get rid of these backpacks. I have a feeling it's going to be a long night."

At 5:30, Phil and Ralph camped out across the street from the building. They were wearing their vests, which held the cameras, and were carrying the collapsible ladder. Cars were exiting the underground garage frequently. When the traffic slowed three quarters of an hour later, they moved behind some bushes close to the entrance. When they were in position, Phil said, "The key is to catch a car leaving that isn't being closely followed by another car. We don't want to get caught in the headlights of the second car. It means we have to wait until the car is halfway out, so we can check to see if it's closely followed."

"Makes sense."

The first three cars exiting had another car right on their tails.

"Is somebody telling them to leave two-by-two?" Phil asked.

"Be patient."

Finally, a car came out, and there were no headlights following. Phil and Ralph ran into the entrance and ducked under the parking garage door as it closed. They moved away from the door quickly and hid behind a pillar. After a car exited, Ralph whispered, "It should be easy to get out. The door opened because the car interrupted the beam of light. I bet you don't have to be as big as a car to make it work."

"Good. Let's hang here until the garage clears some more. Then we can move around."

Thirty minutes later, when there were only three cars left on their level of the parking garage, Phil and Ralph made their way to the door labeled 'Stairway.' The door wasn't locked, so they started the climb.

"Fifteen stories. Right?" asked Ralph.

"Yeah, and I don't know if this one counts."

Luckily for them the doors were labeled, so they didn't have to keep track of which floor they were on. They decided to go slowly and rest twice, at floors five and ten. Ralph reached the first resting place half a story before Phil. Looking at Phil when he arrived, he asked, "You going to make it?"

Between deep breaths Phil said, "I'll make it, but I don't think I can keep up with you. I've never been in great shape, and I guess my age is showing."

"We'll rest here a while. Take a drink." He offered Phil the water bottle he'd been carrying.

"Thanks."

Ralph reached the tenth-story resting place a whole level before Phil, so they enjoyed an even longer rest there. The final five stories were agony for Phil. After they rested, Ralph put his ear to the door. When he heard nothing, he slowly opened the door, and he and Phil entered the deserted hallway. Before they closed the door to the stairs, they made sure it didn't lock behind them.

"It's Sheldon Productions, right?" asked Ralph.

"Yeah, her boss is Nick Sheldon, the son of the president, Graydon Sheldon. It's a family business. Nick is vice president."

They didn't have to search long before they saw the entrance to the Sheldon Productions offices. They put on their latex gloves and approached the door. Much to their surprise, it wasn't locked. "I guess they have a lot of faith in the building security," Phil said.

"Still, it's sloppy. There might be people in other offices who would want to snoop at their stuff. Anyway, it's easy for us. Let's find Nick's office and see where we can plant the cameras."

Movie posters decorated the offices. Phil asked, "Ever heard of these movies?"

"No, I can't say I have. This one's in Spanish, and one there is in Chinese or something. I don't think Sheldon Productions is one of the big guys."

They stepped around the receptionist's desk and went into the corridor to the right. There were several small offices off the corridor. They only had room for a desk, a couple of chairs, and some filing cabinets. At the end of the corridor, they came to an office with Graydon Sheldon's name in big gold letters on the door. They went in and saw two desks in an outer office and another door with Graydon's name on it. They peeked in the president's office. A big desk, conference table, and a mini bar didn't come close to filling the space. The office had a large window with a nice view of the street below.

"I bet Nick has a setup like this on the other side," Ralph said.

"I don't know why I even came in here. Clearly the office belongs to Graydon, not Nicholas."

"Don't fret, Phil. I saw the name, and I didn't stop you. It's natural to be a little curious."

They went back to the main corridor and followed it to the other end. As they'd suspected, the door at the end had Nicholas Sheldon's name in the same gold letters. It was arranged like his father's office, but the view out Nick's window wasn't as nice. Ralph and Phil installed three cameras. Because there was no way to tell which of the desks in the outer office belonged to Cindy, they put up cameras focused on each desk. The final camera went on a sprinkler in Nick's office.

The trip down the stairs turned out to be less difficult for Phil than the assent, but it started to bother his knees toward the end. When they got to the bottom, there were no cars in the garage. "Let's see if interrupting the light beam is enough to make the door open," said Ralph.

Ralph went near the door and waved his hand in the light beam. Nothing happened. He glanced at the floor. "Oh no!" he exclaimed. "There's one of those things that detects cars. You know, like at intersections."

Phil checked the garage floor. "It looks like we're stuck in here."

"We'd better hope someone's working late." Ralph checked his watch. "It's 7:30 now. Maybe someone will still use the garage."

"I wish I could be as optimistic," Phil said. "This floor's completely empty. Granted, there are lower levels, but I'm afraid we're going to be in here all night."

"All we can do is hope. Let's go by the doors, so we're ready if they come open."

"Okay. It's all we can do."

After a half hour of waiting in silence, hoping a car would appear from the lower levels of the garage, they heard the door opening. A car came in. Quickly they positioned themselves to duck under the door after the car.

Outside, they hustled away from the garage entrance.

"That guy must have gone to dinner and then come back to finish some work," Phil said. "I hadn't even considered the possibility the door would open for someone coming in."

"Dinner? Did you say dinner? I'm starving. Let's ditch these vests and the ladder. I need to find a place to eat."

"Fine, but first we'd better email the girls telling them we got the cameras in place."

"No problem. There's WiFi at the hotel."

Chapter Twenty-Five

PHIL AND RALPH SPENT THE next day in New York. They visited Times Square, Central Park, and took the boat out to the Statue of Liberty. They were booked on a 9:00 flight out of LaGuardia, so they got a cab at 6:00. They checked in, made it through security, and were searching for a place to eat when Ralph got a text message from Beth who wanted him to call.

"Where are you?" she asked.

"At the airport."

"You're going to have to turn around. We need you to retrieve the cameras tonight."

"Why?"

"Cindy got on the chat room right after work. She said she had an awful day. She called her boss a sex maniac. She's sure she can't work for him. Something happened at work, and she's really upset. Sherry and I are convinced it's probably significant enough on its own to warrant a sexual harassment complaint. We need to find out what happened."

"Okay. We'll see what we can do. It might be tough. We'll give it a try."

After saying goodbye, Ralph turned to Phil and repeated what Beth had said.

"I'm a hazard on the fifteen-story climb," Phil said. "You should head back right away. Take the ladder and get going. Oh, and give me your boarding pass. I'll settle things with the airline and get us a hotel for tonight. We can meet outside the building when you've retrieved the cameras."

"I don't have enough cash for the cab fare."

Phil reached in his wallet and handed Ralph some money. "That should do it. If I have to, I can use a credit card for my cab. Take off; you don't have much time."

During the cab ride, Ralph tried to remember what time the last car came in the garage last night. He paid the cabbie and hustled to the place he and Phil had used the previous evening. Now came the waiting. Luckily after only five minutes a car approached the entrance to the garage. Ralph ducked inside with no trouble. Surprisingly, the garage still had quite a few cars.

He made it through the door to the stairs without anyone seeing him. While the climb seemed to take longer than before, the camera retrieval went smoothly. He knew right where they were. He headed down the stairs again in less than five minutes.

When Ralph reached the door leading to the garage, he cracked it open and heard people talking. A group of men walked by. Ralph figured the meeting, or whatever had caused all the cars, must be over. Now he didn't know what to do. If he waited until he didn't hear anyone, he'd risk a chance of not getting out of the garage. He figured he'd wait for a gap in the foot traffic before making his move. Then he heard a ding from an elevator followed by another group walking past his door. He waited until the group had passed and made a dash to a pillar. He got to a more secure hiding place by the time the elevator dinged again, letting off another group. By this time a steady stream of traffic flowed out of the garage. Ralph had to wait until he was able to follow the last car.

When he emerged from the garage, Ralph expected Phil would be waiting, but he wasn't anywhere to be seen. He moved across the street from Cindy's building. After fifteen minutes, Phil arrived in a cab in front of the building. Ralph came running. "Where have you been? I got the cameras, and it took me a while to make it out of the garage. I thought you'd be here before me."

"Sorry. Long lines at the airline counter, and hotels were full. Finally, I had to stand in a twenty-minute line for cabs. Anyway, everything went well?"

"Yes, I have the videos. And given how upset the women are, we'd better look at them fast. They'll be waiting for a report."

After Phil and Ralph checked into their hotel, they went to Ralph's room to view the videos. A video focused on one of the secretaries came first. It showed her arriving for work. She had blonde hair with dark roots. She wore a low-cut tight blouse, a short skirt, and high heels.

"It's the way the boss wanted them to dress if I remember correctly," Phil said.

"You're right."

The motion-activated video didn't show much. This secretary didn't seem to do a lot. She typed some and walked to the filing cabinets to put papers away. She also spent quite a bit of time reading a magazine. In the afternoon, they heard a shout from the other room. A man's voice said, "Gwen, come in here." The secretary got up and went into her boss's office. The camera showed her coming back later. A little disheveled, she had a grin on her face. She checked her plentiful makeup and added new lipstick. The rest of the day passed as it had begun. They fast forwarded through it.

"That's Gwen; let's turn to Cindy now," Ralph said as he downloaded the video from the other camera focused on a secretary's desk. Cindy looked young and had long brown hair, prominent cheek bones, a slim waist, and large breasts.

"She doesn't dress the same, despite what her boss wants. I wonder if it's the root of the problem."

"Let's look."

The video trained on Cindy's desk didn't show much more than the one trained on Gwen's desk. She seemed like a normal secretary. At one-thirty on the time stamp a man came in and went to Cindy's desk. He got close to her and stroked her hair. She wriggled away and said, "Nick, don't do that."

Then the man grabbed her arm and pulled her up roughly. He put his arm around her and dragged her away. The two people went out of the camera's field of vision. Next the camera showed Cindy rushing back in with a tear-streaked face. Clearly, she'd been crying, but Phil and Ralph weren't able to detect the cause of the tears.

"The time stamp shows it's five minutes before 2:00. She left our view for twenty-five minutes. I bet we can tell what's made her cry in the other video," said Phil.

The rest of the video focused on Cindy showed her trying to work but not getting much done. Clearly upset, she cried intermittently. She got out of her chair and walked somewhere a couple of times, not back into Nick's office, somewhere else.

"I bet she's going to the restroom," said Ralph. "Her makeup is a little better when she comes back. Then she starts crying again. Something awful must have happened when he dragged her back into his office."

"Let's look at that video."

The camera focused on Nick's office didn't detect any motion until Nick dragged Cindy into the office in the afternoon. When they were both in the office, they separated. She seemed to be cowering, and Nick paced around. Nick Sheldon looked to be fairly short, five-six or five-seven, and he had slicked back black hair.

When he stopped pacing, Nick said, "Cindy, you've got a good job here, but you have to loosen up a little. I like to get along with my secretaries. You don't seem to want to get along."

"It's not that, Mr. Sheldon. It's just all the touching makes me uncomfortable."

"That's what I'm talking about. You need to be more friendly. Friends touch each other sometimes. And I'm the kind of guy who touches some."

At that point, he stroked her bottom. Cindy shuffled away, slapping his hand. Clearly mad at her, Nick rubbed his hand where she'd slapped him. "Okay. I'll show you how a good secretary treats her boss." Then he called out, "Gwen, come in here."

After a few seconds, Gwen came into Nick's office with a quizzical look on her face. "What can I do for you, Mr. Sheldon?" she asked.

Nick turned around and leaned on his desk, facing the two secretaries. "Gwen, it's time to show Cindy how a secretary should act."

Gwen hesitated. "Right here, in front of her?"

"Yes, and Cindy, stay here and watch."

Gwen went to Nick and gave him a big kiss. Then she stepped back, unzipped his fly, knelt down, and performed oral sex on him. All the time Nick stared at Cindy. While Ralph and Phil weren't able to see Cindy's face, they could tell she was crying by the way her shoulders shook.

When Gwen finished, Nick said, "That's how a good secretary treats her boss."

Cindy didn't say anything as she wiped tears from her eyes.

After a few moments of silence, Nick said, "Think about it. Think about whether or not you want this job. I pay my secretaries top dollar. There's no way you'd get another job as good as this one."

Cindy bolted out of Nick's office.

"It sure explains her crying in the previous video," Phil said.

"Call Sherry and tell her what we have. I'm going to edit the video and put it on a thumb drive. I bet the girls will want us to get it to her pronto."

When Phil got Sherry on the phone, he described what they had on the video. "Oh my God," Sherry gasped when Phil described the scene in Nick's office. "I wouldn't come back to work after witnessing that. I wonder what she's going to do."

"I think you guys should call her and tell her we have this video. She should lodge her complaint right away."

"It's after ten o'clock. Should I call her this late?"

"Yes, you should. She'll want to know about the video."

"How are you going to get the video to her?"

"Let me figure it out after your call. Either Ralph or I will take it, or we'll get a messenger or something. Tell her it'll be delivered by seven tomorrow morning."

"Okay. I guess that'll work."

"Call me and report on your phone call. Wait—Ralph, do you have two thumb drives?"

"No, only this one."

"Sherry, Ralph only has one thumb drive, so we can't provide her a backup."

"I heard. Goodbye."

Chapter Twenty-Six

AT SEVEN O'CLOCK THE next morning, Cindy Newsome went down to her mailbox on the first floor of her apartment building. There she found a small package taped to the outside of her mailbox just like the email had said. Weird. Last night's phone call had been brief. The woman said she should check her email and read the message from I. N. H. S. S. S. A. The email had a long explanation. Most importantly, it told her about the package.

She grabbed the package and rode the elevator to her small apartment. She inserted the thumb drive in her computer and got the video on her screen. She didn't like seeing it again. Still, she understood what these people were about. They wanted her to lodge a sexual harassment complaint against Nick, and this video gave her the proof she needed. They didn't want her to use it right away unless she had to.

She'd planned to go into the office and give her two-week notice, but this video changed everything. Getting into her work clothes, she decided to go right to Mrs. Hagerty, the head of personnel at Sheldon Productions. She wouldn't go to her office at all. She never wanted to be near Nick Sheldon again, or Gwen either.

When Cindy got to Mrs. Hagerty's office she hesitated a minute and then knocked on the door. "Come in," said Mrs. Hagerty.

Cindy entered the small office. Mrs. Hagerty, a thin woman with gray hair and a sort of pinched face, glanced up and said, "Hello, you're Cindy Newsome. You got promoted to be one of Nick's secretaries, right?"

"Yes, you're right."

"What can I do for you?"

"I can't work for Mr. Sheldon, I just can't. Is there any way to reassign me?"

"Why? I can't simply reassign you because you asked. Nick picked you out of a large group of applicants. He'd be disappointed if you left him."

Cindy fiddled with her purse for a while with Mrs. Hagerty staring at her. Finally, she said, "Okay. I didn't want to do it this way... I want to file a sexual harassment complaint against Mr. Sheldon."

"Do you have a written complaint?"

"No, I didn't realize I needed one."

"Why don't you go to your office and write out your complaint. I'm not able to do anything without a written complaint."

Cindy started to tear up. "I can't go back to Nick's office. I just can't."

An awkward silence followed as Cindy composed herself. Finally, she made a decision. "Mrs. Hagerty. I have solid proof of sexual harassment. I want to be reassigned immediately."

Mrs. Hagerty looked puzzled. "Solid proof. What solid proof?"

Cindy retrieved the thumb drive from her purse. "It's on here," she said.

"This is very irregular. What are you trying to do?"

"The video on this thumb drive will show you what I have to put up with and why I can't go back to work for Mr. Sheldon. Please look at it."

"You can't go around taking videos of your workplace."

"I didn't take the video. Couldn't you look at it?"

"I don't know if I can."

Annoyed, Cindy said, "The people who took this video said they'd post it on the company website if I didn't get satisfaction. You don't want that."

"Are you threatening me?"

"Yes, I am. It doesn't have to be that messy. Just look at the video."

"I guess I have to. You've given me little choice."

Cindy handed the thumb drive to Mrs. Hagerty and watched her get the file on her computer. The video started with Nick coming into her office yesterday and showed what happened when he dragged her into his office. Thankfully, the people who edited the video did not show all of Gwen's performance. Still, it left no doubt about what transpired. The video ended with Nick's words to her after Gwen had finished.

Mrs. Hagerty's expression didn't change as she viewed the video. When she finished, she pushed her chair back from the desk and gazed at the ceiling. Then she got out of her chair. "Wait here. I'll be back."

"I'd like to take the thumb drive back. I'll get it out of your computer."

"Sure," Mrs. Hagerty said as she left the room.

Cindy put the thumb drive back in her purse. She had no idea where Mrs. Hagerty had gone. As time passed, she started to get nervous. *Has the whole thing backfired?* She didn't like the idea of putting the video on the company website, but threatening to do so certainly worked.

Fifteen minutes after she left, Mrs. Hagerty came back. "Come with me. We should be able to get this straightened out."

Cindy followed Mrs. Hagerty. Much to her relief, they headed away from Nick's office. They walked to the far end of the opposite corridor and entered Graydon Sheldon's office. Mrs. Hagerty nodded to the two secretaries in the outer office and marched right into the president's office. Cindy followed.

Mrs. Hagerty said, "Graydon, this is Cindy Newsome."

Graydon Sheldon, a slightly paunchier version of Nick, rose and motioned to the conference table. "We'd better sit at the table. This won't take long."

When they were seated, Mr. Sheldon continued. "Helen tells me you have a video of Nick and his secretary Gwen."

"Yes, and it's more. He forced me to watch, and he keeps touching me."

"This kind of thing has happened before. Never with a video. We've had more threats to go to some newspaper reporter. I'm going to handle it the same way we've handled it before. Helen, can you see if Linda has the paperwork done yet."

Mrs. Hagerty left the office. Mr. Sheldon and Cindy sat in awkward silence for a few minutes until Mrs. Hagerty returned, bringing a sheet of paper. She put the paper in front of Mr. Sheldon, and the silence continued as he scanned it.

When he finished reading, he said, "Okay Miss Newsome. What I have here is a non-disclosure agreement. It says you will never discuss the reason you are leaving Sheldon Productions with anyone. I am offering you seventy-five thousand dollars if you are willing to sign this agreement."

Cindy was flabbergasted. She didn't have any idea what to say. She didn't earn nearly seventy-five thousand dollars a year. Essentially, they were buying her off. Part of her was thrilled, but part of her didn't like it. Nick wouldn't learn a thing. He'd not be punished at all. He'd keep being a creep.

Mr. Sheldon became impatient. "Are you going to sign?"

"Let me read it," Cindy said.

Mr. Sheldon passed the paper to her. Cindy was well aware a lawyer had drafted it. Basically, it contained what Mr. Sheldon had described. If she signed, she was prohibited from ever talking about the reason she left Sheldon Productions. There was a blank for the amount of the payment she would receive. Finally, she looked at Mr. Sheldon. "I'm not going to sign this until the blank is filled in."

"So, if I fill it in with 100,000 dollars, will you sign it?"

Cindy hesitated. "There's one more thing. I'm going to need a good letter of recommendation from Sheldon. Will I get it?"

"Yes, we can be sure you have a good recommendation. Put my name down as your previous employer," Mrs. Hagerty said.

Mr. Sheldon added, "If it makes any difference, the money will come out of Nick's pocket."

"Yes, it does make a difference. Go ahead and fill in the amount, and I'll sign."

"And you'll give us the thumb drive," Mrs. Hagerty said. "It's the only copy you have of the video, isn't it?

"Yeah. It's the only copy."

Five minutes later, Cindy walked out of Mr. Sheldon's office with a check for 100,000 dollars. The more she thought about it the better she felt. She didn't really want to go through the hassle of a sexual harassment complaint. The way it had all turned out avoided the stress of that whole process. She figured she'd tell the I. N. H. S. S. S. A. people, whoever they were, she'd signed the non-disclosure agreement in exchange for a payment. Maybe it wouldn't make them happy. All things considered, she didn't care.

Chapter Twenty-Seven

THE TEAM ASSEMBLED AT PHIL'S the evening after the men returned from New York. They sat around the kitchen table making ice cream sundaes. Phil started the conversation. "I guess we have to count our New York experience as a loss."

"How so?" Ralph asked.

"We didn't get any evidence about sexual harassment procedures. They paid her off. She never filed a sexual harassment complaint. I thought the whole idea was to show something about sexual harassment procedures. They weren't even involved this time."

"I can see what you're saying, Phil," Sherry said. "Still, we helped Cindy, and she sure needed help."

"She was really freaked out," Beth said. "And it happened fast. We complain about the waiting with the other cases. This one didn't take any time.

"And Phil, I'm going to disagree with you. This one's no failure. It showed another way men get away with sexual harassment. Granted, we didn't demonstrate anything about procedures, but it might be useful when I get around to telling the story of our adventures."

"Okay," Phil said. "I can see. Beth is right. This one didn't take a lot of time. We've got to retrieve the cameras in McKeesport. After that we've got nothing. Is anything in the hopper?"

"Of course. Beth and I are ready to go with another case."

"Give us the particulars," Ralph said.

"Beth is ready to present the case."

"Okay. Lucinda Wallace from a suburb of Atlanta. She works for an insurance company in a room full of cubicles. Her boss, Daniel Reeser, supervises several people in the cubes and comes by often. It's a lot like Sam Turbridge and Rochelle Martin. Every time he comes by her cube, he grabs her. While she tries to avoid him, she can't."

"This isn't going to be easy," Ralph said. "A room full of cubicles won't be easy to surveil. We might not get good video."

"So, you start to back off the first time we suggest a hard one," Beth said with a laugh.

"No. It might be difficult, but I'm not saying we can't do it."

"We'll have to take our ladder for sure," Phil said. "I bet those cube farms have high ceilings."

"You guys are ready for the challenge?" Sherry asked.

"Sure," Ralph said. "I'm just saying we might not be able to achieve the same quality video we got in the other cases."

Phil added, "Yeah, we'll go to Atlanta after we get the McKeesport cameras. It should be easy to get flights to Atlanta."

****

The next night, Phil and Sherry were in their hiding place in the trees beside the school in McKeesport. "We're missing the David Katel lecture," Phil said.

"Yes, I know. It's a big deal on campus. It might have been difficult to get seats. Lots of people are upset about him being invited. I sure hope everyone behaves well."

"Margaret's worried about the reaction."

"They've been clear. The college isn't endorsing him. Still, we're giving him a platform."

"Yes, the Randolph's money put us in a tough position. While I understand the other side, it's okay to let the guy speak. It's not good when a US Senator can't speak on a college campus. We ought to be able to hear him. Even if we don't agree with him."

"I'm glad we've got this job to do. As far as I'm concerned, I like having an excuse to skip the whole thing."

"Me too."

They lapsed into silence. A half hour after the last person left the school, they made their way to the side door they'd entered previously. Picking up the cameras went faster than setting them up, so they were in and out of the building in only three minutes. When they got back to their hiding place, Phil found Sherry laughing again.

"What's so funny?"

"It's like last time. I'm so nervous I have to let it out when we get back here. I guess it comes out as laughter. And it's a little funny—a librarian and a retired college professor breaking and entering. Come on, it's funny."

"I guess I can see it, but it seems dead serious to me. I'm concentrating on getting those lock picks to work. I'm so worried about the details, I haven't stepped back to take the long view. And I've been at this longer than you have. As long as you suppress your laughter until everything is done, it's okay."

Sherry hugged Phil. "I'm aware it's serious business."

They shared a long kiss. After the kiss, Phil grabbed his backpack. "We'd better stop, or we'll never get home."

"What's the hurry?" Sherry asked with a gleam in her eye.

Phil smiled, checked his surroundings, and took Sherry in his arms.

Chapter Twenty-Eight

THE NEXT MORNING PHIL DELIVERED the cameras to Beth. She had the morning off and had volunteered to do the editing. She started with the video of Dorothy McGuire's classroom. Most of the video wasn't at all relevant for them, so Beth did a lot of fast forwarding. After the students left on the second day, a man came into the classroom. Beth increased the sound and backed the video until she got to the man's entrance.

The guy came to Dorothy's desk. Beth saw him well and had a side view of her. He wore a suit and tie and was large, maybe six two and well over two hundred pounds. He had the look of an ex-football player.

He asked, "Have you thought about what I asked?"

"I have, and no, Dave, I won't go out with you. We've talked about it before. You're married. I won't go out with a married man."

"My marriage is finished. Sally and I hardly touch each other. We're only together because of our boys. And I'm sure she's seeing someone. I shouldn't have married her. I can't understand why I did. I didn't love her then, and I sure don't love her now. For all intents and purposes, I'm not married. We shouldn't let it get in our way. You recently broke up with your boyfriend. We both need someone."

"Dave, I'm sorry your marriage is falling apart. Still, there's another reason we shouldn't date. You're my supervisor. It is against school policy for us to date."

"Not a problem. We can keep it secret."

"It won't work. The town's too small. Everyone knows you. Think of all the parents and the other teachers. If you dated a teacher, it would be all over town before you knew it."

"The way you keep putting up obstacles, it looks like you're not attracted to me. I know it's not true."

"I do like you Dave, but not that way. While you're a good colleague, a good principal, I don't want to date you."

The principal appeared to get mad and gave Dorothy a stern look. "I didn't want it to come to this... Your tenure decision is this year. I don't think it's a good idea to get on the wrong side of your principal."

At this point he walked out the door. Dorothy stared after him as he left and then put her head down on her desk for several minutes. When she finally sat upright, Beth could tell she'd been crying.

When Beth got through the videos, she found two more with Dorothy and Dave Johnson. If she hadn't been fast forwarding most of the time, she would have probably learned a lot about the school, particularly with the video from the principal's office. The two other encounters she'd found were basically repeats of the first one. Johnson asked Dorothy out, and she refused. The final encounter, which happened in the principal's office, showed an explicit threat to cause difficulties in her tenure case. Beth felt the three encounters were enough to warrant a sexual harassment complaint. The videos contained none of the inappropriate touching in the other cases. Still, it was clearly sexual harassment.

In the evening, the group gathered at Phil's house to review the videos Beth had edited. The four quickly agreed. Dorothy McGuire had a good basis for a sexual harassment case. The threat to mess with tenure made it clear cut.

"I don't know about grade-school teachers, but tenure at the college is a big deal," Phil said. "I suspect it's the same. I remember being incredibly nervous before I got tenure. And I've seen lots of colleagues go through it. At a college you're at the mercy of the senior members of your department. If you've crossed one of them, they might just sink your tenure case. Of course, there are several layers, so a department can be reversed. It doesn't happen often. I bet the principal is a key player in a grade-school teacher's tenure decision."

"I think it's not as dramatic as at a college," Sherry said. "Colleges make the decision after five years or so. School teachers get tenure earlier."

"Yeah, our tenure decision is made early in a person's sixth year," Phil said. "You work with people for five years. They get to be your friends or your enemies. The worst situation is when you have to vote against one of your friends. I hated making tenure decisions."

"While this is all fine, it's beside the point," said Ralph. "You'll never have to make another tenure decision, Phil. The point is, we can make things better for Dorothy. I think we need to get the email out to her right away."

"You're right, Ralph," Sherry said. "We can use most of the same words we used with the others, and the email should go out tonight."

****

The next night, right before she went to bed, Dorothy McGuire checked her email one more time. She opened the email from the INHSSSA Group. She didn't who they were or what to expect. The internet contained a lot of weird stuff. She didn't delete emails until she knew a little about them, so she read the first paragraph:

> You don't know who we are, but we know quite a bit about you. Most importantly we are aware your principal, Dave Johnson, treats you terribly. We would like to help you with this situation.

After Dorothy read the email through, she didn't have the faintest idea what to think. She read it again, and still it didn't make sense. Who were these people and INHSSSA? She had a terrible feeling this might be a prank or internet scam. Still, they hadn't asked her for anything. She didn't even have to reply to their email or open an attachment. All she had to do was post in the chat room. She couldn't figure out how any danger might be lurking, so she did what they said. She posted a short message saying she'd be happy if they sent the videos.

Chapter Twenty-Nine

PHIL GOT TO HIS WEDNESDAY lunch early. He'd missed the David Katel speech, and he wanted to hear his colleague's reports. Andy strode toward him as he got there.

"You go to the Katel talk, Andy?" Phil asked.

"I sure did. He's one of my heroes."

"Is he as impressive in person as he is on TV?"

"He's a real presence. It came through on TV, and even more so in person. He can really command a room. Quiet descended when he spoke. I was impressed."

"What about the content of his speech? I read the story in the paper. According to Sally, some of what he said didn't seem right. Several things were out-and-out false or at least very misleading."

"I read Sally's story too. I don't know. I was reminded of the difference between what's on my TVs and what you read in the mainstream media. It's different."

"There's more than that," Bert interrupted who'd walked in while Phil and Andy were talking. "Katel and the people on your TVs get many things wrong."

"Like what?" Andy asked.

"Global warming, for one. Katel said it's a hoax. That's not true. All the measurements show the planet is warming. The polar ice caps are shrinking. Sea level is rising. The average temperature is increasing. All the measurements tell us the same thing. Global warming is real."

"Katel is saying people aren't causing global warming, and there's no reason to try to do anything about the climate."

"Then why didn't he say so? And he's wrong, too. What I'm talking about is when he said global warming is a hoax. I was there. I heard it."

The rest of the group had arrived, so they left Andy and went into the back room.

Once they were seated, Phil spoke. "I had to miss the Katel speech. So far, I found Andy loved the speech and Bert didn't. What about do the rest of you?"

"I for one thought he's amazing," William said. "He was more wrong and more sure of himself than anyone I've ever witnessed."

"Yes, you're right," George said. "Because I'm the president of the Faculty Assembly this year, I went to the dinner before the speech. Even at dinner, the guy's astounding. He's absolutely sure he's right on everything. I guess it's an advantage if you can erase all doubt."

"I tried to get the idea across in my article," Sally said. "I said, 'self-assured' and 'firmly held opinions.' You have to admit, the firmly held beliefs make him a compelling speaker."

"What he says is mostly nonsense." Bert couldn't hold himself back.

"It's what's so dangerous about him," Bob said. "He can say complete nonsense in a very convincing way."

"I was unable to be there. Give me examples," Phil said.

"Like I said to Andy, global warming is a good one," Bert replied. "In his speech, he called it a complete hoax. One of the students, a physics major I might add, asked him how much the average temperature would have to rise for him to believe in global warming."

"Yeah, I loved that exchange," Bob interrupted. "He didn't actually give an answer. He simply said the average temperature bounces around all the time. And he then went off on a discussion of ice ages."

"I thought his discussion of the horrors of immigration was awful," Jeremy said. "He argued illegal immigrants are a major cause of crime. I'm sure the data don't support him."

"And another student, one of ours, called him on the crime data," George said. "There's a study showing crime rates among illegal immigrants are lower than crime rates of native-born citizens. Katel didn't want to address the study, so he said 100 percent of them are criminals by the definition of illegal immigrants."

"That's not the point!" Bert argued loudly.

"We know, Bert, calm down," Phil said.

"He made a large number of completely unsubstantiated claims," Sally said. "The European Union is a conspiracy to thwart the interests of the US. Antitrust laws have blocked the expansion of industry in the US. The US Government was behind the 9/11 attacks. I can't remember all of them."

Bob jumped in. "He thinks he's an expert on everything. He even said he's smarter than all the talking heads on TV. And then he spouts lots of completely wrong stuff."

"Before I went to the dinner, I read an article on him," George said. "The authors mentioned a psychological theory they thought described Katel. It's called the Dunning Kruger effect, named after two psychologists. Basically, they demonstrated the less competent you are, the more you believe in your own abilities. Katel isn't smart at all, and that fact leads him to believe he's smarter than everyone else."

"Yeah, your right," Jeremy said. "It explains why he's such a convincing speaker. He believes all the things he's made up or found on a weird website. There's not a glimmer of doubt in any of his pronouncements."

"What you're talking about explains why academics usually make bad politicians," Phil said. "We're trained to doubt. We're trained to see both sides of issues. We are willing to see how contrary evidence would make us changes our minds. Katel is a convincing speaker because he's not like that at all."

"You're right, Phil," Bert said. "And it makes him dangerous. People are enthralled by his delivery. They don't spend enough time analyzing what he says."

"Andy thought him wonderful," Phil said. "How did the rest of the audience react?"

"I saw a mix," Sally said. "A lot of the townspeople I talked to loved him. Others not so much. While not many were as strongly opposed as you guys, a few were close."

"Katel and his like are a challenge to our educational system," William said. "Education, higher education in particular, needs to emphasize the importance of truth. We should train students to understand the difference between facts and opinions. Katel and his like have lots of opinions they claim are facts."

"You're right, William," George said. "I've been impressed with the students I've talked to. They seem very skeptical of Katel. I've been encouraged."

"In the long run then, okay to let Margaret have her big donation?" Phil asked. "Lackey will survive a speech by David Katel."

"Even I might agree," Bert said. "If you're right and most of the students are skeptical, it may even have been good to have Katel speak. Next year, they owe us a speaker I can agree with. Do we have the money to get good speakers?"

"Yes, we do," George answered. "And I might put you on the committee to recommend speakers. Okay, Bert?"

"I'm not sure I've ever said this before," Bert said. "I'd love to be on the committee."

They all laughed as they got up to leave.

Chapter Thirty

RALPH ARRANGED FOR HIS STUDENT helper, Jim, to man the store on Friday so he and Phil could take an early flight to Atlanta. They got a rental car at the airport and headed to the address of Lucinda Wallace's workplace. Atlanta is huge. With all the traffic, it took them an hour and a half to find the place. The building took up considerable space in a suburban office park. They got out of their rental car and walked by the front door.

"It's an insurance processing center, not the kind of place the public accesses directly," Phil said. "There's only one door and a bell to ring if you need to come in."

He and Ralph were unable to come up with an excuse to gain entry, so they walked by inspecting the lock on the door. In the back, the loading dock had the same arrangement. All people making deliveries had to ring a bell to gain entry.

When they returned to their car, Ralph said, "The lock shouldn't be a problem. We need to know when they clear out of the building and hope there's not any kind of alarm."

"You're right. An alarm would cause us problems."

"I'm not sure this kind of building would be alarmed," Ralph said. "It's mostly a paper-pushing place. I doubt there's anything worth stealing."

"I bet the computers are very nice. There's a good market for computers and computer parts."

Ralph slapped his forehead. "Sure, I of all people should have thought of computers. So, we may well have to deal with an alarm. We should rig a camera to try to steal the code like we did in Milwaukee."

"Good idea. It might mean we'll have another day in Atlanta. Better safe than sorry. The place to enter the code appears to be inside, and we might not be able to get a good view through the door. It's a good thing there's a half window in it. We'd be sunk without it."

Early in the evening, when all the cars had cleared out of the office park, Ralph secured a camera on one of the trees close to the door. The next day they saw the tourist spots in Atlanta. They liked Atlanta's aquarium and enjoyed having a day to walk around and admire the city. In the evening, they retrieved their camera and went back to the motel to check the video.

The motion activated camera's first pictures were in the middle of the night. Despite the low light, they saw several people piling out of a van and approaching the building.

"It's a cleaning crew," Phil said. "I bet they come at night to clean."

"Makes sense. I hope we learn something."

The first of the cleaning crew to get to the building, a woman, took out a large set of keys and opened the door. When she turned to the keypad, her body blocked any view of her entry. Next, she leaned out the door. Phil and Ralph could tell she was talking, but they weren't quite hearing her. One of the others shouted out, "*Cinco, quattro, ocho, uno.*" The leader ducked back in the door and returned to the keypad.

"We've got it," Phil shouted. "five, four, eight, one. We got the code."

"I can't say much for the security consciousness of the cleaning crew," Ralph said. "Still it's exactly what we needed. There's no reason to go through the rest of the video. We were really lucky. There's no way we would have discovered the code. We had a bad angle."

After darkness descended, Phil and Ralph parked their car on the street behind the office park and made their way to the front door. Their lock picks worked quickly, and Ralph entered the code. They made their way down a corridor with offices on both sides. When they came to the end, they opened the door to a large room with cubicles. There was another similar room further along.

"Wow," Ralph whispered. "It's a real cube farm. I wonder which one belongs to Lucinda Wallace."

Phil went around one of the half walls and looked into a cubicle. "This one's got a name plate. It belongs to B. Pederson. I guess we'll have to check them all and hope there aren't two L. Wallaces. I'll take this side of the room, and you take the other. If we don't find it here, we can check the other room."

"Okay," Ralph said. "I knew cubicles would be harder."

When they met at the far side of the room, Phil shook his head. "No L. Wallace."

"Me neither," Ralph whispered.

They went into the next room and split up again. About half-way down his side of the room Phil bumped into Ralph.

"I found it," Ralph said. "L. Wallace, and there are little girly touches. It's more likely Lucinda not Larry."

"Great, but we'd better be sure there's only one L. Wallace. See you at the other end."

When they got to the end Ralph said, "Only one."

Phil replied, "None on my side."

"Good. We're in luck. There's a sprinkler close to her cubicle."

The camera went up easily. As in the other cases, the sprinklers were what they needed. They folded their ladder and put the furniture they'd had to move back into place. They were sure no one would spot the camera. As they retraced their steps, they heard the front door open.

They froze and listened intently. They could tell from the Spanish that the cleaning crew had entered. They expected the cleaning crew to came in later; they had the previous night. It didn't matter, though. They had to get out. As quietly as possible, they made it rapidly to the back door. They didn't know what to do with the alarm, so they opened the door and slipped out. Calmly, they walked to their car. They heaved a big sigh when they climbed inside. Phil started the car, and they drove off. As they came to the corner, they saw a police squad car with its lights flashing turn into the office park.

"We must have tripped a silent alarm when we went out the back door," Ralph said.

"If we're lucky, they'll blame it on the cleaning crew," Phil offered. "I thought it was bad luck them coming in. Now it'll probably be a good thing. In any event, we'd better get as far away as we can."

"Too close. We'll have to be careful when we get the camera."

Chapter Thirty-One

A COUPLE OF DAYS LATER, Dorothy McGuire in McKeesport received the package from the INHSSSA people. She saw an Atlanta postmark. She put the thumb drive in her computer and queued the video file. It showed three of her discussions with Dave Johnson. In each case, he'd asked her out and she refused. She'd always tried to be polite, even nice. She wondered if she shouldn't have been so polite. She knew girls sometimes said no when they meant yes. They were playing hard to get. *That's not me.* She was being nice because he was her supervisor. She didn't think it would be wise to yell, "buzz off you jerk, I don't want to date you." As much as she wanted to, she wouldn't say anything like that. Still, on the video, maybe she came across as too nice. It should be beside the point. Dave had threatened to deny her tenure if she didn't go out with him. Sexual harassment clear and simple. The INHSSSA people, whoever the heck they were, were right. She had a good case, and the video would support it. She decided to take a personal day and go to the superintendent's office. She knew a good sub to call, so she decided to take off the day after tomorrow.

Dorothy made an appointment with the head of human resources for the school system for 10:00. She had all her ducks in a row, so she felt very confident. At 10:05—*they always make you wait five minutes,* she thought—she entered Mrs. Wilson's office.

Mrs. Wilson, who was stocky with gray hair, smiled and asked, "What can I do for you, Dorothy?" Dorothy remembered her from the interviews she'd done before she got the teaching job.

"I have a sexual harassment complaint I'd like to file. It's against Dave Johnson, my principal."

"Oh no, not Dave, he's one of Superintendent Squire's favorites. He'll be very upset with this."

A little taken aback by this response, Dorothy stood her ground. "Maybe he doesn't know Dave well. I have this complaint, and I'm following procedure by bringing it here. If my complaint concerned another teacher or an aide, it would go to my principal. Since my complaint is against him, I came here."

"I see you have a written complaint. Can I read it?"

Dorothy handed her the papers.

After Mrs. Wilson had read the two pages, she rocked back in her chair and looked Dorothy in the eye. After a long time, Mrs. Wilson spoke. "This is a serious complaint, and you say it's been going on for a long time."

"Yes, it's maybe been a month or two he's been asking me out. The threats to adversely affect my tenure case are more recent, the last couple of weeks I'd say. He's ratcheting up the pressure."

"We'll have to do an investigation. Is there anyone else who can testify in this matter?"

Dorothy thought for a minute. "No, I don't guess there is. I think he makes sure no one else is around when we're talking."

"Unfortunately, we'll have to talk to him. It's hard to keep these matters private as much as we try. Are you sure you want to go through with this?"

Dorothy got mad. "Mrs. Wilson, I'm making the complaint. I want to go through with it. What he's threatening is serious. Sure, I want to go through with it!"

Dorothy surprised herself. Then she realized she went into the proceedings with an ace in the hole: the video. While she wouldn't use it now, she had it if she needed it.

Mrs. Wilson sensed Dorothy's anger, and she got her back up a little. "Of course, I know it's serious. And we'll start the investigation of the complaint right away. Is that all?"

"Yes." Dorothy walked out of Mrs. Wilson's office. She felt proud of herself for not saying "yes, thank you." She didn't want to thank Mrs. Wilson. Years of polite encounters made the words "thank you" almost a reflex. She'd been able to suppress the reflex this time.

In the evening, Beth and Sherry saw Dorothy's post in the chat room. The process had been started.

Chapter Thirty-Two

DAVE JOHNSON CALLED AN IMPROMPTU faculty meeting for Friday after school. It had been three days since Dorothy lodged her complaint, so he probably knew about it.

The staff convened in the school's auditorium. Dorothy sat beside Susan Browning, a third-grade teacher. Susan had befriended her when she started, and they often conferred on school issues. Susan whispered to Dorothy, "What do you think this is all about?"

Dorothy responded, "I don't have any idea. It's not like Dave to call a meeting for after school."

"Particularly on Friday. Bill and I are going to our cabin for the weekend. I sure hope this isn't a long meeting."

Then Dave Johnson came in. He walked to the front of the auditorium and turned on the crowd. "Come sit in the front you two," he said pointing to the two gym teachers sitting in the back of the auditorium. "I don't want to have to shout."

Amid laughter from the others, the gym teachers moved to the front row. "Thank you," Dave said. Then he walked to the podium and took a sheet of paper out of his inner coat pocket and turned to assembled staff.

"I'll try to keep this brief. I felt I had to speak up. It's come to my attention a few staff members in the school have trouble telling the truth.

There are rumors going around the building about improper behavior. These rumors are unsubstantiated and false. Such rumors can be very damaging to the morale of the whole school. I have always demanded ethical behavior, and I've always thought I got it. Nevertheless, it's come to my attention I might be wrong. We can't have lying here. I won't stand for it."

He paused at this point and stared out into the audience, focusing on Dorothy. He continued staring at her while he spoke. "I don't want to name any names. The person involved is aware of what I'm talking about." He paused then and finally shifted his gaze to the rest of the room. "That's all. Have a good weekend," he said as he walked out of the auditorium brushing off the few teachers who tried to ask him questions.

Dorothy didn't quite know how to react. She got red in the face. Several of her colleagues cast glances in her direction as they walked out. She and Susan walked back toward their rooms. "Why did he stare at us?" Susan asked.

"Let's go into your room. I don't think this is hallway talk," Dorothy replied.

When they got into Susan's classroom, she asked, "What gives?"

"He stared at me, not us. You can't tell anyone. No one else knows. I've lodged a sexual harassment complaint about Dave."

"What?"

"For quite a while he's been asking me for dates."

"He's married."

"I have always turned him down. It's taken a turn recently. He'd out and out told me he'll scuttle my tenure case unless I go out with him. I couldn't stand it anymore, so I went to the superintendent's office. I don't understand quite why Dave called the meeting. Maybe he's trying to set me up as a liar."

Susan put her arms around Dorothy. "The whole thing's terrible," she said. "You're a terrific teacher. There's no way your tenure case will be even close. He can't stop it."

"Are you sure? He's the principal. And today's performance doesn't make me feel good. There was no way to miss his anger."

"I guess you're right. I bet he's been sure no one else is around when he's asked you out."

"Unfortunately."

"So, it's going to come down to your word against his. And he's starting a campaign to ruin your credibility in the building." Susan looked at Dorothy, expecting her to be very upset, but it didn't look like it. She asked, "Why are you smiling?"

"It won't work. I have evidence proving what I claimed."

"Evidence? What kind of evidence?"

Dorothy explained about the email from the I. N. H. S. S. S. A. group and the video they'd sent. The story amazed Susan. If the video was good, she understood Dorothy's confidence about the outcome of her complaint. Before they parted, Dorothy made Susan swear not to tell any of this to a living soul.

Chapter Thirty-Three

PHIL WENT ALONE TO ATLANTA to do the camera pickup. He got into the door with his lock picks and the code. There was no evidence the camera had been disturbed. He punched the code in again when he departed through the front door and hustled to his car. The police didn't show this time.

When he got back to Lackey, Phil went to Ralph's store and gave the camera to Ralph. Beth had volunteered to do the editing for this case, too.

In the evening Ralph heard a scream from the spare room where Beth had started working on the video. "What's wrong?" Ralph asked as he ran into the room.

"Oh my gosh, you've got to see this," Beth said.

"What is it?"

"Here, I'll back it up to the start."

Ralph pulled a chair beside Beth.

"It's the night cleaning crew. Keep watching."

They saw two of the cleaning crew come in and fan out in the room. One of them ran a vacuum cleaner and then went into the other room. The other one wiped off the computer screens and dusted the cubicles. After the vacuuming guy left, another man came in and closed the door.

The man came up behind the woman cleaning the cubicles, put one arm around her and covered her mouth with his hand. He whispered something in her ear, then he loosened his grip and turned the cleaning lady around. Ralph hadn't paid much attention to her. She appeared to be young. She had a shocked and frightened look on her face as she stared at the guy. He didn't give her much time to think. He attacked her again, pushing her backwards on the desk in the cubicle and hiked her skirt. He tore off her underwear, hitched his pants down, and raped her.

"No wonder you screamed," Ralph said. "This is awful!"

"I haven't seen any further." Beth paused the video. "I was fast forwarding through the bit with the cleaning ladies. Then I saw this. What are we going to do?"

"I don't know. The police should see this. It's nothing we can deal with. This is rape as clear as can be. It's not sexual harassment. It's out of our league."

"It's hard. We don't know who the cleaning lady is, and we don't know who he is."

"He must work at the place. The building's locked, and there's a security code. He must be an employee. No one else is able to get in. We should be able to find out who he is, and the cleaning lady shouldn't be difficult. There aren't many of them. They work for an outside firm, I suppose."

"We can't go asking questions at office cleaning firms."

"I guess you're right. We'd better bring the other two in on this."

"I'm calmer now. I think I can finish my job. I'll edit the video. I'll put this episode separate from anything involving Lucinda Wallace. We can show the edited version to Phil and Sherry tomorrow evening." Beth sighed. "It'll be interesting to see their faces when we show them this bit."

"You're sure you're okay to do the rest of the editing? I can do it if you want."

"No, I'm okay now."

The next evening the two couples gathered at Beth and Ralph's place.

"We got an interesting video for you," Ralph said. "Beth's got it loaded to show through our TV."

The first video showed Lucinda Wallace at her computer in her cubicle.

Soon a man came up behind her. He asked her a question, and they both peered at her computer screen. The man put his hand on Lucinda's upper arm. She shook him off. The hand then went down to her rear end and he gave it a rub. She turned on him, and he walked away smiling.

"He reminds me of Sam Turbridge," Sherry said. "He thinks he can touch her any time he wants."

"Yeah, and there's more," Beth said.

The edited videos showed ten more similar encounters. Usually he grabbed her backside. A couple of times he stroked her breasts. Obviously, Lucinda didn't like the attention. Her body language made it clear. She tensed each time the guy came into the room.

"It's a clear-cut case," Phil said. "Unwanted touching if I've ever seen it."

"Yes, and he's Daniel Reeser. He's her direct supervisor. We checked on the firm's website. They have pictures of all of the bosses," Beth said.

"I guess we should compose the email to Lucinda," Sherry said.

"No wait," interrupted Ralph. "We've got another interesting video clip this time."

"What is it?" Sherry said.

"Watch," Beth said. "You won't believe it."

The video started with the cleaning crew coming in and working. When they got to the entry of the rapist, Ralph said, "It's Grover Brown, the district supervisor of the insurance company. I found him on their website. He's in charge of this building and some others. I bet you're wondering what he's doing there in the middle of the night."

"I guess you'll show us," Phil said.

"Oh my God!" Sherry gasped when the rape started.

They watched in silence as the video continued, leaving nothing to the imagination. They were witnessing rape, no question about it. The four conspirators sat in silence. No one knew quite what to say.

Finally, Phil broke the silence. "This isn't a job for the In Hissa group. It's a job for the police."

"Fair enough," Ralph said. "How do we get it to the police? We can't simply walk into a police station and give them the video. They'd ask a ton of questions we wouldn't want to answer."

"So, you've got no interest in being charged with breaking and entering, huh Ralph?" Sherry said.

"Not to put too fine a point on it, yes," Ralph replied.

After a long pause, Phil said, "I don't think we need to make a decision tonight. You two dropped a bomb on us. We're going to have to do some serious thinking about what we can do. I wonder what the police in Atlanta would do if they got an anonymous package in the mail with a thumb drive in it."

"Maybe it would work. I like your first impulse better," Sherry said. "We need to take time and figure out what to do. This isn't an easy one."

Chapter Thirty-Four

AS SHERRY DROVE HOME, SHE wondered how they were going to handle the rape. *The perpetrator's a bigwig in the insurance company. We can't proceed as normal.* The sexual harassment complaint might land on his desk, and nothing would happen. And rape's much worse than sexual harassment. They had to deal with the rape. At that point in her musings, two cars going incredibly fast passed Sherry. As they flashed by, Sherry thought she saw the passenger in the second car leaning out of the window and shooting a pistol at the car in front.

Sherry didn't know what to do. Her curiosity piqued; she increased her speed. They were approaching a curve in the road, and she didn't think the two cars in front of her would be able to manage it at their speed. Sure enough, when she slowed to go around the curve, the lead car had flipped off the road. The other car had managed to stay upright, and its passengers were getting out. Sherry stopped about two hundred feet behind the two cars. She pulled out her phone, planning to call the police but changed her mind and started filming the scene in front of her.

Two men had guns. They went to the overturned car and hauled out the driver and his companion. They then shot the men from the other car. Sherry suddenly realized she recognized one of the shooters—Bob McFall from the farm down the road from where she lived. After the shooting, the shooters dragged the two bodies off the road. Then Bob turned around and looked at Sherry. *Oh my God,* thought Sherry. *He's going to recognize my car.* The other guy saw her car too, and he pulled out his pistol and began shooting at her. A shot hit the windshield on the passenger side, shattering it and spraying a few small shards of glass toward Sherry.

In a panic, Sherry jammed her car into reverse and backed away fast. She heard a couple more shots, but they didn't hit her car. After backing up about 200 yards, she shifted into drive and turned on to a farm road. While her compact sedan wasn't great on dirt roads, Sherry sped. She knew this farm road, a shortcut to her house. She seldom used it. A closed gate was situated at the far end of the road. At the gate, she slammed on her brakes and hurried out of the car. She glanced back down the way she'd come. *Bob probably knows this road, too.* No one was coming. She drove through the gate and stopped on the other side. She had always been taught to close gates behind her.

When Sherry got to the main road, she half expected Bob and the other guy would be waiting for her. Luckily, they weren't there. Driving quickly to her house, she ran in the front door shouting for her mother. When she found her in the kitchen, she ran to her saying, "Mom, we've got to pack a few things and get out of here in a hurry."

"What? Slow down, dear. What are you saying?" her mother said.

Sherry took a deep breath. "On my way home, I witnessed a shooting. Bob McFall, you know, from down the road, and someone else ran two people off the road and then dragged them out of their car and shot them."

"Oh my God. How terrible!"

"Yes, and I'm sure Bob recognized my car. They took a few shots at me as I drove away. We've got to get out of here. They're aware I witnessed what they did, and they're sure to come after me. Go upstairs and put a few things in a suitcase. We can find a place in town to spend the night."

Gladys Ahearn didn't climb the stairs quickly. Sherry had started throwing things in a small bag. A car pulled up, so she ran to the window. It was Bob McFall and the other guy. Thinking quickly, Sherry moved to the side of the window. She'd have been a perfect silhouette if she kept standing in front. She told her mother to stay away from the windows.

"What's happening?" asked her mother.

"They're here!" Sherry yelled.

She looked out the window again and saw Bob and his friend get out of their car and take out two big gas cans, two boards, and a hammer from the trunk of the car. One of them went to Sherry's car and splashed gas on it. He then backed away and threw a lit match on the car. It went up in flames with a big whoosh.

Gladys had come to peek out of the other window. "They set your car on fire!" she said with panic in her voice.

"I have an idea about what they're going to do next. They're going to try to burn us out. We've got to get to the basement fast." Sherry took her mother's hand and hustled her toward the stairs. As they made their way down the stairs, they heard banging on the front and back doors.

"They're boarding the doors," Sherry said.

"What?"

"Keep moving Mom, we've got to make it to the basement. It's going to be the only safe place real soon."

The two women made it down the steep stairs to the basement. They didn't turn on any lights. Being sure her mother was settled, Sherry said, "You wait here. I'm going to go back and get the things we'll need. They're going to set the house on fire soon. Don't worry, I can get us out of here. Now we have to wait."

Sherry hurried up the stairs. She spied a figure walking beside the house. The smell told her he'd poured gasoline on the side of the house as he walked by. She sprinted to her bedroom, unlocked her drawer, and grabbed her laptop. Next, she retrieved two spare blankets from the closet. Carrying her load, she ran back down to the kitchen and grabbed a mop and a broom. As she headed toward the basement stairs, she heard another whoosh and flames leaped toward the windows. She dumped her stuff at the bottom of the basement stairs and hurried to her mother.

"We're going to be okay, Mom. In a little while, we're going out the storm doors. Those guys won't be able to stay too long. They might wait to see if we try to jump out a window. After a while though, they'll have to leave. They don't want to be here when the fire attracts other people.

Sit tight. Okay?"

Her mother nodded. Sherry bolted up the stairs to the living room and retrieved her purse. She wanted the cell phone. It had the videos that would put Bob and his friend in jail. The house burned on all sides. The heat was intense, and smoke seeped in. The whole house was going to burn in a hurry. It contained a lot of memories. She'd grown up there, and her mother had lived there for more than sixty years. *Now's not the time to think about such things. Survival's more important.* She hoped her plan would work. She hurried down to the basement.

In the basement, Sherry went to check on her mother. She looked frightened and so frail. Sherry hugged her. "We're going to be okay, Mom. I need to soak these blankets in water and wrap ourselves in them before we try to go out."

"How will we get the storm doors open? Won't they be on fire too?"

"I've brought the mop and broom. I'm going to use those to push the doors open—I won't have to touch the doors. We should wait a bit longer to be sure the guys who started the fire have cleared out. I'll call Phil, so he can come get us."

Sherry dialed Phil's number. When he answered, she said, "Phil, this is an emergency. I need you to come to my house as fast as you can. Don't come all the way to the house, stop about 100 yards from the house on the edge of the woods. My mom and I will come out of the woods."

"What?"

"Our house is on fire, and we are about to escape. Come get us at the edge of the woods. Do you understand? Oh, and bring two big towels."

"Yes," answered Phil. "The edge of the woods. Your house is on fire?"

"I'll explain when you get here. Right now, I've got things to do, and you need to drive. Come fast."

The heat from the fire had made its way to the basement. Luckily, the smoke hadn't gotten thick. Sherry figured it was time to make their getaway. She got one of the blankets and went to the sink and turned on the water. She soaked the blanket and then brought it to her mother. "When the doors are open, wrap yourself in this," she instructed her mother. Then she went back and soaked the second blanket.

With the blanket over her shoulders, Sherry took the broom and the mop and approached the storm doors. They were tough to open from the basement under any circumstances. She knew the guys who'd set the house on fire had blocked the front and back door. They only got two boards out of their car, so they probably hadn't thought about the storm doors. Sherry went up a step toward the doors and gave a strong push with the mop on the middle of the right-hand door. Much to her surprise, the mop went right through the door, and little bits of burning wood showered down toward her. She jumped out of the way and quickly put the burning pieces out. For her next attempt, she pushed on the middle of the doors where there were two layers of wood. She shoved hard and the left door came open. Sherry stepped back as flames temporarily covered the opening. When the flames died away, she went back and pushed open the other side. Sherry was elated to see the backyard.

Sherry went back to her mother. "Come on," she said. "Let's wrap ourselves in these blankets and get out of here."

"Fine with me. It's getting hot."

Sherry wrapped her mother in the blanket. "Can you walk?"

"I'll have to," Gladys answered.

Sherry got her purse and the laptop and wrapped herself up. Taking her mother's hand, she approached the opening. The fire burned around the edges of the storm doors, and they had to bend to avoid it as they got out. Sherry went up first, kicking burning boards out of the path. Her mother followed, clinging to Sherry's hand. When they cleared the building, Sherry said, "We're out, we can take off these blankets now."

As they shrugged off the blankets, they heard a siren. "The fire truck's finally coming," Gladys said. "I bet the neighbors called them. Should we go and tell them what happened?"

"No," Sherry replied. "Come on; I told Phil to stop at the edge of the woods. We don't want to talk to the firemen."

"Why not?"

"Bob McFall and his friend wanted to kill us. It's best if they think they succeeded, at least for a while. If they know we got out of the house, they'd come after us again."

"Oh. This sure is a mess. My poor house!"

Chapter Thirty-Five

AS SHERRY AND HER MOTHER waited for Phil, the firemen worked. It took them quite a while to get the blaze under control. From her vantage point, she saw the house had almost completely burned. Only two of the walls were still standing. Because of the firemen, anything inside would be soaking wet. While they might be able to salvage some things, it didn't look good.

Phil pulled up fifteen minutes after they'd entered the woods. The two women piled into the back seat. Sherry said, "Good, you remembered the towels. Here mom, wrap yourself in this towel. You've gotten a chill."

"Please tell me what's going on," Phil pleaded.

"In due time," Sherry responded. "First, make a U-turn and get us back to town."

When they'd made it a half a mile from the farmhouse, they passed two police cars parked by the side of the road with their lights flashing. Phil said, "I'd have made it to your house earlier if I hadn't been slowed down by those guys on my way here."

"They are investigating the wreck," Sherry said.

"What wreck? Can you tell me what this is all about?"

Sherry had been turned around, checking the rear window. She shifted forward and finally said, "We're not being followed, so I can relax and explain things." She told Phil the story, starting with the cars passing her.

When she got to the part where the killers shot at her, Phil gasped. "You're all right?"

"Yes, my car windshield shattered. There's more to it."

Sherry continued with her story. When she got to the escape from the burning house, Phil asked, "Did you call the police?"

"No, I didn't have time. I drove like mad getting away, and then they came and started the fire before I could react. I only called you. My main priority was getting the two of us out of the burning house without getting shot. After we escaped, I guess I should have called the police. I didn't think about it. I only wanted to get away from there. There will be time to call the police when we get back to town."

"They'll have questions. They have a wrecked car, two dead bodies lying beside the road, and a fire caused by arson. It's more action than our police department gets most years."

"I'm worried about Bob McFall. Clearly, he knows I witnessed what he did. I hope he thinks we both burned in the house."

"I hope it worked," Phil said.

"I've got the goods on the men who did it. I videoed it all on my cell phone. I'll feel better when Bob McFall and his companion are in jail."

"Should I take you straight to the police station?"

"No, take me to your house. I want to get mom settled. I'll call the police from there."

"Your mom can have the guest room. You can take my bed; I'll sleep on the couch. Come to think of it, the police may not have anyone to question you until morning. The police station is closed. There are only two or three people on duty after hours, and they're probably investigating the car accident and shooting."

"I bet you're right. Take us to your house." Sherry sighed. "Right now, the adrenalin is draining out of my system. I've been so keyed up ever since those two cars came racing by."

Phil drove into his garage and let the two women out. When they got in the house, he showed Sherry and Gladys the guest room. He only had to move one pile off the bed to make it presentable.

After he'd shown Gladys the guest bathroom, they went out in the living room. Gladys surprised them both when she spoke with a twinkle in her eye. "There's no need to put bedding on the couch, Professor. You and Sherry can sleep in the master bedroom."

"Mother!"

"Do you think I'm a fool, darling? It's been written all over your face for several weeks now."

"I should know I can't keep anything from you," Sherry said.

"You'd better call the police before we go to bed. I'll get the number," Phil said.

When Phil came back with the number, Sherry stopped him. "First, let me show you the video on my phone."

Phil looked at the video completely through once, and then said, "Let me see it again. Which one is Bob McFall?"

"The one in jeans and a red t-shirt," Sherry answered.

After his second look, Phil said, "You're fairly far away, and it's not always in focus. Still, it's good enough to tell what's going on. Also, I bet there are ways of enhancing the video. I bet the police will be very happy to see this. It's time to call them."

Sherry dialed the police. The dispatcher took down her information. After determining no one was in immediate danger, the dispatcher told her the police weren't able to do anything until morning. All the officers were out investigating a car wreck. Sherry gave Phil's address and phone number. When she had the information, the dispatcher told them to expect a call from the police the next morning.

After Sherry told Phil about the response, he said, "It's a little anticlimactic. I guess it's what happens at night in a small town. They can't have a very large police force. We'd better get to sleep so we're ready for them in the morning."

In the bedroom, Phil gave Sherry a t-shirt to use as a nightgown. Sherry came into Phil's arms in bed. They shared a long kiss. Then Sherry pulled away. Phil could tell she was crying.

"What's wrong?" Phil asked.

"Nothing. I'm decompressing. Hold me."

Phil took her in his arms. It seemed right to fall asleep together.

Chapter Thirty-Six

THE NEXT MORNING, THE POLICE called at eight o'clock and said they'd be there in half an hour. Sherry and her mom were a little rumpled. They only had the clothes they'd worn the day before. They both did a little primping in anticipation of the police coming.

Gladys said, "I guess we'll have to get ourselves a whole new wardrobe. Our old clothes won't be fit to wear even if they weren't burned to a crisp."

"Leave it to you to look on the bright side," Sherry said.

"Every cloud has a silver lining."

"And you'll be the one to find it."

At five minutes after eight, a Lackey police car parked in front of Phil's house. Two people got out, the police chief and a young woman. As they watched them get out of the police car, Phil said, "The guy's the police chief. I don't have any idea who the woman is." They were a mismatched pair. The police chief was big, probably a little too big, and red faced. The woman was petite with short blonde hair. She wore a navy-blue business suit.

Phil let them in and made introductions. "Chief Richardson, this is Sherry Ahearn. She's the one who made the call last night, and this is Gladys Ahearn, her mother. I'm Phil Philemon, we've met before."

The chief shook hands all around. "Nice to meet you." Turning to the woman, he continued, "And this is Melissa Jacobson. She's a special agent with the FBI."

"FBI?" Phil and Sherry echoed.

"Yes," the chief said. After an awkward pause, he added, "Is there a place to sit down? This might take a while to sort out."

Phil gestured toward the living room, and they went in. He, Sherry, and her mom took seats on the couch, and the chief and the FBI agent sat in the chairs facing them. When they were seated, the FBI agent spoke for the first time. "Your report last night mentioned Bob McFall. He's a person of interest to us. Actually, he's a fairly small fry, all things considered. Can you tell us what you saw?"

Sherry answered, "I can tell you, and then I can show you. I got a good video on my phone." Sherry told her story, starting from the two cars zooming past her. Both the chief and the FBI agent took notes. After she finished, Sherry showed the phone video.

"Very quick thinking, Ms. Ahearn. Videos like this make our job much easier. I can verify it's Bob McFall in your video. We don't know the other one's name. He's a guy they call 'Hench' on our wiretaps. We are in the process of identifying the two bodies. We suspect they're from a rival gang."

"Are there gangs in Lackey?" Phil broke in.

"No," the FBI agent said. "These are not local gangs."

"There's more to my story," Sherry said.

"Okay, proceed," the FBI agent urged.

Sherry filled them in on what happened after she drove back to the farmhouse until she arrived at Phil's house.

"Again, I have to compliment you, Ms. Ahearn. I take it you wanted them to believe you'd died in the fire?"

"Yes. I'd been pretty sure Bob McFall recognized my car out on the road. And his coming to our house with the gas cans cinched it. If we'd jumped out a window or gotten out of the house any other way, they would have shot us. We had to wait."

"Chief, we need to follow through on Ms. Ahearn's plan. Can we get the cooperation of the fire department? We need them to report they found the remains of two bodies in the fire."

"What?" Chief Richardson asked.

"The main thing is we have to get the heat off Ms. Ahearn and her mother. If Bob McFall thinks they died in the fire, he'll act like he's in the clear. Chief, go to the fire department right away and get their cooperation. Tell them to say they found the remains last night after all the spectators left. And, just a minute, we'll probably have to get the local mortuary involved too."

"I don't understand," Phil said. "Why fake their deaths? Won't Bob McFall be in jail? Sherry's video should be enough for you to pick him and his compadre up and throw them in jail."

"It's not simple. Like I said, Bob McFall and this Hench are small fry. We want their bosses. If they think they're in the clear, they'll lead us to their bosses. We don't want them arrested. We need them free. We're close to cracking a much bigger case." Then she turned to Chief Richardson and said, "You understand what you need to do?"

"Yes." The chief got out of his chair. "I'll take the cruiser and come back to get you when I'm done."

After Chief Richardson left, Sherry said, "Suppose the fire department fakes finding two bodies in the farmhouse. Where do Mom and I go?" Looking at the FBI agent, she continued, "I'm sorry, I didn't catch your name."

"Melissa Jacobson. Call me Melissa."

"So, Melissa, where do we go?"

"We can take you to a safe house out of state. You'll be away from here, and we'll get you everything you need."

Gladys looked up. "It'll be a lot. We don't have anything. We lost everything we owned in the fire. I bet we can't salvage anything."

"We'll take care of it."

"What about insurance? You had insurance, didn't you?" Phil asked.

"Yes, we did. And I guess my brother Trick would be able to collect if we died in a house fire. That won't work. We're not dead."

Phil jumped in again. "I had to have a death certificate to collect on insurance on my wife. You won't have a death certificate. It's complicated, and what about Sherry's job?"

At this point Melissa interrupted. "We can deal with all the details. We probably won't have to have you in a secure location very long, maybe two or three weeks. We have people who've done this kind of thing before. I'll call, and our people will work out all the details."

"What about a memorial service? Lots of people in town are aware Sherry and I are close. It's a small town. And Gladys has lived here a long time. It's hard to keep secrets."

"Stay calm. We'll probably move you two women tonight, so no one sees you leaving. Today you have to stay away from the windows and don't contact anyone. Phil—it's Phil, isn't it—go about your business as usual."

"My story is a friend I'm very close to just died in a fire. How can I go about business as usual? It would seem very odd to people in town. I probably should go out to the farm to investigate the house. I'd go there if they actually died. And what about Sherry and Gladys's friends? It's going to be very difficult to carry out this charade."

"The best advice is to try to stay away from people. I guess you should go check out the farmhouse. Be sure to act depressed," Melissa said. "Come back here and closet yourself in the house with everyone else."

"I'll have to answer the phone. What do I say?"

"Keep it simple. The two deaths are a tragedy. You're in grief. You haven't heard anything about any memorial service. Details will come later. Buy time."

"My brother Trick is a chief of police in South Carolina. He has to be told this is all false. It would tear him apart if he thought we both died. You can trust him," Sherry said.

"Okay," answered Melissa. "I'll get word to an FBI agent in his area, and he can brief your brother. We should keep the circle small. The more people involved, the more likely it is someone will make a mistake."

"What's Bob McFall involved with?" Sherry asked.

"No, in fact especially you can't be told," Melissa replied. "You may well be asked to testify, and you shouldn't be aware of the rest of the case. If we can land the big shots, it'll be all over the papers. You'll find out about it for sure. Now if you'll excuse me, I've got several phone calls to make. Is there a room without an outside window where Sherry and her mom can stay?"

"Only the bathrooms; however, the curtains in the guest room and the master bedroom are quite thick. I don't think anyone can see in," Phil replied.

Gesturing to Sherry and her mom, Melissa said, "You two should go in one of those rooms. When I get details, I'll tell you more about what's going to happen."

Sherry and her mom retreated to the master bedroom, and Phil followed them. Sherry closed the door and took Phil aside. "I guess this puts me out of commission on our project," she whispered. "I bet the FBI is going to want to restrict my internet access. The three of you are on your own."

"What are you two whispering about?" Gladys asked.

"Oh, it's nothing, Mom."

"You may be able to use the chat room," Phil whispered. "We'll have to see how your situation turns out." Phil broke away from Sherry and went to her mother. "Mrs. Ahearn, is there anything in particular I should try to find at the farmhouse? Is there anything that might have survived the fire?"

"I wonder what everything looks like. Take pictures if you can. The barn may be okay. Stack any salvageable stuff there."

"I wonder how they're doing getting the fire department to go along with the story," Sherry said. "I bet it's hard. Most of the firemen who respond to fires out where we live are volunteers. They're going to have to get the word out to a lot of people."

"We'll let them worry about it," Phil said. He went back to Sherry and gave her a hug. "I'm going to miss you."

"It won't be long, Phil. Mom and I might like a vacation. Mom in particular. She hasn't taken many vacations."

"So, who's finding a silver lining now?" Gladys asked.

"I'm my mother's daughter," Sherry quipped.

"Actually, I'm the one who has it hard," Phil said. "I've got to do an acting job. Maybe we should finesse the memorial service by saying your bodies are going to be buried in South Carolina near Trick. I keep thinking of other details. I sure hope Melissa is right, and the FBI people can coach me. I've never done anything like this before."

"None of us have done anything like this before. I can understand why you're nervous. You'll do fine. You've been through a similar event before. You know, with your wife. It's not the same. Still... similar."

"This time it's different. I went into a tailspin after Mary Jane died. Come to think of it, I stayed in the house quite a bit doing nothing. My friends from my lunch group practically had to pry me out of the house. Depression took over. Maybe I can hide out here a lot."

Sherry replied, "You're probably right. We'll have to wait for the FBI people and listen to their advice." They were interrupted by the ringing phone, and Phil went out to the living room to answer it.

Melissa blocked his way to the phone. "Don't answer. We need to see who it is."

After five rings, they heard the message. Frank Jenkins, the head librarian. He asked if Phil knew anything about Sherry's whereabouts. She was supposed to be at the library at eight thirty, and she hadn't shown.

"It's okay," Melissa said. "Let them wonder."

Chapter Thirty-Seven

AT TEN O'CLOCK, PHIL RETURNED Frank's call, saying he didn't know anything. He promised to go out to the farm to figure out what had happened to Sherry. They both agreed normally Sherry would call in if she had to miss work. At eleven, Phil left to go to the farm.

In the daylight, Phil saw the skid marks on the road where the two cars had tried to manage the curve but no other evidence of a wreck. Somebody had cleared the mess. When he got to the farmhouse, it was almost completely destroyed. He spotted a red official-looking car parked by the barn. Phil drove over and parked by it. The car belonged to the fire chief.

Phil got out and walked to the fire chief. "Hello," he said when he got beside the man. "I'm Phil Philemon. One of my friends, Sherry Ahearn, and her mother Gladys live in this house. Do you know where they've gone?"

"I'm afraid they didn't survive the fire," the chief said.

"What!" Phil put as much panic in his voice as he could muster.

"It's a tragedy. No, murder. The fire clearly resulted from arson. Gasoline started it. And the doors were nailed shut. Look on the bottom of the front door. The guys who started the fire wanted to kill the people in the house, and they sure did."

Phil was impressed by the way the fire chief sold this lie. "Where were the bodies? I'm not sure why it matters. I guess I'd still like to know."

"We found the bodies huddled together in the basement. I guess they went there to get away from the smoke. We took the remains of the two women to the mortuary in town."

"Any idea who started the fire?"

"No, arson is often difficult to spot. Not in this case. Whoever did it ran around the house with a gasoline can. Then they threw a bunch of matches at it. The fire engulfed the house from all sides. The thing is gasoline and matches aren't exotic. Anyone can get them. I bet gasoline cans are somewhere on every one of the farms around here, and everyone has matches. While the arson was easy to spot in this case, we've got no idea who did it."

Phil managed to produce a tear. "I can't believe Sherry's gone," he said as he turned away from the fire chief.

"It's a real tragedy. It must have been horrible when the two women found the doors blocked."

Phil turned his tear-stained face back toward the chief. "A tragedy, yes." He then walked away, faking more tears. He went toward the woods, hoping it looked like he was trying to compose himself. After several minutes, he walked to the house and took pictures from several angles.

He went back to the fire chief and asked, "What's going to happen to all this?"

"I guess the farm will pass down to the family." Pointing to the charred remains, he continued, "There's probably nothing worth having. In any event, we'll leave it alone. Sometimes people find important stuff in the ashes."

"The only heir would be Sherry's brother Trick—Richard Ahern—I guess. He lives in South Carolina. I suppose the police have contacted him."

"I guess. We don't get involved with those details."

"I'd better go back to town. Sherry had a lot of friends. I hate to be the one to have to tell them about this."

"I'm really sorry."

When Phil got back to the house, the assembled crew had grown by one. Sherry introduced a round-faced, red-haired guy as Samuel Hopkins, a US Marshall. He'd been called to help with the details of Sherry and Gladys's temporary relocation. Half eaten lunches were on the table. Apparently, Sam had brought sandwiches.

Phil filled them in on his discussion with the fire chief, even bragging about the tears he'd been able to produce. Melissa seemed quite pleased with the performance of the fire chief.

At one point, Phil said, "I had a thought at the fire site. Trick should probably come here. With Sherry and Gladys dead, it's his property. Wouldn't it be more realistic if he came here? He should want to try to determine if anything can be salvaged. And maybe he'd want to put the property on sale. He'd have a lot to deal with."

Gladys responded, "You're right. He grew up there, too. I'd like it if he had the job of going through the ashes."

"Yes," Sherry added. "It would be natural for Trick to want to check things out. Now, Phil, you need to get some lunch."

After Phil wolfed down a sandwich, he went to his computer and downloaded the images from his camera. As he scrolled through the pictures to get to the most recent ones, Melissa stopped him at the pictures of the doors at the McKeesport school. "Why take pictures of doors?" she asked.

"Oh, it's a random shot," Phil said. "Here they are," he announced and got out of the chair. "Sherry, why don't you sit in front of the computer. I'll get a chair for you, Gladys."

After they'd looked at three of the five photos Phil had taken, Gladys spoke up. "It's a God-awful mess. It's a total loss."

"I'm afraid so, Mom."

Phil added, "The fire chief said they wouldn't touch anything. He said at times people find important stuff when they stir the ashes. He figured whoever inherited the property would want to do a thorough search before clearing away the remains of the house."

Sherry got up from the computer after the last picture. She had tears in her eyes, and she rushed into the bedroom. "Let her go," Gladys said. "It's been hard on her having to worry about me, and what with people trying to kill her... She grew up in that house. She'll be okay. At times a person needs a little cry."

About fifteen minutes later, Sherry came out of the bedroom. Phil rushed to her and put an arm around her. "I'm fine," she said. "It just got to me."

Melissa came to the couple. "Ms. Ahearn, you've been incredible. Your quick thinking has provided us important evidence, and you saved your life and your mother's too. I'm sure McFall and Hench would have shot you if you'd gotten out of the house any other way."

"Thanks, and call me Sherry. I don't deserve much credit. I acted on instinct most of last night."

"Well, your instincts are good ones. Let's take a look at what Sam has for us."

Samuel Hopkins and the others sat around the kitchen table. He had a couple of folders on the table and opened one of them. "Here is a house in Georgia. We've used it a few times. It's in a little town. It's a very walkable place. We'd get you a car. You wouldn't have to use it very often. Take a look at the pictures."

After viewing the pictures, Sherry said, "I didn't expect this would be like a real estate sales job. Okay, what else do you have?"

"The other one is further away—in Nebraska. It's a similar situation, a small town easy to get around in. Here are the pictures."

"This all is real nice," Gladys said. "Actually, I don't like either of them. I think it's time for me to experience one of those old folk's homes... a retirement community, I guess."

"Mom!" Sherry said in surprise. "You wouldn't hear of the idea when I tried to get you to move close to me in State College."

"I had my house then. Now I don't. I might not like a retirement community. Still, I want to try one out. While you're wonderful, you don't want to live with your old mother all the time. You and Phil want to be frisky more often than you get a chance. It doesn't work with us living together."

Sherry blushed. "You heard the woman. Do you have anything with a retirement home nearby?"

"And my son lives in South Carolina, right outside Hilton Head. Is it possible to find me a place in a retirement community near there?"

"Mom, you can't order what you want."

"Why not?"

"Let me get on the phone," Sam said. "We might be able to find something for you. Would an apartment near the retirement home work for you, Sherry?"

"Sure."

The phone rang. Phil recognized Ralph's number. Ralph sounded panicked. "One of my customers told me Sherry's house burned down, and she died. Is it true?"

"Yes, it's true. I got a call from the library. Sherry hadn't come to work. I went out there and found the house burned down. I saw the fire chief. He told me both Sherry and her mom died in the fire. I'm in shock now. I don't have any idea what to do."

"Is there anything Beth and I can do?"

"No. The police have contacted Sherry's brother in South Carolina. How did your customer find out about it?"

"Yeah, she heard it on the radio—the local station."

"I'm probably not going to be coming to the store for a couple of days. I'm sorry. I'm not able to deal with the public at this point."

"I understand."

Phil hung up and said to Sherry, "Ralph. One of his customers heard about the fire and the two deaths on the radio."

Things were settled three hours later. Gladys had found a nice-looking retirement community in South Carolina near Hilton Head, and Sherry would live in an apartment in a town fifteen minutes away.

Phil received several calls as the news spread across town. He perfected his depressed-sounding response. He thought people bought the charade hook, line, and sinker. When they got a chance in the afternoon, Phil and Sherry slipped into the master bedroom and conferred about their project. They decided Phil would have to bring Beth and Ralph in on the ruse. Sherry wanted things to proceed as normal. Beth should send the email to Lucinda Wallace to get started. Also, they should try to identify the rape victim and keep trying to figure how to get the police involved. Finally, they agreed Beth should check the chat room for any messages from Sherry. Sherry figured she'd be able to get access to a computer even if email might be prohibited.

At ten that night, they didn't put on the porch light as Sherry and Gladys slipped out the back door into a black FBI van. Before leaving, Sherry gave Phil a long goodbye kiss.

Chapter Thirty-Eight

ONCE SHERRY'S EYES ADJUSTED TO the light, she looked to the front seat to see the driver. Much to her surprise, it was Melissa. She said, "I'm surprised you're here, Melissa."

"Yeah... I'm surprised to be here, too."

"This isn't part of your usual assignment?"

"No, this is special," Melissa snapped. "I don't want to talk about it. Sit back and relax. We're stopping at a motel in a couple of hours. Try to sleep if you can."

Sherry wondered what had put Melissa in such a mood. It didn't seem like the right time to ask, so she didn't try. She sat back and recognized how tired she felt. She'd been keyed up all day. She smiled to herself. Playing dead tired her out.

****

In Lackey the next morning, Phil arose early and went to Beth and Ralph's apartment. Beth opened the door. After she let Phil in, she threw her arms around him and said, "Oh Phil, I'm so sorry." Tears streamed down her face.

"She was such a great person," Beth said. "You must feel awful."

Phil extracted himself from Beth. The next moment Ralph had him in a bear hug. "I don't know what to say. First Mary Jane and now Sherry."

Phil slapped Ralph on the back, stepped out of the hug, and said, "It's okay."

"What?" they echoed.

Phil held up his hands to calm them. "It's complicated. First and foremost, Sherry's not dead."

"The radio and today's paper." Ralph hurried to the kitchen table to get the newspaper. "And one of my customers said he'd seen the fire department delivering what must have been the remains to the mortuary."

Phil raised his hands again. "Calm down. I'll explain. Why don't you go to the couch? Be calm, everything's fine."

When Beth and Ralph were seated on the couch, Phil sat down in a chair facing them. Carefully, he explained the whole thing, starting with Sherry's drive home the night before last. He finished with Sherry and Gladys's departure last night.

"Amazing," Beth said. "Sherry had the presence of mind to get down to the basement with the house burning around her. She didn't try to crawl out a window and escape."

"No, she figured the two guys were probably outside waiting for them to try to escape. She had to wait them out. They wouldn't hang around too long. Eventually a big fire attracts attention. A neighbor called the fire department. Sherry said she heard the fire engine coming when they'd just left the house."

"How'd they get the fire department to fake finding two bodies?" Ralph asked. "There are a lot of volunteers who helped put the fire out."

"They were good," answered Phil. "When I talked to the fire chief yesterday around noon, he said they'd found the bodies in the basement after they got the fire out and most of the crew had left. Because it supposedly happened late, they only had to bring a few of the full-time people in on the plot. I guess someone in the mortuary knows too. And now I'm letting the two of you in. It must stop here. Nobody else."

Beth spoke up. "How long will this have to go on? I don't like the idea of having to lie to people."

"The FBI isn't sure. They estimated two or three weeks," Phil said. "You two won't have to lie to people too much. Don't broach the subject.

And when another person does, agree with them when they say it's awful. You'd be surprised at how few people will say anything. People don't like talking about death. People who are aware you were friends of Sherry's will avoid you. They won't want to talk about it."

"It won't be too bad for us, Beth," Ralph said. "Phil is going to have the tougher time. Lots of people are aware of their relationship." Then he turned to Phil and asked, "What are you going to tell your lunch group and your other college friends?"

"I'm going to mope around and try to avoid people. I'm going to copy what I did during my bout with depression after Jake McMahan's trial. I'll spend a lot of time in my house. Don't expect me at the store for a couple of weeks. I've already fielded several phone calls. I've gotten good at sounding shocked and sad."

"So, what's this big case the FBI is working on?" Ralph asked. "I know Bob McFall a little. He doesn't impress me as a criminal mastermind."

"No, apparently McFall is a fairly small piece of the entire thing. They wouldn't tell us what it's about. They said Sherry might be involved in a trial, so it's better for her not to have any knowledge of the rest of the case. Apparently when it breaks, it'll be all over the news."

After a short lull, Beth asked, "What does this do to our other project?"

"Sherry wants us to continue as normal. She said you should send the email to Lucinda Wallace."

"What about the rape?" Ralph asked.

"Sherry and I still don't have the faintest idea what to do about it. Sherry suggested trying to discover the name of the victim. If we can, we'd have to figure out how to get the information to the police. Basically, we need more information before we can do anything."

Ralph said, "I've been wondering if maybe we can send the video to the head of the cleaning crew. If I can locate the supervisor, he or she will know the victim. What do you think?"

"It might be the way to go... yeah, good idea. Maybe if we develop a relationship with Lucinda, she can help us find out about the cleaning crew. It might work. When we're back in touch with Sherry, we'll get her opinion."

"I'll check out the net. You're right, Lucinda might be the easiest way,"

Ralph said.

"Guys, don't forget—there's one in the works. We haven't heard anything from Dorothy McGuire, the teacher from McKeesport," Beth said. "She should be learning about how the school system is dealing with her sexual harassment complaint."

"Wow, what with the Atlanta video and Sherry's mess, I almost forgot about Dorothy. She hasn't been active in the chat room, has she?" Ralph asked.

"No, there's not been anything from her for a while. Still, her case has been in the hands of the superintendent or whoever for more than a week now," Beth answered.

"It would be nice for her to tell us how it turned out. I wouldn't think it'll be a big deal," said Phil. "The video was clear. Her principal has to be removed."

After they dealt with the details in the email they wanted to send to Lucinda Wallace in Atlanta, Phil went home to hide out.

Chapter Thirty-Nine

SHERRY AND HER MOTHER ARRIVED in South Carolina in the early afternoon two days after they left. The drive had been long. Throughout, Melissa didn't say much. They stopped at the retirement community first. Trick and a representative of the retirement community were there to meet them. Gladys thought the apartment looked nice. While the apartment was much smaller than the farmhouse, she seemed willing to give it a try. Clothes were in the closet, and the kitchen cupboards had dishes. Melissa and Sherry left after a half an hour.

On the drive to her new apartment, Sherry tried to see if Melissa would open up. "You seem uptight. What's happening?"

Melissa responded, "I didn't like being taken off the case."

"I can understand. I was surprised when you were the one driving us. I can't think it's the kind of duty you're used to. Don't the Marshalls deal with witness protection? Why were you reassigned?"

"You're not going to stop asking questions, are you?"

"No, please tell me what's going on."

"Okay, later. We're here now. This is your apartment complex."

Sherry looked around at the apartment complex—a set of not very new garden apartments. They went into the office to introduce themselves.

They got the key to apartment 6B quite quickly. Apparently, somebody had already arranged things.

A little sedan sat in 6B's parking place. Melissa checked, and the keys were in the car. She gave the keys to Sherry. The apartment, on the second floor, had a balcony. The furnishings were nice, and again, there were clothes in the closet. Sherry and Melissa poked around a little, and then Sherry said, "This is all satisfactory for a short stay. I can't say any of these clothes are ones I'd pick."

"At least they should fit. Remember you gave us your size."

"Yeah, I remember," Sherry said. "What do I do for money?"

"Oh, after I give them a call, someone will come by with cash. We'd like you to avoid using a credit card until this is all completed. Also, you are not to contact anyone. No phone, no email, no nothing."

"What about Phil? He's aware of everything. Can't I email him?"

"No, absolutely no one."

Sherry gave Melissa a look. "You run a tight ship. Phil's going to wonder what's happening."

"I'm sorry. There are rules. While you're not like the typical person in witness protection, rules are rules."

"Okay, I guess I understand. Now I want to change the subject. I want to hear why you've been so grumpy."

"I guess you deserve to hear. Not here, though. I need a drink. I bet there's a bar somewhere."

Sherry and Melissa located a bar on the end of a shopping strip five blocks from Sherry's apartment complex. After they got seated and ordered drinks, Sherry said, "Why were you reassigned?"

"I guess it might be good to tell someone, but you can't tell a soul."

"I won't tell anyone. I don't know anyone here, anyway."

"This assignment is very unusual. You're right, the Marshalls normally handle witness protection. The problem is my boss, Larry Clarkson. He's the agent in charge of the investigation. He and I both had motel rooms in Lackey. The other agents involved were staying in Henderson. I didn't think anything about it. Maybe I should have."

"He hit on you."

Melissa seemed a little shocked. "Yes, how'd you guess?"

"I've had my fair share of trouble with men. When you were the only other one staying in Lackey, weren't you suspicious?"

"Yeah, perhaps I should have been. I guess I'm not tuned in. Anyway, when he knocked on my door the night before I met you, I thought he wanted to talk about the case. He didn't. He had a bottle in his hand and wanted to have a drink. While I should have known it wasn't right, I let him in. He's my boss, after all. And he's probably fifteen years older than I am."

"Aren't their rules about fraternizing in the FBI?" Sherry asked.

"Yes, there are, but the FBI is still a very male dominated place. And where do you draw the line? There's nothing wrong with going out for drinks with the people you're working a case with."

"He wanted more than a drink."

"You're right. I figured it out after the first drink, and I flat turned him down. He tried to argue. I was firm, and he left. I figured there wouldn't be any repercussions, but the next afternoon, right before you were about to leave, I got the call to be your driver. I'd been reassigned. They gave a phony story about the driver not showing, but I know different. Larry had exacted his revenge." There were tears in her eyes when Melissa finished.

Sherry didn't quite know how to respond, so she sat there and nursed her drink. Finally, Melissa composed herself and said, "I guess I don't know where the line is... I mean, between being friendly in a professional situation and being too friendly. I thought I had things straight. Evidence suggests I didn't. Maybe I should invent a boyfriend. Or better yet, a girlfriend."

"Melissa, I wish I knew how to help. I'm not full of good experience. In fact, most of my experience is similar. I've had bosses hit on me. It happened so often I quit a lucrative career in business to be a librarian. The one thing I know is you can affect men's reactions by changing what you wear."

"How do you know?"

"I went to library school right after I'd had a few very bad experiences in the business world. I decided to adopt what I called the dowdy look. I wore sloppy clothes to hide my figure, I let my hair grow out, and I didn't wear makeup. And I stopped having trouble with men."

"We sort of have a uniform and dress standards."

"I understand. Still, it's possible to make subtle changes. Maybe wear your blouses one size larger, not tight. And wear your suit skirt a little longer. You can make small changes to make yourself less attractive. In your case, it might be hard. You're a very good-looking young woman."

"I see what you're saying. Still, aren't you advising me to avoid the problem, not take it on?"

"You're right. All I'm saying is I made those kind of changes and they worked for me. They might work for you."

"I suspect you've given me good advice. The advice came a little too late, however. Right now, I'm thinking about lodging a complaint against Larry. I wonder whether it will do any good."

Sherry almost told her about the In Hissa group at this point. Instead she said, "I hate to say this. My experience suggests you won't have much luck. You don't have any witnesses. The case will come down to your word against his, and the woman almost always loses in those situations. I lost the two times I lodged formal complaints about similar things."

"Reassigning me in the middle of things is very suspicious. And having me do a Marshall's job too."

"Still, I bet Larry is well liked by his supervisors. And I bet they're men, right?"

"Yes."

"While I hate to say this, your chances aren't very good."

Melissa looked glum. "I guess you're right. The way the system works is wrong. Guys get away with so much. It's plain not fair."

Sherry wanted to tell her about what they were doing. Again, she restrained herself. She nodded and finished her drink.

Chapter Forty

LATE IN THE AFTERNOON, FIVE days after Sherry and her mother left for South Carolina, a small sedan parked in front of Phil's house. Trick Ahearn, Sherry's brother, got out, retrieved his suitcase from the trunk, and walked to the front door. Trick, who Phil had met once, resembled Sherry—the same strong cheekbones and big dimples. Phil, who'd seen him coming, opened the door before Trick rang the doorbell.

"Welcome," Phil said, taking the suitcase and shaking Trick's hand. "Good flight?"

"Okay. The flight from Pittsburgh to Henderson bounced a little. Thanks for letting me stay here, Professor Philemon."

"Phil, please call me Phil. No trouble at all. Did the FBI pay for your flight? They should have."

"Actually, they did. At first, they balked, but then Melissa, Agent Jacobson, squawked at them, and they covered the flight. I didn't want to push them further. It's why I asked to stay here."

"You're going to have to do a lot of playacting here, you know—the grieving son and brother. My place will give you somewhere to come and relax."

"I guess you're right. I should be able to do the play acting. In my job, I've seen people I can use as models. Though we don't deal with too many murders, I've dealt with some. I know how devastated people can be. Then again, some people face these situations stoically. I'm going to be pretty stoic."

"My approach is to ignore people as much as possible. I deal with some of them on the phone. Otherwise, I stay here. You might not have that luxury."

"No, I'll be out a bunch. I have to deal with a real estate agent, the insurance agent, the bank, and the mortuary. And then there's the farm. I'm not anxious to be the one who has to go through the charred remains of the house."

"I'd like to help you," Phil said.

"You got it. I hoped you'd offer. I understand you've been out to the house."

"Yes, I saw it the day after the fire. Everything was covered in a black goop. I guess a mixture of ashes and water. It should have dried out by now. We haven't had any rain this week."

"Good."

After a pause, Phil said, "Let me show you to the guest room," as he grabbed the suitcase and led Trick into the hallway.

For dinner, Phil ordered in pizza and made a salad. Over dinner, Trick filled him in on what had happened when Sherry and her mother got to South Carolina. He said Gladys liked the retirement community, and Sherry had a reasonable apartment. Both women were treating it like a vacation. Still, they'd be happy if the vacation didn't last too long.

As the discussion about South Carolina ran out of gas, Trick blushed and said, "Oh, I forgot, I'm supposed to tell you Sherry misses you a lot. And she gave me a letter for you. I have it in my suitcase."

When Phil got the letter from Trick, he put it in his pocket. "I'll get to this later. I think there's a Pirate's game on TV. Want to watch?"

"Sure."

The next morning, Trick arranged to return for lunch. After lunch, they'd go out to the house. When Trick finished his breakfast of cold cereal, he headed out to see how many of his planned stops he would be able to finish in the morning.

At lunch Trick said, "You were right, play acting all the time can be difficult. I don't know how many people recognized me and gave their condolences. The experience resembled a funeral more than anything else. I'm glad I can come here and let my hair down."

"How'd your visits go?" Phil asked.

"A real estate agent, Bill Simons, is going to come by when we're out at the house this afternoon. We decided to put the property up for sale. I talked with the women. Neither of them wants the property, so I was straight with Bill, no faking."

"I wondered if they'd want to rebuild. Honestly, I didn't know."

"No, at this moment, they don't want to rebuild. Actually, I think I'm going to put a high price on the property. They don't want the farm to sell fast. That'll give them a little time to be sure they want to sell."

"What else did you accomplish?"

"I went to the mortuary to sign the papers to get the cremated bodies shipped to South Carolina. Completely bogus, but the process went off like a charm. The mortuary people were primed. The bank was different. I didn't have a safe deposit box key, and the procedure for dealing with that kind of situation involves a proof of death and a court order. I didn't expect to get into the safe deposit box. I know the rules. My trying should be good for the charade."

"How about the insurance agent?"

"I got there too. The insurance claim for the house is a legitimate claim, no problem. Both Sherry and my mom have small life insurance policies. I told the insurance agent I'd mail her death certificates when I got them. We can straighten all that out when Sherry and my mom come back to life."

"Wow, you were efficient," Phil said. "You took care of the whole list."

"If the idea was to make people believe Sherry and my mother are dead, I believe I did."

"And some of the visits were useful too. You wanted to sell the property, so putting it on the market now makes sense. And the insurance claim on the house is real enough."

"Will we need more than one afternoon out at the house?" Trick asked.

"I don't know. Why ask?"

"The return on my reservation is open. I'd like to leave tomorrow if we get our work done this afternoon."

"Sure. Make your reservation for tomorrow. If we don't finish out at the house today, I'll be happy to finish later. Go ahead and call the airline. You might be able to get an early flight."

Phil and Trick drove Trick's rental car out to the house. They'd loaded the car with a couple of rakes and a shovel from Phil's garage. When they got to the ruins of the house, Phil opened his door and stepped out. Trick sat there. When Trick finally got out of the car, he stammered, "I didn't think this would be so hard."

"It's the house where you were raised."

"Yes, but there's no house there now. And the footprint looks so little. I remember the house being gigantic."

"You want me to do this?" Phil asked. "I can come back later and search for stuff."

"No," said Trick. "Thanks for the offer. No, I can help. So, you figure we rake and take a closer look if the rake runs into anything solid."

"Yeah that ought to work."

Phil and Trick began. They found some things that hadn't burned. They found lots of pottery shards and bent and distorted metal. Two plates were all in one piece. They also kept the knives, forks, spoons, and assorted serving pieces from a set of silver. While not in any shape to be used, they could be melted down. Little things like the jewels from rings or necklaces they'd been asked to search for were probably in the ashes. Finding them would most likely take a more careful sifting, but they might get lucky.

When they'd been toiling away for an hour, the real estate agent came. Trick went off with him. He wanted to show him the three plots of farmland Gladys still owned. No one in the family had farmed the land for a long time. The rent for the land provided most of Gladys's income.

As Phil kept working, the tines of his rake caught on something hard. He felt down with his gloved hand and blew off some of the ashes to reveal a small green stone. His rake had snagged the remainders of a gold chain. He bent down closer and blew away more ash. There were two more green stones visible. He'd found the emerald necklace, the one piece of jewelry Gladys and Sherry most wanted to find. The chain had melted and had missing sections, but the emeralds were unscathed. Phil guessed the necklace had been in a box, and the necklace more or less stayed together when the house collapsed.

Phil didn't find anything else worth reporting—a few more spoons and one tea cup. When Trick and the real estate agent got back from their drive, the real estate agent started hammering in a For Sale sign by the side of the burned-out house. Phil shouted to Trick, "Look at what I've found!"

"What is it?".

"Come see."

When he got to Phil, standing by the little pile of keepers, he exclaimed, "Oh my God, you found the necklace." Trick jumped up and down and offered Phil a high five.

Phil removed his glove and slapped Trick's out-stretched hand.

They worked at their rakes for another half hour before quitting. There was no sense in Phil coming back tomorrow or any other day. They'd managed to rake through every part of the ruin. They probably had missed some things, but finding the necklace made the day a big success.

They took turns taking long showers when they got home and then drove to Henderson for dinner at Phil's favorite restaurant. Trick had managed to get an early flight the next day, so they said goodbye early the next morning. Right before Trick left, Phil gave Trick a letter to pass on to Sherry.

Chapter Forty-One

THE DAY AFTER TRICK LEFT, in McKeesport, Dorothy McGuire got a letter from the office of the school superintendent. The short letter said her complaint had been dismissed. They found no evidence to substantiate the claims. While the INHSSSA people had told her to expect this, it still hurt. She knew Dave had denied everything, so they'd rejected her complaint. She didn't worry. She still had the video. She'd talk to Mrs. Wilson and show the video. It would make them change their minds.

Dorothy made arrangements for a substitute and another appointment with Mrs. Wilson at the school superintendent's office. She had the thumb drive with her. She'd reviewed the video in the morning. She felt confident when the secretary ushered her into Mrs. Wilson's office.

Mrs. Wilson did not seem happy to see her. She said curtly, "Take a seat, Ms. McGuire."

After Dorothy sat down, Mrs. Wilson continued. "I presume you got the letter from the superintendent?"

Dorothy nodded, and Mrs. Wilson said, "The letter's crystal clear. Your case is closed. The matter is settled. Why are you here?"

"I am not satisfied with the outcome. It wasn't just. Why didn't you believe me? I presume it came down to my word against Dave Johnson's.

So why take his side and not mine?"

"I will not discuss this with you. The case is closed."

"I want to appeal."

"There is no avenue for appeal. I repeat; the case is closed. You are already on shaky ground with the superintendent. It would be best for you to never mention this matter again. Please leave."

The outcome stunned Dorothy. *No avenue for appeal. Why not?* When Dorothy started to speak, Mrs. Wilson got up and stood by her door, gesturing for her to leave. In shock, Dorothy finally stumbled out the door. She was crying by the time she got to her car. She hated herself for crying. She felt so hopeless.

After she got herself under control, she knew she had to talk to someone. Susan. She had to call Susan. She would be still in school, so she'd have to wait. Dorothy drove back to her apartment and tried to keep herself busy with TV. Finally, fifteen minutes after the students were let out of school, she called Susan's cell.

"Dorothy, why weren't you in school today?"

Dorothy, a little taken aback when people were quick with caller ID, said, "Susan, I need to talk to you. Can you stop by my apartment on your way home? It won't take long."

"What's this about?"

"My complaint against Dave. I don't want to talk about it on the phone. Please, can you drop by for a short talk?"

"Okay, Bill doesn't get home for a while. I can do the lesson plans at home. I'll be there."

"Thanks!"

When Susan arrived, Dorothy had her read the letter from the superintendent. "It's pretty short and to the point. I guess it's sort of what you expected, isn't it?" Susan asked.

"Yeah, I guess. I didn't come to school today because I went into the office to talk to Mrs. Wilson—the head of personnel. I wanted to lodge an appeal."

"I remember. You were ready to show them the video those people sent you."

"Yes, right. Wilson practically threw me out of the building. She said the case is closed, and there's no avenue for appeal."

"Why? We're union. You should be able to take your case to the union."

"Remember who the building union representative is."

"Whoops, Clayton Dennis, and he's about Dave Johnson's best friend in the world. You're right. He wouldn't help you. There's no way he'd cross Dave. Wait, let me see the video while I think about what we can do."

"Okay, it's not long."

Dorothy got the video on her computer. After Susan watched it, she said, "It's clear as can be. While watching the second scene, I had a thought. At this point, you're trying to appeal a decision made by the superintendent, right?"

"Yes."

"So, who's his boss? The school board, right? Squires works for the school board. They hired him, so you should be able to appeal to them."

"Wouldn't I be out of place to go over the superintendent's head? I mean; I'm already complaining about my boss. Now I'd be complaining about my boss's boss."

"Dorothy, you don't have many options. I agree the union's not going to work. It's the school board or nothing else. And the video is clear as can be." After a pause she continued, "I have an idea."

Later in the evening, Dorothy and Susan approached the house of Claire Montgomery, a member of the school board. As Susan explained to Dorothy, her husband worked for Ernest Montgomery, and she'd met Claire at several staff parties. While they weren't exactly close friends, there was a good chance Claire would be willing to talk to them.

Claire Montgomery opened the door and led them to the living room. Claire's money showed in her clothes. While Claire's hair was gray, her age wasn't obvious. She looked good. Dorothy had been impressed with the house when they parked in front. The inside impressed her more. Susan and Dorothy sat on a massive leather couch, and Claire sat across from them.

Susan took the lead. "Claire, we know this is very irregular. It's an unusual situation. As I said on the phone, Dorothy is one of my fellow teachers. And she has lodged a sexual harassment complaint against our principal."

"Dave Johnson?" Claire interrupted.

"Yes," Susan said. "Anyway, Dave has been asking Dorothy for dates. Of course, she's refused him. He's married. And most recently he's threatened to interfere with her tenure case if she doesn't go out with him. It's what triggered her complaint."

"So, what happened?" Claire asked.

Dorothy picked up the story. "I got a letter from the superintendent saying they are taking no action. They dismissed the case. In essence, they believed Dave's denials and not my account. I went to see how to lodge an appeal. The head of personnel, Mrs. Wilson, said there's no avenue for appeal."

"I'm sorry. It's not the board's role to get involved in matters like this," Clair said. "This type of thing is correctly delegated to the superintendent. I can't be of any help."

Susan broke in at this point. "Dorothy has evidence to prove her version of events. And if there is no avenue for appeal, how can she present this evidence?"

"Why didn't you bring this evidence forward in the first place?" Claire asked.

"It's complicated," Dorothy answered. "Things will proceed faster if I show you the evidence. It's a video. Then we can talk about where I got it and why I didn't present it earlier. Here, I brought a laptop. I can show the video."

"Okay, I guess," Claire said.

Dorothy showed the video to Claire, who watched in silence. When they reached the end of the video Claire said, "It clearly shows him asking for dates, which is outlawed, right?"

"Right, supervisors cannot date their direct reports," Susan said.

"And then he threatens to make trouble for your tenure case," Claire continued. "It's completely unprofessional. You have an open and shut case, so why hold back this evidence? Where did you get the video?"

"It started when I got an email from an anonymous group. They call themselves the I. N. H. S. S. S. A. Group. It stands for 'it's not he said she said anymore.' Anyway, they said they had this video showing Dave

Johnson treating me badly. Their instructions were to go through the regular sexual harassment procedures and only use the video if I didn't get satisfaction. I followed their wishes. I never thought I'd have no way to appeal the decision."

"Who are these people?"

"I have no idea. I only know two things. First, they monitor a chat room I frequent. Second, the package with the thumb drive containing the videos came from Atlanta."

Claire asked, "Do you know anyone in Atlanta?"

"Only one of my cousins. I don't believe he'd have anything to do with it. We're not close. I'm not even sure he has my address, though I guess he'd be able to get it from my aunt."

Filling the silence that followed, Susan said, "I'm sorry to be dropping this in your lap, Claire. We didn't know where else to turn. We couldn't leave things where they were."

Claire finally spoke up. "I can see why. You've put me in a real fix. I've never run into anything like this. It's not going to be easy." After a pause, she continued, "Would you mind if we talked about this with my husband? I rely on him for advice very often, and Susan, you've met Ernest. He runs a large company, and he has dealt with his fair share of personnel problems."

"It sounds reasonable," Susan said.

"Sure," Dorothy added.

Susan and Dorothy left the Montgomery's house an hour later. Ernest Montgomery had listened to the whole story and watched the video. First, he quizzed the two teachers about why they hadn't taken this to their union representative. Though he didn't like their answer, he understood. After considerable discussion, Ernest convinced Claire the sexual harassment procedures at the school system were poorly written. Good procedures should always have an avenue for appeal. If the complaint accused a co-worker, not the principal, the principal would be the first to decide, and his or her decision would be appealed to the superintendent. The procedures hadn't contemplated a complaint against a principal. As things stand now, he advised using the entire school board as the appeals committee.

When Dorothy got home, she realized she hadn't posted anything to the INHSSSA people. She posted a short message saying her initial complaint had been denied, and she was in the process of trying to figure out how to appeal the decision. The details didn't matter. She'd been honest, if a bit cryptic.

She tried to sleep. The whole thing depressed her. She guessed she shouldn't have been surprised at Dave's attempt to paint her as a liar. The problem remained—it appeared to have worked. In subtle ways, her colleagues were avoiding her. Now maybe she wouldn't be able to use the video. She hoped Claire Montgomery could come through for her.

She hadn't thought it would be easy to go through the business of a sexual harassment complaint. She'd been right. So far, her experience had been awful and more complicated than she'd anticipated.

Chapter Forty-Two

BETH READ DOROTHY'S POST AND told Ralph about it. She figured they'd tell Phil when he came for one of his frequent early morning visits. All three of them looked forward to the visits. They used them to compare notes on their attempts to act sad about Gladys and Sherry's death. Phil had been right. Few people asked direct questions. They did face questions about the lack of a memorial service. They'd all stuck to the party line. Sherry's brother in South Carolina would bury the ashes there. Phil had been able to head off plans by the librarian to have a service in town.

****

In Atlanta, Lucinda Wallace ran across the email from the INHSSSA group a day after it arrived. She read it through. At first, she considered discussing it with her boyfriend LeRoy. They'd moved in together only four months ago. While things were fine, she didn't want to rock the boat. LeRoy had a bad temper. She'd seen it a couple of times. She didn't want him to go after Dennis. LeRoy had joined the Atlanta police force a couple of years ago. If he went after Dennis, he might lose his job. She should go through the procedures at the company like these people said. If they had what they said they had, she should be able to nail Dennis.

Lucinda made a short post to INHSSSA asking them for the video. She didn't mind not knowing who they were or where they were from as long as they sent the video. They told her not to ask, so she didn't. She found getting this process started exciting. Dennis made coming to work unpleasant. Except for him, she liked the job.

****

In Lackey, Beth found Lucinda's post, and she and Ralph loaded the two thumb drives. Phil volunteered to go to Harrisburg to mail them. He didn't like staying at home and sounding grieved on the phone. Lots of people had called, and he was tired of the whole charade. The FBI had told him not to contact Sherry at all, and her letter said email was forbidden. He found the whole thing frustrating. The trip to Harrisburg would interrupt the routine. He decided to drive. While it wasn't a great drive, he liked driving. It would get him out of the house.

****

In South Carolina, Sherry'd been able to spend time with her mother, Trick, his wife, and their two kids. She didn't get to see her niece and nephew too often, and she enjoyed them. It resembled a family reunion, even if not planned. She'd had a long talk with Trick about what had happened.

The FBI had followed through with the cash Melissa had promised, so she went to a local bookstore and bought a stack of books she'd wanted to read. She and her mother had taken a shopping trip to add to the wardrobe the FBI had picked out for them. She liked having so many new clothes.

She did spend time checking the *Female Friends* chat room. She saw the posts from Dorothy in McKeesport and Lucinda in Atlanta. It appeared to her things were progressing. She also found a couple of candidates for their project. She'd shared with Beth the duty of finding the next person to help. She hoped she'd be back in Lackey before they'd have to pick the next person.

Also, much to her relief, her mother adapted to the retirement home. Gladys had met several people there, and she'd joined the knitting club. She ate in the dining room in the main building every night. She invited Sherry to one of the dinners. Sherry found the food good, and it surprised her that so many people knew her mother's name. Despite wanting to, Sherry didn't tell her mother "I told you so." In any event, this retirement community seemed right for her mother. When this finished, she wasn't sure her Mom would want to move back to Pennsylvania.

Sherry wondered how much this all cost. The FBI had covered the expense so far. If her mother wanted to stay, they'd have to take over the expense. Sherry guessed they'd be able to afford it. They'd get the insurance on the house, and they'd probably sell the farmland.

She also had several more meetings with Melissa. Much to Melissa's annoyance, she had been assigned to be their guide while they were in South Carolina. She opened up to Sherry about how peeved she still was with Larry. She didn't like being reassigned right toward the end of the case. She felt sure the case would break soon, and she'd be stuck in South Carolina. She didn't think Sherry and her mother needed constant supervision. Sherry agreed with her.

The only alarming thing about her meetings with Melissa was learning the FBI kept track of her internet usage. Melissa let this slip one evening after they'd been in South Carolina for more than a week. They were back in the bar they'd visited a couple of other times.

After their drinks came, Melissa took out a notebook. When she found the right page, she asked, "What is I. N. H. S. S. S. A?"

Sherry panicked. Luckily, Melissa had been referring to her notebook to get the acronym right. This gave her a chance to collect herself before Melissa looked at her. "What? I don't know what you're talking about?" "It's I. N. H. S. S. S. A," Melissa repeated as she checked her notebook again.

"I have no idea. Why are you asking?"

"We regularly check the computer usage of people who are new to witness protection. You remember I told you not to email anyone. You wouldn't believe how many people ignore our instructions. We've had to move people who emailed their friends their new address."

"I guess it doesn't surprise me. A few of the people you put in witness protection aren't the sharpest tacks in the box. I haven't emailed anyone, not even Phil, who knows all about what's going on."

"Yes, you haven't used email. Still, like I said, we've been monitoring your computer. I mentioned the crazy acronym because it's associated with lots of the posts you viewed in a chat room." Again, she checked her notebook, "*Female Friends*, yes, *Female Friends*."

"I don't get it—I look at lots of posts in *Female Friends*. I guess I've seen the acronym. I never thought anything about it."

"We have people who keep track of clicks, and they sent me the question about the acronym. Their analysis suggested you went to posts mentioning the acronym a large number of times, more than they figured would randomly happen."

Sherry responded, "It's weird. I'll have to check the next time I'm on the site. Let me tell you, it freaks me out. You're checking on my internet usage. You don't want me to send anything, and I haven't. I can't see how it's anyone's business what I view on the internet. Is there anything wrong with the *Female Friends* website?"

"No, there's not," said Melissa. "In fact, I'm halfway tempted to post about my experiences. I don't think I will yet. Maybe later."

"Look, I frequent the chat room because it's interesting. Lots of women are having troubles like yours—many even worse. In the past I've written posts offering support to them. Sexual harassment and sexual violence are big problems. I don't know anything about any acronyms."

"Okay. It's no big deal. Those analysts who check on these things were probably bored. If you have lots and lots of data, you can find trends when there's really nothing there. I'm sorry it freaks you out. It's standard operating procedure."

Sherry put her hand on Melissa's arm to reassure her. "It's nothing. It surprised me. I'm sure your procedures make sense for most of the people in witness protection. It's probably sensible to keep everything in place even for perfectly law-abiding citizens like me and my mother."

"Thank you for understanding."

Sherry sipped her drink, hoping she'd effectively defused the situation. She'd have to watch herself. She probably spent more time on the INHSSSA posts than the others. She'd have to change the way she clicked through the site. She knew she shouldn't avoid those posts completely. It would be as suspicious as spending too much time on them.

Chapter Forty-Three

THE SMALL PACKAGE ARRIVED FOR Lucinda Wallace in Atlanta. LeRoy would be home early that night, so Lucinda hid the package in her underwear drawer. She wanted to review the video without LeRoy being present. *There's no telling what he'd do if he saw Daniel pawing me like he does.* LeRoy's job got him out of the house early, so she'd use the hour she had in the morning to view the video. Luckily, they lived close to her work.

The next morning, after LeRoy left, Lucinda got the package from her dresser. There were two thumb drives. She put one back in the package and stuck it in its hiding place. It was odd to view her cubicle from the top. The first scene showed Daniel coming behind her and fondling her breast. Clearly, she leaned away from him and attempted to swat his hand away. Sexual harassment involved unwanted behavior. No one viewing the video would ever think she wanted him to grab her.

When she finished the video, she had no doubt she had a good case. The INHSSSA people, whoever they were, had captured eleven instances when Daniel had tried to fondle her. She'd been able to block a couple of his attempts, even rushing away one time. She had him dead to rights. Lucinda understood sexual harassment complaints often came down to conflicts between what the woman said and what the man said. Maybe a coworker had witnessed Daniel grabbing her. But the walls on the cubicles were tall and getting anyone to testify against their boss might not be easy. This video changed everything. She didn't need anyone else to support her story. She ejected the thumb drive and put it back in her dresser.

Lucinda spent the rest of her morning time on the company website checking into the procedures for submitting grievances. The company had a clear policy. They even had a lengthy statement about sexual harassment. She took notes about what she needed to do. Checking her watch, she realized she needed to hustle to make it to work on time. She folded the notes and put them with the package containing the two thumb drives. She liked what she'd discovered.

The next morning, when LeRoy left, she typed a statement describing her sexual harassment complaint. The company website contained little guidance about what had to go into the complaint. She tried to stick to the facts—lots of unwanted physical contact. She gave two examples. She thought the statement probably could be better. Then again, maybe it didn't matter. Lucinda was sure she'd get a chance to tell her story. The whole thing wouldn't ride on how well she'd written the complaint. She decided to use one of her morning breaks at work to call personnel to make an appointment. She'd go outside and use her cell phone.

Lucinda got through to the right person at personnel after describing what she wanted to two secretaries. She made an appointment for five-thirty. The person she talked to, a Mrs. Ferris, said she'd call Lucinda's work to get permission for her to leave a half hour early. The main headquarters were across town. Lucinda hoped she'd make it on time for her appointment. Atlanta traffic was usually horrible around rush hour. She didn't take her afternoon break and told Daniel about skipping the break to add time to her early departure to try to get ahead of rush hour. When he asked her about why she had to go to personnel, she said, "It's nothing you should be concerned about." It didn't bother Lucinda to lie to the jerk.

Lucinda had good luck with traffic and got to the company headquarters fifteen minutes before her appointment. She sat in the lobby and perused a magazine. The magazine didn't hold her interest. She looked around at the other people waiting. A few of them were young. They were probably applying for jobs. Others were older, and Lucinda wondered what they'd come to personnel for.

At five twenty-five, Lucinda went to the receptionist and said she had an appointment with Mrs. Ferris. The receptionist picked up her phone, gesturing for Lucinda to wait. "Mrs. Ferris will be here in a minute," she said as she put down the phone.

About three minutes later, a tall, well-dressed black woman came out of one of the doors and asked, "Lucinda?"

"Yes, I'm Lucinda."

Mrs. Ferris came over, shook Lucinda's hand, and said, "I'm Kathleen Ferris. Please follow me back to my office."

Lucinda followed Mrs. Ferris down the hallway into her office. They were on the tenth floor, and the office had big windows. "Wow, what a view. You must have difficulty getting any work done. All I can see are the walls of my neighbors' cubes."

"Yes, I have a great view. You get used to it. Actually, I don't look too often anymore." After a pause for them to get seated, Mrs. Ferris continued. "I understand you have a sexual harassment complaint."

Lucinda gulped. "Yes, against my boss, Daniel Reeser. How do we proceed? Do you want to hear about it, or should I give you the written complaint?"

"Why don't you tell me first. I can read your written complaint later."

"Okay. The whole thing is fairly simple, I guess. We work in cubicles and Dennis comes by frequently. Lots of times people have questions for him, and other times he's coming by to check on us. I guess I'd say he's a hands-on manager. And that's the problem. He's too hands-on. Almost every time he comes to my desk, he puts his hands on me. If I'm standing, my backside, and if I'm sitting, my breasts. He's very sexual. Often, he leans into me and presses against me with his crotch. And not every once in a while. It happens multiple times a week. Finally, he's asked me out several times. I always turn him down. He knows I live with my boyfriend, but he doesn't stop."

"I see," said Mrs. Ferris. "You've come to the right place. It sounds like you have a solid complaint. Now, let me read what you've written."

Lucinda took the complaint out of the folder and gave it to Mrs. Ferris. At one point during her reading, Mrs. Ferris used a pen to make a notation on Lucinda's complaint. "Together with what you told me, this makes your case quite clear. This is how things will proceed. Wait— first, you didn't mention any witnesses. Are there witnesses? Do your colleagues witness this behavior?"

"Honestly, I can't tell. The walls on the cubicles are high. There's no way anyone else got a good view of what he's doing. And I haven't talked to anyone about his behavior Still, I can't believe I'm the only one he molests."

"I guess we'll have to interview your colleagues. The process will be messy. Anyway, here's how we proceed. We do a thorough investigation. Besides interviewing your colleagues, we will have to talk to Mr. Reeser. He'll be aware he's under investigation because of your complaint. After our investigation, we issue a formal report."

"I figured everyone at work would find out about it. Is it possible to keep my name out of it?"

"We try to, but still sometimes people figure out who's behind the complaint."

After a few moments of awkward silence, Lucinda said, "I bet I can guess how this is going to turn out. He'll either claim he didn't do anything—in other words, I'm a liar, or he'll say I encouraged him—I'm a skank. I've heard about this kind of thing. Even though he's the accused, I'm the one who'll be on trial."

"I wish you were wrong. We try not to do that. Nevertheless, sometimes we can't avoid it. I can't promise anything. I guess the question is this: knowing what you know, do you want to continue?"

Lucinda thought, *The videos are clear. What I'm talking about happens. I'm not a liar. And I'm not encouraging him. I'm no skank.* While she wished she could show the videos now, the email had been clear. Only use the videos if she didn't get satisfaction from the normal process. She looked at Mrs. Ferris. "Yes, I want to continue. No one should have to endure what I've had to endure."

"I agree, and I'm glad you're willing. We need to weed out men like Reeser." Mrs. Ferris walked Lucinda out to the reception area. When they got there, Mrs. Ferris turned to Lucinda, shook her hand and said, "This should be completed in a couple of weeks. While the process might be hard for you, you're doing the right thing. If you have any questions at any time, here's my card. Feel free to call me."

Lucinda hustled to her car. She had to create a story to tell LeRoy. The meeting had been short. Still, she'd be home about an hour later than usual. She texted him, telling him she'd been held up at personnel. She'd tell him they had to straighten out paperwork. She'd complain about useless paperwork. He'd be sure to sympathize.

Chapter Forty-Four

SHERRY READ LUCINDA'S POST ABOUT starting the sexual harassment process. She didn't linger. She'd adopted a rule of trying to keep her speed close to constant as she clicked through the posts in the chat room. Beth also saw the post and reported the news to Ralph. The next morning, they told Phil.

"I'm getting tired of this whole thing." Phil said as he nursed the coffee Beth had made for him. "The drive to Harrisburg only provided a short diversion. I'm bored at home. The phone calls have slowed down. I'm considering going to my Wednesday lunch tomorrow. It's maddening not to be able to contact Sherry. We know absolutely nothing about what's happening with her."

"Are you sure you can continue the charade with people, especially ones you're used to talking to," Ralph asked. "You've got the easy task staying inside and avoiding everyone."

Beth jumped in. "Ralph's right. I've found it hard telling lies like this. I've had to tell a whole bunch of people it was a horrible tragedy. The house burning down was a tragedy. I try to concentrate on the house when the people are clearly talking about the two deaths."

"Haven't you spoken to almost everyone you'll have to speak to? The phone calls have almost stopped."

Ralph and Beth looked at each other. "I haven't had anyone mention anything about Sherry or her mom in a couple of days," Ralph said.

"Me neither," Beth added.

"I'm going to come out of hiding. At least tomorrow I can go to my lunch group. I've already talked to all of them on the phone. I know I'll have to look sad. I should be able to pull it off."

"Okay, Phil, be careful," Ralph said. "I sure wish the FBI would wrap up this case."

"Amen," Phil said.

The next day, Phil got to Andy's a little late. He made sure his clothes were slightly wrinkled, and he ran his hands through his hair, messing it up. Andy rushed to him when he entered. "Oh Phil, I'm so sorry. You two were such a nice couple. Fridays aren't the same without you two."

Phil accepted the hug, and replied, "Such a shock. One moment she's here, the next she's gone."

Andy said, "Your group's already in back. You're brave to come so soon after Sherry's death."

Phil gave him his best downtrodden look. "Yeah, I've got to get on with my life."

Phil's lunch group all rose when he came in. Phil stopped them. "Sit back down. Treat me normal. I don't want to talk yet. I want to be around people for a while. I know from before I'll be going through stuff for a long time. So, what's the topic of conversation? Anything but me."

Bert spoke up. "We're back on one of our old quandaries—trying to figure out what causes the deepening split in our country."

"Bob's trying to convince us the split's all about news sources," Jeremy said.

"Well I'm right," Bob said. "If you get your news from some places, you don't get the same stories you'd get from other places. What about those TVs in the regular restaurant? If your news is slanted, left-wing or right-wing, makes no difference, your views will be slanted."

"How many people watch the news?" William asked. "While I know there's a group of activists who hang on every news report, most people don't regularly watch any news or read a newspaper."

Sally jumped in. "You're right, newspaper readership is down everywhere. TV cut into readership a long time ago. Now the internet has taken another cut. I don't know how long we're going to be able to stay in business."

"Yeah, still those who're keyed into the news, what William called the activists, affect all the people around them," George said. "In political science we call them opinion leaders. Not everyone has to be plugged into the news."

Jeremy spoke next. "It's not only the different news outlets. There's a split by education level, by income, by urban-rural, and there are strong regional differences. There's more to it than where you get your news."

"Yeah, and you forgot about belief in science," Bert said. "People seem to want to be ignorant. Why can't they believe science? Ignoring global warming is stupid."

"The difference we're talking about comes down to this," Bob said. "A lot of the debates are people talking past each other because they don't agree on what objective reality is. You can't have a sensible debate unless you share the same sense of the facts. And if you're like David Katel, you don't worry about checking your facts."

Phil didn't participate, but he liked being with his group. He'd seen too much TV and read too many books in his enforced stay at home. Still, he didn't smile, as much as he wanted to. He kept a sad look on his face as the discussion went on around him. As usual, the group didn't reach many conclusions and often the discussion repeated itself. But he felt comfortable—glad to be back.

Chapter Forty-Five

THE SAME DAY IN MCKEESPORT, Dorothy McGuire got a call from Claire Montgomery. Claire told her she'd convinced the executive council of the McKeesport Board of Education to have a special meeting to discuss her case. After considerable discussion, the Board chair came around. In a case like Dorothy's there needed to be an avenue for appeal. The special meeting was scheduled for seven p.m. on Thursday, tomorrow.

Dorothy arrived at the school board office at six fifty-five. She was glad to see Claire. She went to her, and they shook hands. Claire leaned toward her and said, "I'm nervous about this. I sure hope it goes well. I'd have egg on my face if it flops."

Dorothy responded, "Thanks so much for arranging this. I'm nervous too. The video evidence should be convincing."

"I hope you're right."

Claire and Dorothy stayed in the background as the four members of the executive committee filed into the meeting room. Superintendent Squires arrived last. Claire and Dorothy followed him into the room. Dorothy looked at the members of the committee—three men and one woman. She didn't know any of their names. Claire led her to a table facing the board members, and they sat down.

The school board members sat behind the imposing u-shaped table. They weren't sitting together. After a minute, Dorothy realized they were all sitting behind placards with their names on them. The chair of the school board, Mr. Gillespie, sat in the center. Mrs. Knudson, the vice chair, sat beside him. The other two members, Mr. Lewis and Mr. Hornwig, were behind their placards. Dorothy saw an empty seat behind the Mrs. Montgomery placard. *It must be where Claire sits at regular board meetings.* Mr. Squires took a chair at the far right-hand end of the table.

Mr. Gillespie, the chair, started the meeting. "We're all here now, so we can start. This is an unusual situation. Claire, you requested this meeting, can you tell us why we're here?"

Claire stood and stepped to a podium facing the board. "We're here because of a flaw in our grievance procedures. When an employee has a grievance against a fellow employee—for example, a janitor who can't get along with a teacher—the grievance is first heard by the building principal. If the principal's decision is appealed, the appeal goes to the superintendent who has the final say. When an employee has a grievance against a principal, the grievance is heard by the superintendent. Then there's no room for an appeal. I guess this has never happened before—a teacher who wants to appeal the superintendent's decision in a case against her principal. As you and I discussed, the executive committee of the board seems like the right group to hear the appeal."

When Claire paused, Mr. Gillespie said, "Right, it is proper for there to be an avenue for appeal of any decision. And after this, I will be starting a process of amending our procedures manual to take care of this oversight. Now we are a bit ad hoc. Nevertheless, my bet is we'll pass legal muster. Does anyone have any questions?"

He paused and looked at all the board members. No one had any questions, so he continued. Addressing Dorothy, he said, "I understand you are Dorothy McGuire, and you would like to appeal Superintendent Squire's decision. Would you please explain the basis for your appeal?"

Dorothy took the place at the podium where Claire had been. She read from a sheet of paper she'd prepared. "Members of the Board, I am grateful for this chance to appeal the decision on the sexual harassment complaint I made against Dave Johnson, my principal. I have evidence—

new evidence. When this evidence is presented, I believe the board will see fit to change the decision."

At this point, Mrs. Knudson interrupted, "Excuse me. Unless this new evidence just came to light, you can't appeal. Appeals are only valid for procedural errors or claims of bias."

"I agree. Usually you're right, Janice," Mr. Gillespie said. "I reviewed our procedures and unfortunately there is no statement specifying the basis for the appeal of a personnel decision. I think we have to admit this evidence."

Mrs. Knudson seemed upset. "I guess you're right. Still, I have to agree with you. We need to have a close look at those procedures."

"And we will. Would you continue, Ms. McGuire?"

"My complaint is simple. Dave Johnson asked me for dates on several occasions. I turned him down. First, he's married. I'd never date a married man. Second, he's my direct supervisor, and it is against school policy for us to date. I decided to file a formal complaint when he said he'd make trouble for my tenure decision if I didn't agree to date him. I explained all this in my written complaint."

Dorothy paused, and Mr. Gillespie interrupted. "Let's pause there and hear from Superintendent Squires. What did you do when you got Ms. McGuire's complaint, Geoff?"

Mr. Squires replied, "We treated it very seriously. Ms. McGuire told us there were no witnesses to back her complaint. We talked to Mr. Johnson, and he categorically denied the allegations. As in many of these matters, we had conflicting information, and the way I see it, a person is innocent until proven guilty. We dismissed the complaint."

Dorothy got mad. "The way I see it, I said one thing, and Dave Johnson said another thing. The way things turned out, you believed him, and you didn't believe me. He's innocent until proven guilty. What am I—guilty until proven innocent?"

"I can tell you're upset, Ms. McGuire. It won't be productive. You said you had new evidence. What is it?"

Dorothy took a deep breath. "It's a video. I have it on this thumb drive." She held the thumb drive.

Claire stepped in at this point. "Fred, you're our technical wizard. I bet you can get this on the screen."

Mr. Lewis rose from his chair and gestured to Dorothy. "Sure, give me the drive. What's the file called?"

"McGuire. It's the only thing on there."

Fred Lewis got the video on a screen behind Dorothy and Claire. All the board members had a good view. It started but without sound. Dorothy glanced at Claire. Claire said, "The sound is important Fred, start it again and increase the sound."

Mr. Lewis complied. The board members were clearly fascinated by what they were seeing. Dorothy could tell they were paying attention.

When the video finished, Mrs. Knudson started the questioning. "Either we owe you a big apology, Ms. McGuire, or this video is doctored, and we should fire you on the spot."

Dorothy jumped to her feet. "The video's not doctored!"

Mrs. Knudson fired back, "Then how did you get it, and why didn't you bring it forward when you submitted your first complaint?"

Dorothy explained about the email from the INHSSSA group. She had copies of the email ready for the board members and Mr. Squires. After everyone had a chance to read it, she explained she'd asked the INHSSSA group for the video. She didn't want to do anything until she saw the video. Maybe it was a hoax. When the video came, she decided to follow their instructions.

"So, you don't know who these people are?" Mr. Lewis asked.

"No. I haven't the faintest idea who they are."

"Excuse me, I don't know if I can speak," Claire said.

"It's okay go ahead," Mr. Gillespie said.

Claire continued, "I have no idea who they are as well. They seem fairly crafty. She can't email them, and if they're right, no one can trace their emails."

"How'd you get the thumb drive?" Mr. Lewis asked.

"It came in a small package in the mail."

"Was there a postmark?"

"Yes, Atlanta."

"It's a clue."

"Excuse me, Fred," Mr. Gillespie said. "This is all beside the point. What we have to decide is whether this evidence is sufficient to overturn the decision in this case. It's what's before us now." He paused and then continued. "Superintendent Squires, do you have any comments?"

The superintendent looked up from his copy of the email. "I find this entire thing extraordinary. First of all, I didn't know anything about it. Second, our school buildings are locked, and no one is able to come in and install cameras without being seen. This must have resulted from, what's the right phrase... breaking and entering. That's it. These INHSSSA people are crooks."

"Doesn't this evidence make Ms. McGuire's case?" Mrs. Knudson said.

"If it's not faked, I guess it does. You yourself brought up the idea it might be doctored."

Mrs. Knudson continued, "Ms. McGuire explained how she got the video. And it seems very authentic to me. I recognize Dave Johnson's voice. And it's clearly him. No offense, Ms. McGuire, I doubt you have the technical skills needed to fake a video like this. You've got to change your decision, Mr. Squires."

"Not so fast, Janice," Mr. Gillespie said. "I have to poll the entire committee when we're ready. What do you have to say, Gregory? You've been silent all night."

Mr. Hornwig rocked back in his chair. "I think much of this is irregular, plain and simple, irregular. Nevertheless, I can't see how we can sustain the superintendent. The evidence is overwhelming. We can't have principals behaving like this Johnson person."

"Mr. Lewis?"

"I concur with Greg. We must change this decision."

"And I agree as well," Mr. Gillespie concluded. "Ms. McGuire, the board will uphold your complaint on appeal. We have to decide what we're going to do about Dave Johnson. There's one thing I can tell you for sure. He will have no role in your tenure decision. And Claire, thank you for your role in this. Without your efforts, we wouldn't have gotten to the bottom of it."

He looked around at the rest of the executive committee and said, "I guess we're adjourned at this point. We'll have to confer with the whole board to decide with Superintendent Squires what we are going to do about Dave Johnson."

On the way out, several of the board members told Dorothy they were sorry for what she'd been put through. She found it easy to be magnanimous. She thanked them and hugged Claire. When she got to her car, she felt like a load had been lifted off her back. She retrieved her cell phone from her purse and called Susan.

Chapter Forty-Six

ON FRIDAY, SHERRY SAW DOROTHY'S triumphant post when she checked *Female Friends*. Though she felt good about what she'd read, the experience wasn't the same. She wasn't able to share the feeling of accomplishment with the rest of the group.

Later she got a call from Melissa. She told Sherry the case would be breaking soon. The news stories would be big. They arranged for a lunch the next day.

After they'd ordered, Sherry spoke. "Can you tell me? When will the stories come out? Can I go home?"

"Hold on. I may have been premature. While I was told the raids would happen last night, they've been postponed. I can't tell you anything yet. I'm sorry. I guess I called you out here on false pretenses."

"When are the raids, or whatever, going to happen? I'd like to be able to go back to my normal life, to my friends and my job."

"If my sources are good, the whole thing should break soon. I'm not sure when."

"I don't like this waiting around. I feel so useless."

"Your mother seems to be enjoying herself. I don't think she's going to want to go back to Pennsylvania with you."

"Yes, I guess she and I will have to talk. The FBI is picking up the tab for our stay here. Eventually we'll have to pay if Mom wants to stay in the retirement community. I don't have the faintest idea how much the place costs. I guess we'll have the insurance on the house, and if she's going to stay here, we'll sell the farmland. I hope we'll have enough."

"I don't know. I bet you'll be okay. And you're right. We made a special arrangement with the retirement community for your mother. If I'm right about the details, normally a resident buys the apartment. We're only renting month-to-month. We'll have to work out the details when the time comes."

"I hope it comes soon."

"We all do. Believe me. We all do."

Their lunches arrived, and the discussion stopped. When they'd finished eating, Melissa said, "I've been looking at the *Female Friends* chat room we talked about before."

Sherry tried to stay calm. "Have you found the site useful? I thought it might be good for you. Give you a chance to work out your issues."

"I haven't posted anything yet. I have to say, though, I find the notion that other people share my same problems helpful."

"I check out the site for a similar reason. I have to admit, I've never posted either."

"And you remember the I. N. H. S. S. S. A. stuff I asked you about before?"

Sherry tried to sound normal when she replied. "Yeah, what about it?"

"Well, I paid attention to those posts since we talked about them. The posts with the strange designation seem to be half of a conversation. Like the people posting are reporting to their bosses. And there's a pattern. First, the person asks questions. Then they say they got a package. The next thing is about a sexual harassment complaint. Finally, there are posts about appeals. While not all the posts follow this pattern, there are similarities. I found the pattern weird."

Sherry was shaken. After a brief silence, she felt she had to stay in the conversation. "Like I said, I hadn't paid any attention to the I. N. H. S. S. S. A. posts. After you asked about them, I did notice those posts. I didn't see any pattern like you did. What do you think's going on?"

"I don't know. I alerted the technical guys, and they're going to look at the posts more closely."

Sherry got more nervous at this point. "Is there any hint of illegal behavior here? Doesn't the FBI cover criminal behavior? How is this an FBI issue?"

"We don't see how there is anything illegal going on. And you're right. Criminal behavior is our main business. Still, we keep track of suspicious stuff on the internet. You'd be surprised at how many wackos tell everyone in their chat rooms about things they are going to do. We've been able to head off lots of crimes by monitoring the internet."

"I wouldn't think *Female Friends* would be the kind of chat room you'd monitor."

"It isn't. Like I said, the tech who checked on you got interested. He saw you were spending a lot of time on those posts. Remember I asked you about them? Anyway, he had time on his hands, so he looked at a bunch of the posts. He told me the posts were funny. I took a look, and, as I explained, I found a pattern in the posts."

"I'll grant you they seem weird, but I didn't see the pattern you did. Would that pattern warrant an FBI investigation?" While worried, Sherry tried to keep her voice calm.

"Probably not. I've got time on my hands, so I followed up on the tech's suggestion. Nothing is likely to come of it. Just weird, I thought."

"After you get rid of me and my mom, will you be assigned to another case?"

"Yeah, I've been thinking about that subject a lot. I'm going to ask for a new assignment when this is finished. There is no way I want to go back to Larry Clarkson's unit."

Sherry wanted to keep the discussion on this new topic. "How does the assignment process work? Can you ask to be reassigned at any point? How much choice do you have in the matter?"

"The FBI has a complex system. We do have choices. We can request assignments. Like in any big organization, you don't always get what you want. The Bureau has to balance your skill set with current openings, your requests, and your most recent evaluations come in to play, too."

"Too bad. I don't suppose Larry's going to be inclined to give you a great evaluation. I hope the result isn't a bad assignment for you."

"I guess that could happen. I feel like making a sexual harassment complaint against him. Then again, such complaints don't often work. The whole thing would come down to his word against mine. I'd probably lose. Filing the complaint would backfire on me. I'd be sure to get a terrible assignment. We have bad posts. There are FBI agents in Alaska, you know."

Sherry thought about reminding Melissa she shared a lot with the women on *Female Friends* but had second thoughts. "I think I told you before, I made two sexual harassment complaints, one in business and one in graduate school. Neither of them did any good. If you only have your word to go on, those complaints can backfire like you said."

"I know. Innocent until proven guilty. Lots of bad behavior isn't punished because of the presumption of innocence. I understand, and I guess it's good. In this kind of case, though, the presumption of innocence doesn't work to the woman's advantage."

The lunch conversation moved on to other topics after this. They left after an hour and went their separate ways.

When Sherry got to her apartment, she felt concerned. She couldn't alert the rest of the group about the FBI looking at what they were doing. It was clear what they had to do. They had to ditch using In Hissa. She and Beth had been so happy with themselves for inventing the acronym. The acronym couldn't be pronounced. Now that fact turned out to be the fatal flaw.

Chapter Forty-Seven

THE NEWS OF THE BIG FBI raids on the human trafficking ring broke two days after Melissa and Sherry's lunch. The raid led to arrests in several cities, and there were also arrests in rural locations, including Lackey. Apparently, local barns were used as holding places for young women who were being moved around the country. The gang moved their captives frequently, so the police had a difficult time tracking their activities. The three in Lackey saw FBI agent Larry Clarkson's press conference announcing the arrests on CNN.

The arrest of Bob McFall and the other guy, Henry Marietta, whom no one knew, resulted from a joint effort of the FBI and the Lackey police. The news spread through the community rapidly. When Phil, Beth, and Ralph heard about it, they did their best to act surprised. They faked shock that a local person would be involved in such a sensational crime. Several people said they thought they'd seen suspicious activity at McFall's farm. When asked why they didn't contact the police, they stopped talking in a hurry.

Phil went to Beth and Ralph's for dinner. They had champagne.

"You've got another bottle for when Sherry returns?" Phil asked.

"Yes, we do. When do you think she'll be back?" Beth asked.

"I don't know. One of the worst parts of this whole thing has been being out of contact with her."

Beth smiled. "Yeah, you've been out of all kinds of contact with her."

Ralph jumped in, "Beth, I'm surprised at you."

"It's okay," Phil said, blushing a little. "Yes, I've missed her in lots of ways. I hope she gets home soon. Something's been bothering me, though. Maybe they will keep a witness like Sherry incognito until the trial. I bet they worry about losing their witnesses. I may have to wait until then. Who knows when it'll happen."

"I bet they don't want to keep her," Ralph said. "If I remember right, they said Bob McFall was a small fry in this investigation. There's not much chance anyone will go after a witness in his case. The way you described it, the video should be enough to convict him. All they need Sherry for is to say when and where she shot the video."

Phil felt relieved. "I bet you're right. If so, I'm going to have to figure out how to explain Sherry's reappearance."

"Won't the FBI issue a statement?" Beth asked. "They should publicly thank Sherry. She went through a lot of disruption for them."

Phil's cell phone rang. He checked the caller ID—Sherry. "Hello stranger."

"It's so great to hear you, Phil."

"I'm at Ralph and Beth's. Wait a moment, I'm going to tell them who's calling." He yelled, "It's Sherry." Then he turned back to the phone. "Do you know when you'll be home?"

"It should be in a couple of days. There's a lot to do here. My mom is going to stay. She's taken with the retirement community. It's a good place for her. And I don't have a car. The FBI might let me keep the rental I'm using now. I'm not sure. There's a lot to accomplish. For example, I don't have a suitcase, and I bought a bunch of new clothes. Now I've got nowhere to put them."

"Gosh, I hadn't thought about all those details. So, Gladys is going to stay in South Carolina?"

"Yes. Trick is close. It will be good for her grandchildren to get to know her better. I'll miss her but I can visit."

Phil broke in, "You can stay at my place when you get back. At least if you want to."

"I was hoping you'd ask."

"Definitely, you can stay as long as you want."

"Wow, an open-ended commitment. I like it."

"It's great to hear you."

"You too," Sherry said. "Now I've got to go. Someone's at my front door. Tell the others we should keep our project on hold. Talk to you soon. Goodbye."

"Goodbye," Phil echoed. Then he turned to his friends, who were hovering. "She'll be able to leave in a couple of days. Her mother's going to stay in the retirement community in South Carolina. She has a lot of details to figure out."

"I heard you offer her your house for when she gets back. So, you'll be living together, too," Beth said. "I hope it's what you wanted."

"Yes, it will be fine. No, I think it will be great."

Ralph said, "People will talk. You know how people in Lackey are."

"Let them talk. They're already aware Sherry and I are a couple."

"Anything else in the call?" Beth asked. "We only heard half of it."

"Nothing important," Phil answered. "She has lots of details to clear up. All her stuff burned in the fire. Though she's bought new clothes, she doesn't have a suitcase. And she doesn't have a car. Lots of details, nothing too important." Phil paused. "No, wait, right at the end, she said we should put our project on hold. Nothing more, no context."

"Okay," Ralph said. "We're not doing anything now. The Lucinda Wallace thing is in her hands now. There's no reason to do anything. I wonder why she wanted to put things on hold?"

"It doesn't matter. She can tell us later," Phil said. "It's doubly good we weren't thinking about embarking on another one yet. And we still don't know what to do about the rape. It'll be easy for us to comply with Sherry's cryptic comment."

"No problem," Beth said. "Now we have all the more reason to pop the cork on the champagne. Let's get to it."

****

Four days later, at about noon, Sherry parked her little sedan in front of Phil's house. He'd been waiting by the window, so he ran out to greet her. They hugged and kissed. Then he said, "Let me get your suitcase. You bought one, didn't you?"

"Two," Sherry said as she popped the trunk.

Phil grabbed the suitcases and brought them into the house. He went into the master bedroom and put the suitcases down. "I've cleared out half of the closet. Not too forward of me, I hope."

"No, it's not," Sherry replied as she grabbed Phil in an embrace. "I'm thinking of being really forward with you," she said as she kissed him.

An hour later, they walked to Andy's for lunch. Along the way, they were stopped by a couple who'd read the newspaper story. When they got to the restaurant, Andy accosted them. "Back from the dead, are we?" he said. "You're still real good looking. It must not have been too traumatic—dying and all."

"Thanks for the compliment, Andy. Actually, I think Phil had the harder time. He had to fake my death and hang around and act all sad about my passing. I got a short vacation. I had a good time."

"Phil did a fair job. We didn't see him much. He had a real hang-dog look about him the one time he showed for the professor lunch."

"Enough of this, Andy," Phil said. "The lady's hungry. She had a long drive."

After lunch, they walked back to Phil's house. Sherry unpacked and then called the library to arrange to go to work the next day. The head librarian had a lot of questions. Sherry thought her boss sounded a little miffed to have been out of the loop about her fake death. He calmed down when she told him only Phil had the whole story.

After her call to the librarian, Sherry found Phil sorting out things in his refrigerator. "I didn't get this cleaned out, sorry," Phil said.

"Okay. We can put it off. There's something I want to talk about."

"What's up?"

"On my long drive, I recognized I know you pretty well. Still, there's a big hole. You've never told me anything about Viet Nam. What did you do in Viet Nam? I'm aware you got shot. I've heard the story and seen the scars on your leg. I don't know anything more about it. You don't talk about it."

The question surprised Phil. "I guess I don't talk about it much. I kind of walled it off from the rest of my life."

"I want to hear about it," Sherry said with a pleading tone.

Phil took a deep breath. "All right. It's best to start by saying I didn't think we should be in Viet Nam in the first place. You're a little younger than I am, so it didn't hit you as much. I opposed the war. I did a little protesting, nothing big. It didn't bother my draft board. When I got my draft notice, I thought about running to Canada."

"Why didn't you go?"

"Two things. First, it would have crushed my parents. Second, the more I thought about it, the more I felt a sense of duty. I mean, my father and my uncle fought in World War II. I'm a citizen of this country. You owe allegiance to your country, even when they're wrong."

"You were noble."

"I don't know. Anyway, I got drafted. While I had the option of volunteering for the Navy, the Air Force, or as an officer in the Army, I wanted the shortest stint. All the other options meant more years away from graduate school and my career. And I figured, as an honors graduate of a good college, the Army would find a job for me involving brains not brawn."

"You weren't right?"

"No. In fact, when you tried to figure out how they assigned us from basic training, the following rule worked. If you'd been in college for two years or more, including a couple of guys with graduate degrees, you were assigned to AIT, Advanced Infantry Training. And everyone from my AIT unit got orders to go to Viet Nam."

"Tell me about it."

"We flew there on chartered airlines. They'd taken out the first-class seats, so there were a lot of us jammed in. In Saigon, we got parceled out to the various units needing replacements. As a result, most likely you got assigned to a unit that had recently lost people. In my case, they'd lost quite a few in a big battle. They'd seen a lot. When I got to my unit, I thought they looked funny."

"Funny? I don't understand."

"Well, you've probably heard about Army training, how they make you polish your shoes and make your bed just so. It's all about spit and polish. Troops in Viet Nam had none of it. Half of the guys weren't wearing full uniforms. They were a ragtag group. Lots of things were a little flakey. For example, I got the impression it would be smart for me to give one of the big machine gunners the morphine in the first aid kit I'd been issued in Saigon. I'm not sure I made a friend then. At least I avoided making an enemy. It seemed smart because the machine gunner, who everyone called Chicken Hawk, carried a big Bowie knife."

"I've seen movies about Viet Nam, and I know what you're talking about. You didn't have any chance to see those movies before you got there."

"Right. So, one of the first days as we were walking along, the front of the column was shot at. I heard the shots, and I followed the guy assigned to break me in. We ran for cover and got in position to shoot. Nothing more happened. After things calmed down and the shooting stopped, I remember being proud. I hadn't panicked. The whole thing seemed strange, surreal. People were out there trying to kill me."

"So, you didn't have to shoot your rifle then."

"Not then. Actually, I didn't have to shoot very often. We did a lot of what were called 'cordon and search' operations. We'd go early in the morning, about three-thirty, and surround a village. At daybreak, one of the platoons would roust everyone in the village out of their hooches. When we'd collected all the people, our ARVN interpreter would question them. Often he had us put the young men we found on helicopters for more questioning."

"So, the kind of operation involved in the My Lai massacre?"

"I think so. In the My Lai case, after they collected the people, they shot them. We just asked them questions. Anyway, we did a lot of those operations. A few times, we got to be the guards at an LZ. Whoops—the Army and its acronyms—a landing zone. We liked it, because we didn't have to carry our packs every day. Most of the time, we worked hard. The higher ups always wanted us to move, so we did a lot of hiking. We could never sneak up on anyone. We made too much noise. As we were marching along, we got shot at several times. We'd all dive down and shoot back at where we thought the shots were coming from. We wanted to make the guy stop shooting—make him run away."

"Frightening?"

"A little, but then I got shot."

"I suppose it changes your perspective."

"One of the interesting things was the difference between what headquarters wanted and what troops like me wanted. When we got shot at, the order would come on the radio from on high: 'maintain contact.' Let me tell you, maintaining contact seemed really wrong. I wanted to break contact as soon as possible."

"If you had to describe your experience in a few words, what would they be?"

"Hot, sweaty, hard work, and fear. We hiked a long way with very heavy packs. And scary, particularly at night. I remember being frightened to death the first night I got there. Luckily, I didn't experience any pitched battles. And my tour lasted only five and a half months before I got shot."

"Thanks. I can tell you don't like talking about it," Sherry said. "It's hard for me to see you as a soldier. You don't seem the type."

"No, I'm not the Army type. When I needed to, I was able to play their games, but I only played. I wasn't committed. Like I said, I walled it off from the rest of my life. I hardly ever think about it. I know there are people whose wartime experiences changed them for life. It hardly changed me at all. I guess I'm lucky."

Chapter Forty-Eight

PHIL AND SHERRY WENT TO Beth and Ralph's for dinner. After they exchanged hugs and popped open the second bottle of champagne, Sherry had them all sit down. "I've got news about our project."

"Yeah, you asked us to put things on hold," Beth said. "What's up?"

"Melissa, the FBI agent, sort of babysat me and Mom in South Carolina. And we became friends. One time, when we were out for a drink, you could have knocked me over with a feather when she asked me about I. N. H. S. S. S. A."

"What?" everyone exclaimed.

"They monitored my computer use. Remember, I wasn't allowed to email any of you."

"I found it frustrating," Phil said.

"One of their technical people detected me spending more than the normal amount of time on the In Hissa posts in the chat room. And Melissa asked me about it."

"How did you react?" Beth asked.

"Fortunately, because the acronym we chose is so weird, Melissa had to look down at her notebook when she asked the question. I had myself under control before she looked at me. I denied knowing anything about the acronym. I told her I checked out *Female Friends* often because the subject matter interested me. She sympathized. She's having troubles with her boss. It's why she got reassigned to babysit us in South Carolina."

"Wow, they were keeping track of your clicks," Ralph said. "That's not easy to do. I'm not sure I would know how."

"I considered not going back to the chat room again," Sherry said. "Then I realized such a change would seem suspicious. When I did go back, I tried to keep my time on the posts consistent with their size."

"Did anything else come up?" Phil asked.

Sherry responded, "Yes, and it's why I wanted you to put things on hold. Melissa told me the tech had gotten interested in the In Hissa posts. The two of them characterized the posts as half of a conversation. And basically, they're right. While they don't know what's going on, they might figure out before long."

"Yeah, Dorothy McGuire's last post had lots of details. Enough details to tell them what the whole thing's all about," Beth said. "We'd better cease and desist."

"No, I don't want to stop what we're doing, and I don't think we should. First, I wanted to change the acronym. Ralph never liked it."

"Now you don't want to?" Phil asked.

"No. If we change the acronym right after Melissa and I talked, they'd get suspicious. So, we have to use it very carefully. Though maybe we can phase it out later, we have to do at least one more using our current procedures."

"I see, but I'm not happy," Beth said. "The last thing we want is the FBI looking into what we're doing. This makes me way nervous."

"I know what you're talking about," Sherry said. "I didn't get any sleep the night after I learned the tech guy had become interested in those posts. I've been wondering about the whole thing a lot. I had trouble not telling Phil before we got here."

"So now I understand the question about Viet Nam," Phil said, giving Sherry a look.

"Maybe," Sherry answered. "I'm interested. Really."

"I don't know what that's all about... we've been careful," Ralph said. "I'm pretty sure even the FBI can't trace the emails back to us. We shouldn't be worried. I agree. We should do one more with In Hissa, and then we can change the way the women address their posts."

"I wish I had your confidence, honey," Beth said. "This whole thing makes me nervous."

Phil said, "Let's eat. The dinner's probably getting cold. We'll be hashing this out for quite a while. There's no reason to have to make a decision yet."

Chapter Forty-Nine

TWO DAYS LATER IN ATLANTA, Lucinda Wallace got a call from Mrs. Ferris in personnel. They agreed on an appointment for the afternoon. Lucinda put one of the thumb drives in her purse. She wanted to be ready when the decision went against her. She thoroughly expected to lose.

When they got into Mrs. Ferris's office, Lucinda said, "This past week and a half haven't been easy at work. I think everyone there knows what's going on. Several of them, particularly the men, have been avoiding me, or worse, giving me dirty looks. I'm glad this is almost finished."

"You can't say I didn't warn you," Mrs. Ferris took a piece of paper out of a folder. "And I'm sorry to say you are unlikely to be pleased with the outcome. Here's the report."

Lucinda took the paper from Mrs. Ferris. They had done an investigation. Mr. Reeser had denied the allegations, and there were no supporting witnesses. They denied the complaint.

Lucinda looked at Mrs. Ferris. "So, his word against mine, and he won. Right?"

"I guess you've given a fair summary. These things are difficult. You said there were unlikely to be any witnesses. And no other female employees said they had problems with Mr. Reeser. I'm sorry. There's nothing we can do. You must have known it was a longshot when you filed the complaint."

Lucinda smiled. She did have a backup plan—a good one. "Mrs. Ferris, I have more evidence. I think it will make you reconsider this decision."

Mrs. Ferris looked puzzled. "What?"

"My new evidence will show you I'm the one to be believed."

"This is very irregular. I don't know if it's appropriate."

"Can't I appeal?"

"I guess so. Why put yourself through more grief?"

"Because my new evidence will make my case. Here, let me show you. There's a video on this drive. We can show it on your computer." When Mrs. Ferris still looked bewildered, Lucinda motioned for her to move aside. Mrs. Ferris didn't budge. "You want to put the thumb drive in my computer?"

"Yes."

"We're not supposed to do that. We don't want to introduce a virus into the system."

"There's no virus on this. I know. I put the thumb drive into my computer." Lucinda paused. Then she had an idea. "We'll run a scan on it before you open any files. If you have the same company software I have, you have that capability."

"Okay, I guess. Can you show me how?"

Mrs. Ferris scooted over to let Lucinda access her computer. Lucinda carefully showed Mrs. Ferris all the steps needed to do the virus scan on the thumb drive. After they both were sure the thumb drive was clean, she started the video.

When Daniel came to her cubicle, Lucinda said, "That's Mr. Reeser, Daniel." Otherwise they watched in silence.

When the video finished, Lucinda couldn't help herself. "I told you I had good evidence. You saw him with his hands all over me. And not just once."

"Yes, I understand what you're saying. And I can tell from your reaction you don't want to be touched." After a pause, Mrs. Ferris continued, "This brings up lots of question and maybe some legal issues."

"What questions?"

"The first, I guess, is how'd you get the video?"

Lucinda explained about the email from I. N. H. S. S. S. A. and their instructions.

"So, you're saying you didn't have anything to do with creating the video. Someone else, this anonymous group, shot the video. They put the cameras at your office."

"Yep."

"Then we have the problem with the legality of the evidence."

"This isn't a court case. I don't understand how legality comes into play."

"Let me explain. Suppose we use this evidence to overturn our decision. We would then discipline Mr. Reeser, maybe fire him. In a discipline case, he would have a right to know about the evidence we have. He might even get a lawyer. He would sue for wrongful dismissal. The courts might well get involved."

"Mrs. Ferris, I don't want to play hardball with you. Still, there's more to what these people told me. They said if I didn't get a settlement to my liking, I should tell them, and they'd put the video on the company's website. I don't think you want the entire internet to view the video."

"This video?"

"Yes. It would clearly be a sensation."

"Let me get this straight. You're making a direct threat. You're trying to blackmail us."

"Wait, wait. Let's back up a bit. You have the evidence. The video shows I'm being sexually harassed."

"Yes..."

Lucinda interrupted, "I don't understand why there's any hesitation. You've got lawyers too. They should ensure you get rid of Daniel. What he does to me isn't right. And I don't think the company wants supervisors like him. I want the company to do the right thing."

"Okay, I'm starting to understand. I don't like threats. Anyway, I'll have to talk to my supervisor about this. And he'll want to get legal involved. Can I have the thumb drive?"

"Yes."

"I don't know how long this will all take. I'll write a report and get the process started. I might not get back to you for a couple of weeks. You have my card. Call me if you have any questions."

"There's one more thing," Lucinda said. "At the end of next week, we have our monthly evals. Given what's happened, Daniel is going to give me low marks. That affects my salary. Is there any way to make a change?

"I'm sure there is."

"Thanks." Lucinda stood, ready to leave. As they walked out toward the front office, Lucinda said, "Look Mrs. Ferris, I'm sorry to drop all this on you. You're only doing your job."

Mrs. Ferris smiled and shook Lucinda's hand when they got to the front office. "Most of my work is routine. This is a mess. In a way, I'm excited. I wonder what the front office's going to do."

"Me too," echoed Lucinda.

Chapter Fifty

THE NIGHT AFTER LUCINDA WENT to talk to Mrs. Ferris, Beth and Sherry saw Lucinda's post and told their respective partners.

At Phil's house, Phil said to Sherry, "This time we might have to carry through with the threat about showing the video on the company website. While I never liked our threat, I understand why we needed it. The thing is, I don't want the FBI involved. If they're still monitoring In Hissa posts, they've heard about videos. It'll be a big deal if we put the video on the company website. They might put two and two together."

"You're right. I sure hope we don't have to follow through on the threat. Still, we can't hang Lucinda out to dry. We have to follow through for her sake."

"I suppose so," Phil said. After a pause he continued, "And again, we're stalled on the project. We've got two things going, but they're stalled. Lucinda has to get the results of her appeal. On the rape, Ralph is completely stumped. He hasn't made any progress on finding anything about the victim."

"Yes, this whole business has its fits and starts. If we want to go ahead, Beth and I have a good candidate for our next one."

"Where is she?"

"Texas, one of the suburbs of Dallas."

"It should be easy to get there. Lots of flights go to Dallas."

"Let me tell you about her. Her name is Darcy Nunez. She is the receptionist in a doctor's office. Two days a week, she's responsible for closing the office. On most of those days, one of the doctors, Robert Sector, waits for her. Despite the fact he's married, he asks her for dates. And he wants to get physical. He tries to put his arm around her and kiss her. She resists. Like the others, she's afraid he'll either get violent or fire her if she doesn't cooperate. She's upset."

"It sounds familiar. A man in a position of power hitting on a subordinate."

"You're right. It's the kind of thing a lot of the posts on *Female Friends* are about. It's a big problem in all kinds of workplaces. There's probably lots more out there. We're only exposed to the ones who post chats."

"Does she say which doctor's office it is? Dallas is a big place."

"It shouldn't be a problem. We have the doctor's name, so we can find the office."

Phil slapped himself on the forehead. "Idiot," he said. "Of course, we can find the doctor. And I guess there might even be a picture of Darcy. Don't lots of doctor's websites show the entire staff?"

"You're not an idiot. You shouldn't say that about yourself."

"What's the doctor's name again? I'll see if I can locate him."

Sherry answered, "Robert Sector."

About ten minutes later, Phil called Sherry to come look at his computer. "I found him. He's an orthopedic specialist. Here's his picture."

"A clean-cut, All American guy," Sherry said.

"I guess so. And here's Darcy Nunez."

"She's good looking. I like the long dark hair, and she has a nice smile."

"It's odd. We didn't have any notion of what the people looked like before. Maybe because we haven't tried to find them. We might have been able to find a picture of Dorothy what's-her-name, the school teacher. I bet lots of schools have websites with pictures of the teachers."

"We could have looked on Facebook, too, but Beth and I figured we might leave a trail. We explicitly decided not to use Facebook."

"Anyway, the website has the address and even an interactive map showing us how to get to the office. We've got good information."

Chapter Fifty-One

THE NEXT DAY PHIL AND Ralph decided they'd be the ones to go to Dallas. They got a flight on the weekend. They got to the Dallas-Fort Worth airport early in the evening, rented a car and found a motel on the same side of town as Sector's office. After checking in, they drove to the doctor's offices. The clinic building took up a large portion of an office park. There were six doctor's names on the sign.

Ralph said, "I don't see any reason to wait. The lock on the front door doesn't look intimidating."

"I'd prefer going around to the back door." Phil said. "The place is all lit up. It would be easy to see us if we come in the front door."

"Okay, if there's an alarm, my new gizmo will let us bypass it."

"Won't we attract attention? Won't the police come to see what's wrong with the alarm?"

"Their response, or lack of response, depends on what kind of alarm's involved. In almost all cases, my device should make it look like the alarm is turned off. If the alarm's tied into the police station, the police are unlikely to respond to an alarm being turned off. They only respond to tripped alarms. If the alarm's tied into an alarm company, they are likely to act the same way. We shouldn't have anything to worry about. Still, the device is new, so there's risk. We have to be fast."

"This time, we're installing the small cameras and the separate microphone. Installing two things is likely to slow us down."

"That's why there are two of us."

Phil didn't like change. "I know the mic and cameras will be harder to spot. Still, I hate to change when everything's worked so well. You're sure they will give us the good quality we've had in the other cases?"

"They did in the trials. You were there. We all agreed this would be an improvement. You seem uptight—are you okay? As far as I'm concerned, we should get rolling."

"Yeah, I'm nervous," Phil said. "No one is stirring around here. I guess you're right. We should make our move. Let's park the car around back. I hope we can be in and out in a hurry."

Ralph pulled the car around to the alley behind the doctor's office. Before he entered the alley, he turned off his headlights. He came to a stop beside the back door of the offices. They checked their equipment, gave each other a thumbs-up, and got out of the car. Ralph picked the lock while Phil monitored the surroundings. Ralph opened the door and disabled the alarm with his new device. With a broad grin on his face, he motioned for Phil to come in.

The doctors' offices were like a rabbit warren. Lots of little rooms and several twisty corridors. They moved quietly, and after a few wrong turns, found their way to the receptionist's area. There were several desks, and they had no idea which one Darcy occupied. While they inspected all the desks, there was no way to detect which one belonged to Darcy. They ducked down and knelt on the floor.

"I'm going to have to install two cameras, one on each end," whispered Ralph.

"Will one microphone do?"

"Yes, put the microphone there." Ralph pointed.

They mounted their equipment using office chairs to get to the sprinklers on the ceiling. They were sure to wipe footprints off the chairs. They only needed three minutes to get everything mounted. A minute later they were in the car headed out of the alley.

Phil scanned the area as they approached the street. "No one's coming. I guess we got away with disabling the alarm."

"No sweat. They may wonder what's up when they get there in the morning. No big deal. Alarms go wonky all the time. Anyway, we should be at the airport waiting for our plane by then."

At their late dinner, Ralph asked, "How's everything going with you and Sherry? I know there were some adjustments when Beth and I started living together."

"Generally, things are okay. I think it's harder on Sherry than on me. Most of the furniture in my house came from Mary Jane. The whole thing is hard on her, losing all the stuff she always had. Now she's got to live with the things some other woman bought."

"Doesn't she have anything of her own to work in somehow?"

"No, she got rid of her furniture when she moved in with her mother. I don't think she minded at the time, but now maybe she regrets being so hasty. Maybe I'll ask her if she doesn't want to replace some things. Not everything I have is in tip-top shape."

"As you know, almost everything in our apartment belonged to Beth. I didn't bring much more than my clothes and my computer. And come to think of it, she's changed my wardrobe, so most of my clothes aren't the ones I brought."

"Sherry and I have only been together for a week. To answer your original question, things are going well. We like each other a lot. It hasn't been difficult to adjust my bathroom behavior. I take a shower in the morning, and she takes one in the evening. And I haven't had difficulty adjusting to someone else in the bed."

"Good. What with the fire and all, you two were sort of thrown together."

"I got no complaints. I hope Sherry doesn't."

The next morning, they flew back east.

Chapter Fifty-Two

WHEN THEY ARRIVED HOME FROM Dallas, Phil drove to Ralph's apartment. As Ralph unloaded his suitcase from the trunk, Sherry came out of the front door.

"What are you doing here?" Ralph asked.

"We need to have a meeting. We've got good news."

When Phil and Ralph entered the apartment, they kissed their respective women. Then Phil asked, "What's up?"

Beth answered, "We heard from Lucinda Wallace. She's thrilled—the insurance company changed their mind. They have decided to fire Daniel Reeser, the guy who's been bothering her. We don't have to put the video on the company website."

"Good. I bet the threat had something to do with them changing their decision," Ralph said.

"We'll never be sure," Sherry said. "I believe the video did the trick. Clearly, sexual harassment is going on. People can recognize it when they see it."

"Great news, no matter what," Phil said. "We have a real string of successes on this project, but we still have the rape to deal with. We're stalled there."

Sherry spoke at this point. "Actually, that's what we want to meet about. Beth and I have an idea."

Phil looked at Ralph and said, "We're all ears."

"Okay, we figured we might be able to use Lucinda. Her post announcing the firm's decision glowed. We should be able to get her to help us. Beth and I composed an email to her we'd like you two to read. Basically, we should take the video of the rape to her. We ought to be able to get her help identifying the cleaning company. After we learn who they are, we can send the video to them. Right now, we're stymied because we don't even know who they are."

"I'd be nervous going to Atlanta to meet with her," Ralph said. "Is that what you're proposing?"

"Yes, Honey," Beth replied. "Sherry has volunteered to go. Basically, honesty is the best policy. When we meet her, we'll remind her we installed the cameras to catch Daniel Reeser in the act. Then we'll show the other video we got by accident. She'll be shocked. We'll tell her we just want the name of the company who cleans their building. She should be able to find out."

"It seems risky," Ralph said.

"No." Sherry responded. "Lucinda likes us. We did her a big favor, and she's incredibly grateful. She'll help us. And we aren't actually asking for much."

"I want to go, too," Phil said. "It'll be better to have two of us. This is a tricky business, meeting with one of the people we've helped. Remember the FBI is sniffing around. Two people in disguise will be better."

"Nice offer, Phil. You don't have to. I can handle it alone."

"I'm sure you could. Still, we'll blend in better as a couple. A woman traveling alone might be conspicuous."

Sherry nodded. "Okay, I understand, and I would be happy to have you come."

"And Ralph can fetch the cameras and microphone from Texas. He doesn't need me. Everything went smoothly there."

"Gosh, we didn't even ask," Beth said. "We have so much confidence in you two."

"Sure," Ralph said.

"I guess we'd better see this email you propose to send to Lucinda," Phil said.

The two guys reviewed the email. They suggested changes to accommodate the inclusion of Phil. And they nitpicked a bit on the wording. The whole process didn't take long. The email suggested meeting right after Lucinda's quitting time at Louie's, a restaurant close to where Lucinda worked. For identification, the email said Lucinda should find the woman in the orange blazer sitting with a man with a white beard.

"Let's look at the restaurant," Ralph suggested.

"Okay, we found the restaurant online. I'll find their website," Beth said.

After they'd checked out the restaurant's website, they were satisfied. It looked like a nice place. Maybe a little more upscale than they suspected Lucinda might frequent, but not too out of line. Also, the booths had high backs, good for a private conversation.

****

Lucinda felt very good about how her sexual harassment complaint had turned out. Several women at work surprised her when they came to her and congratulated her. They said they'd seen Dennis being awful to her, and he'd hadn't been nice to them either. Lucinda had to hold herself back from asking why they'd been silent during the original investigation. She knew, of course. Fear. She decided not to be nasty. On the other hand, a few of the men in the office didn't seem at all pleased with her. She guessed she'd have to live with it. She hoped the mood would pass soon.

When she got back to her apartment two days after learning about Dennis's firing, LeRoy accosted her.

"What's this I hear about you and a sexual harassment complaint? The other cops down at the station seemed to know everything. I'm living with you, and I've heard nothing."

Lucinda could tell he was mad as he would have been if she'd told him about it in the first place. "The process is finished. I told you I didn't like my boss, Daniel. Well, his actions got so bad I filed a complaint. And I won my case. No big deal. They fired him. A couple of the other women told me he'd been doing the same stuff to them."

"What kind of stuff?"

"Oh, silly stuff, brushing by them when he doesn't need to, grabbing them, and patting their rear ends. Lots of unwanted touching. No problem anymore. He's been fired."

"The way I heard it, you were the only one who complained."

"Your information's good. I filed the complaint."

"So, how'd you win your case? Sexual harassment is hard to prove. Did the other women support your story?"

"Look LeRoy, I don't want to talk about whole business. It's over. The good thing is, I have a new boss. I don't have to worry about Daniel. Leave it alone."

"Lucinda, you didn't tell me. I can't understand why."

Lucinda went to LeRoy and gave him a hug. "I'm sorry. I suppose I should have told you. I didn't want you to worry."

"If I'd have known the guy bothered you, I'd have taken care of it."

"And gotten in trouble with the police force. You're still on probation."

"You're telling me I shouldn't stand up for my woman?"

"No, I'm asking you to let it go."

"Okay. Still, I don't want to hear any more surprises like this again."

"Fair enough," Lucinda said as she kissed LeRoy.

The next morning, Lucinda saw a new email from the INHSSSA people. They wanted to meet. They had a favor they wanted to ask. She remembered her promise to LeRoy. She decided she'd have to talk to him.

That evening Lucinda told LeRoy the whole story. She even showed him the video. She had to calm him down again. She convinced him Daniel had been punished enough. Finally, she showed the last email and asked him what she should do.

"I'm not sure," LeRoy said. "These people, whoever they are, have been incredibly nice to you. They went out of their way to get you the evidence you needed. I'd see what they want."

"That's sort of what I figured too. I'm happy you agree."

"Meeting them only seems right. You don't have to do what they want if you don't want to."

"Right. I'm nervous about what they might want. While they were doing me a big favor, they had to break into the building to set up those cameras. Breaking and entering. They didn't steal anything. Still, what they did's against the law."

"You're right. Shit, I'm the policeman. I should have thought about that. If they ask you to break any laws, flat out turn them down."

"I will. Definitely I will."

"In fact, maybe I'll come to Louie's and watch this meeting. If you have any trouble, or they suggest anything illegal, you signal me."

"Okay," Lucinda said. "I'll post a chat agreeing to the meeting. I like the idea of you being there too. Thanks."

Chapter Fifty-Three

PHIL AND SHERRY PACKED CAREFULLY for their trip to Atlanta. They planned a four-day trip and flew south on Thursday, which gave them time to get everything in place and not worry about airline delays. Their meeting with Lucinda was scheduled for Friday afternoon.

On Friday, they arrived at Louie's at four forty-five. The place hadn't filled yet. They got a booth on an end, which suited them fine. Sherry had on her orange blazer. She'd put streaks of blonde in her hair. Also, she wore a fake stomach and padding on her thighs. The padding added at least forty pounds. Both Phil and Sherry wore glasses. As a final touch, Phil had added a cane and a limp. If they ran into someone they knew, they wouldn't guess who they were.

At five after five, they recognized Lucinda as she walked in. She had on slightly more formal clothes than in the videos. Lucinda scanned the booths and gave them a little wave as she approached their booth.

"Hello, Lucinda," Sherry said as they shook hands.

Lucinda hesitated because the way they were sitting put her back to LeRoy at the bar. She had no choice, so she finally sat down facing the two. "I guess you're not going to tell me your names."

"No, we're not," Sherry said.

One of the servers came and asked for drink orders.

When the drink orders were completed, Sherry said in a low voice, "We're so happy your sexual harassment complaint got settled to your satisfaction."

"Me too."

"As you're aware, we put up cameras to get you the evidence you needed."

Lucinda nodded.

"In the process, we captured another image we found very unsettling. We'd like to show you the video and ask you a simple question. It's all we need—the answer to a simple question."

Lucinda looked puzzled, and then she said, "Okay."

Sherry took out her phone, started the video, and gave it to Lucinda. Lucinda looked intently. She sucked in her breath when the rape became obvious. When Lucinda returned the phone, her hands were shaking.

Sherry gave Lucinda a little time before she spoke again. "This happened at night. The woman is one of the people on the cleaning crew. They do your building at night, and I bet you recognized the man."

"Yes. Grover Brown—he's the big boss."

"Right. This stuff, rape, is out of our league. We've been trying to get the name of the cleaning company."

"I can probably find out," said Lucinda, who had calmed down after her initial surprise.

"It would be a big help," said Phil, who'd been silent until then. "We want to send a copy of this video to them. They can take it to the police."

Lucinda didn't respond. She reviewed her options. If she raised her hand, LeRoy would be here in a few seconds. These people wanted to get this information to the police. Why not do it through LeRoy? There was no reason not to use him, so she raised her hand.

"What's going on?" Phil asked.

Lucinda answered, "I have a friend who can help us."

Phil and Sherry exchanged a panicked look. There were stuck.

A man about Lucinda's age slid into the booth beside her.

Lucinda made the introductions. "This is my boyfriend, LeRoy Andrews, he's on the Atlanta police force. LeRoy, these people don't want to use their names. They're the ones who helped me."

Phil and Sherry shook LeRoy's outstretched hand nervously.

"LeRoy, these people provided me incredibly useful video evidence. I want you to see what else they got when they were gathering evidence for me."

"Okay," said LeRoy.

Sherry interrupted, "Lucinda, this is not the way we wanted to proceed."

"You wanted the police to have this."

"Yes, not this way."

Phil put his hand on Sherry's. "We don't have much choice."

"Okay," Sherry said. "Here's how it's going to go down. I have a thumb drive with the video I showed you. My friend and I are going to leave. As we're leaving, we'll give you the thumb drive. You can explain it all to LeRoy. Got it?"

"I see what you want." Lucinda said. "I guess it can work."

Sherry got up and moved to allow Phil to get out. Though rattled, Phil had the good sense to grab his cane before he slid out. When they were both standing, Sherry reached into her purse, took out a tissue and used it to extract the thumb drive. She handed it to Lucinda. "Here it is. Be sure it gets into the right hands," she said. Then Sherry grabbed Phil's hand, and they hurried out of the restaurant.

After they were well away from the restaurant, Phil finally broke the silence. "Well, that didn't go as planned. It was good with the tissue and all. I never would have thought about fingerprints. Still, I didn't like the whole thing."

"The policeman got a good look at us. His superiors are going to know what we looked like."

"I'm not too worried about being identified," Phil said. "I'm sure the disguises are good. The policeman's going to be way off on how much you weigh. My wig and fake beard are good, even if I do say so myself. And my limp looked convincing. Nice touch the way you helped me get in the car."

"Thanks. I hoped it would help."

After a few minutes, Sherry started the conversation again. "What do you think the cop's going to do with the video?"

"I have no idea. Whatever he does, it's going to suggest a lot of questions. If he hasn't already, he's going to ask Lucinda a bunch of questions about who we are. I hope the answers don't get back to the FBI. They're already paying attention to In Hissa. The acronym might get into a crime report now."

"Isn't it only a tech? I wonder how far into FBI files our acronym actually is?"

"I'll bet Mr. Policeman, Lucinda's boyfriend or whatever, had already heard about us. She'd probably told him. She had to tell him about us to get him to be there at the bar ready to come when she signaled."

"Yeah, it's too bad she had the connection. I guess we should have checked out the boy friends."

"We knew there would be risks, and I guess particularly with the tape showing the rape. Still, I'm not sure this could have turned out worse."

"Oh, lots of worse things might have happened. We're not arrested. We can ditch these disguises soon. Don't be so gloomy, Phil. It might turn out fine. And there's nothing we can do about it now."

Once they got back to their motel room, they shed the disguises. Though they were a little jumpy the whole time they were in Atlanta, they managed to see a few of the sights. They both were happier when they got back to Lackey late on Sunday.

Chapter Fifty-Four

PHIL AND SHERRY LEARNED RALPH had encountered no trouble retrieving the equipment from the doctor's office in Dallas. He and Beth had spent quite a bit of Sunday editing the video. While they had some difficulty syncing the audio and video, they managed to get the job done.

When Phil and Sherry arrived for an early meeting Monday morning, they stopped Beth from showing the Dallas video.

"In a minute or two. First, we want to report on our trip to Atlanta. It didn't quite go as planned," Sherry said.

"What happened?" Ralph asked.

"We got to the restaurant and met Lucinda. After we showed her the video and she recovered from her shock, we told her what we wanted. Then she signaled this guy, a policeman, and he came to our booth. It turns out her boyfriend is an Atlanta policeman."

"Oh my God, what did you do then?" Beth asked.

"Sherry's quick thinking saved us," Phil said.

"I shouldn't get any special credit," Sherry said. "Anyway, I told them I had a thumb drive with the video Lucinda had seen, and we were leaving. Then we got up. The last thing I did was hand over the thumb drive. And Phil and I high-tailed it out of there as fast as possible."

"We have no idea what happened after we left. We were going to give the thumb drive to them and hope they'd get it to the police. We didn't want to give it directly to the police, but the whole thing was taken out of our hands."

"You were wearing your disguises, I presume."

"Yes, and I think they were good," Phil said.

"I sure hope they were," Beth said. "I bet you were nervous."

"You bet," Phil said. "It's done now. We've been monitoring the *Atlanta Constitution,* and there's been nothing about it to this point. It's like our V project. We did what we did and then started monitoring the papers."

"You want to look at our newest video now?" Beth asked.

"Sure, on to the next one. Atlanta's done. At least our part of it is done," Sherry said.

Beth started the video. The first part showed the workplace. There were several women behind computer screens. The one they recognized as Darcy sat behind a desk in front of a sliding glass window. Patients came to the window, Darcy took their IDs and insurance cards, and got them checked in for their appointments.

"I know the scene," Phil said. "It's like any doctor's office."

"Yeah, watch what happens next," Ralph said.

The next scene showed Darcy moving around the office gathering stray papers. The other women in the first shot were gone.

"This is one of the days she had to close the office," Beth said.

After a few seconds, a doctor, or at least a man in a white coat, came into view. Beth increased the volume, and they heard him say, "Hi Darcy. Have a good day?"

She replied, "Not too bad, Dr. Sector. Anyway, I'm tired. I want to get out of here in a hurry."

"Come on, Darcy. Please call me Bob. No more of the Doctor Sector business."

"I wish you wouldn't come around when I'm trying to close."

The doctor went behind her, put his arms around her, and said, "You know you like me. I don't know why you're fighting it."

Darcy wriggled out of his grasp and backed away. "Please, you know I've got a boyfriend. I'm not interested in dating."

"Let me change your mind." The doctor reached for her again.

She evaded his grasp, and much to the disgust of the people watching in Pennsylvania, she went out of range of the cameras.

"It's not much," Phil said. "The other times, we had stronger cases."

"Wait, there's more," Beth said.

The next scene came from the other camera. It was a different day. Darcy had on a different outfit. This time Dr. Sector came behind Darcy and grabbed her breasts. Again, Darcy wriggled away. Finally, she shoved the doctor away as she turned around and glared at him.

When he recovered from being shoved, the doctor came at her again, growling, "You want to play rough, eh?" He then grabbed her wrists and held her arms down to her sides and tried to kiss her.

Darcy finally escaped his embrace by kneeing him in the crotch and running away. The doctor bent over in pain. Darcy didn't appear in the video again.

"That's it," Beth said. "They didn't appear again. I don't think Darcy closed again."

"Well, it's an open and shut case," Sherry said. "My only question is whether we should send her the video right off like we did Barbara Fairchild in Salt Lake City. It's not exactly the same. He's not hit her yet. Still, he's one step away."

"You're right," Beth said. "We should send the video right away and tell her to use it. This doctor looks to me like a guy who might get violent."

"It's one of my first impressions when I saw this video," Ralph said.

"I concur," Phil said. "You've probably got a copy of what you sent Barbara in Salt Lake City. It worked. Put the video on a thumb drive. I'll go someplace and mail it this afternoon."

Phil went to upstate New York to mail the small package—only about a two-hour drive, *no sweat*. As he had in the past, he handled the package with latex gloves. No one came near the machine he used. He weighed the package and put on the required number of stamps before mailing it. The whole process took about three or four minutes. As he got into his car for the trip back, he realized traveling tired him these days. He and Sherry had traveled back from Atlanta the previous evening, and now he'd taken this car trip.

Chapter Fifty-Five

IN DALLAS, DARCY NUNEZ OPENED her email before dinner. She thought she'd delete a bunch of it before Mario Alvarez, her boyfriend, got home. She found a strange email from someone called the INHSSSA Group. She opened the email out of curiosity. She started reading but stopped when Mario came in the front door. She went to greet him.

"Hi honey," she said as she gave him a hug and kiss.

When he started to try to turn it into something else, she wriggled away laughing. "Wait, big boy. It's time for dinner. We can get around to what you're interested in later."

After dinner, Mario plopped down in front of the computer. "What's this?" he said looking at her screen.

"It's an email from a group I've never heard of."

"Yeah, it says you don't know them, but they know about you... and one of the doctors, Doctor Sector, treats you terrible." Mario turned to look at Darcy. "What are they talking about?"

"Let me see," Darcy said as she scooted Mario off the chair. "It's my email," she said. "You can look over my shoulder."

They both read the email in silence. When they finished, Mario asked, "Who are these people?"

"I haven't a clue. I've never heard of them before."

"Are they right? Is this doctor bothering you?"

"Yes. It started out as nothing. He thinks he's irresistible. A big flirt. I laughed him off. Then he started waiting around on the days I closed, and he got more aggressive."

Darcy looked at Mario. He'd become agitated, so she continued, "It's not a big thing. I can deal with guys like him. You're getting mad. I can tell. Don't."

"I don't like this doctor hitting on my girl!" Mario said. "I should show him how to behave."

Darcy sensed Mario's growing anger. She got up and put her arms around him. "This is no big deal. Please calm down."

After a while, she returned to the computer and said, "Let's read this email again. These people are trying to help me. Maybe they're right. Maybe I should file a sexual harassment complaint. They said they had video evidence."

"I don't think a sexual harassment complaint will do any good. Don't those usually backfire on the woman?"

"I guess so. They say they have good evidence they're going to send me."

"I don't like this whole thing," Mario said. "I don't like it at all."

Darcy put her arms around Mario again. She held him tight and started to sway side-to-side. After she could tell he turned from angry to eager, she said, "Let's get to the bedroom, and I'll convince you you've got a real good girlfriend."

Mario followed her willingly.

Chapter Fifty-Six

TWO DAYS LATER, IN DALLAS, Mario used his afternoon break to check the mail at the apartment. Luckily, he had only a short drive from the construction site. The first day, he didn't find any package, so he left the mail alone. The second day, he found it. He decided to go in to look at the video.

He only had a chance to view the video once. What he saw infuriated him. The doctor didn't just ask Darcy out. He grabbed her and tried to kiss her. Mario got so upset he didn't know what to do. He paced around the apartment with all kinds of thoughts swirling in his head, checked his watch, and ran out the door. He'd catch hell from his boss if he didn't get back on the job site fast. He took the package with the thumb drives with him. He'd figure out what to do about it later.

After work Mario was upset—silent and brooding. *It's not like him at all,* Darcy thought. Finally, she asked, "What's got you so bugged? You seem bothered."

"It's the email you got," Mario replied. "Who is this Doctor Sector? And what's he doing?"

"Sector is one of the doctors in the practice. He's new. I think he went to med school a little late, so he's not as young as a new doctor usually is. Anyway, he's been in the office for about six months."

"And what's he doing to you?"

"It's only when I'm alone late, when I'm closing. Most of the rest of the time, there are lots of people around. During normal hours, he's busy. Anyway, when I'm there alone late, he comes around and asks me to come out for drinks. And a couple of times he's tried to cop a feel. It's real juvenile stuff, and he won't take no for an answer."

"That's it, mostly. Asking for dates, and what did you say, copping a feel?"

"Yes. I've been wondering about it. The people who sent the email must be monitoring a chat room I post on. It's called *Female Friends*, and people do a lot of complaining about bosses who harass them. I've probably mentioned Sector's behavior a couple of times. In fact, it's the only way they could have found out."

"He's not trying to grab you all the time?"

"No, not all the time."

Mario went silent. He knew the whole truth. *She's making it sound much more innocent than it is.* He'd seen the video. He didn't know what he'd do. Somehow, he'd punish Sector. No one should treat his woman that way.

****

The next morning in Lackey, Beth mentioned to Ralph she hadn't seen a post from Darcy saying she'd received the package. "It's odd. All the rest of them acknowledged receiving the package. She should have the video by now, but we've heard nothing from her."

"The mail isn't always reliable. I wouldn't worry about it yet. If we don't hear anything in a couple more days, we can email her and ask what the problem is."

"Okay, it's odd. All the other times, we've had very faithful correspondents. And we were very clear in our email. We wanted to hear back from her. Maybe we should talk to Sherry and Phil about this," Beth suggested.

"Let's not bother them yet."

****

Back in Dallas, Mario schemed. His schedule made it hard. Usually, he got off work after the doctor's offices were closed. Then he remembered Darcy saying Sector stayed late when she had to close the office. Darcy had to stay late on Wednesday, tomorrow.

Mario had checked out the doctor's website, so he knew what Sector looked like. On Wednesday, he parked where he had a good view of the part of the lot where the staff parked. At this point, Darcy's Kia and a few other cars were the only cars left. Soon, there were only two cars in the lot, Darcy's Kia and a white BMW 3-series. The BMW had to be Sector's car. He got out of his pickup and walked a little closer. He wanted to be sure the BMW belonged to Sector.

After he'd been in his hiding spot for ten minutes, Darcy came out. She jumped into her car and left in a hurry. A couple of minutes later, a man came out. Mario got a good look at him. He matched the picture of Dr. Sector. Mario hustled back to his pickup and followed the BMW as it left the parking lot.

Mario tried to be careful as he followed the doctor's car. At one point he had to park, because the doctor stopped in a Starbucks. After the doctor purchased his coffee, he got in his car and scooted into a gap in the traffic too small for Mario to follow. When Mario did get across traffic, the doctor's car was way ahead. Even though Mario gained considerable ground, he still had a block to make up when the white BMW turned right. Mario made the same turn and saw the white car turning into an apartment complex.

Mario turned into the apartment's lot and pulled his pickup right behind the parked BMW. The doctor got out of his car with his Starbucks cup in one hand. Mario jumped out. "Dr. Sector, I want to talk to you."

"What?" the doctor said with a confused look on his face.

Mario walked up right in front of him. "You've been hassling my girl, Darcy, and I want it stopped."

"Look man, I don't know what she's been saying. She must have a big imagination."

"You calling her a liar?" Mario moved even closer to Sector.

"Hold on." The doctor raised both his hands to ward off Mario.

"You're hassling her, grabbing her, and trying to kiss her. No one touches my girl!"

"I'm doing no such thing!" Dr. Sector backed away from Mario.

"You are too."

"Calm down. I don't have any idea what she's been saying. It's not true."

"You're the liar," Mario yelled as he stepped forward and shoved Dr. Sector in the chest.

Dr. Sector fell down hard. His café mocha flew out of his hand and spilled on the street. With the doctor on his back in front of him, Mario thought about kicking him, but then the doctor reached into his coat. Mario dived on top of him and grabbed for the pistol Sector tried to pull out. They struggled. Mario was stronger than the Doctor. As a result, he got the gun pointed away from himself. The gun went off. The noise deafened him. Though Mario was stunned and couldn't hear anything, he held on. Then he felt liquid on his hands where they were holding the gun. Blood.

Mario rolled off the doctor and looked at him. Red blood spread across his whole shirt front, and his eyes weren't focused. *Oh my God*, Mario thought, *He's going to die.* He staggered backwards, still staring at the doctor.

After a minute, a guy came beside him and said, "What's going on here?"

Mario replied, "We were having a fight, and he reached for a gun. It went off. He shot himself."

"Oh my God," said the man. He approached the body and put his finger on the doctor's throat. "There's no pulse. He's dead," he reported.

Confused and frightened, Mario said, "What do we do?" He stood beside his truck. "Should I move my pickup?" He wanted to get away as far as possible. It wouldn't work. More people crowded around.

Even though the guy who got there first was making a cell phone call, he still responded to Mario. "No, don't change anything. I'm calling 911. They'll want to know everything."

Mario stood to one side as the neighbors gathered. It appeared a few of them knew Dr. Sector. After a brief look, most of them turned away. Several of them seemed hostile to Mario. These folks lived in a fancy apartment complex. Mario, in his work clothes, didn't fit in. He looked down. He had blood on his shirt and his hands. No wonder they were giving him hostile stares.

After five minutes, a police car pulled in, followed by an ambulance. The guy who'd called the police took charge. He showed the doctor's body to one of the policemen. The other policeman tried to move the crowd back, and the EMTs rushed to the body.

The man talking to the police pointed at him, and the officer came over.

"What happened here?" the cop asked.

"The man down there and I got into a fight, and he pulled a gun. I dove on top of him and while we were fighting for possession of the gun, it went off. He killed himself with his own gun."

"This your pickup?"

"Yes," Mario replied.

"What's it doing parked this way?"

Mario gulped. "I'll admit I followed the guy here. He works where my girlfriend works, and he's been hitting on her. I came to tell him to stop. Then he disrespected her—called her a liar—so I shoved him, and he fell over the curb. The next thing I know he's going for a gun. So, I dove on him and tried to get the gun. I didn't want it pointing at me. Then the gun went off. That's how it happened, honest."

"Okay, stay here." The officer walked over to the man who'd called and asked, "You seem to be in charge here, did you see what happened?"

"No," the guy said. "I live on the other side of the building. As I got out of my car, I heard a shot, so I came around to investigate." Pointing at Mario, he continued, "I saw him getting off the body. What he said to you matched what he said to me. They fought, and the dead guy pulled a gun on him. They were wrestling for possession of the gun when it went off."

The officer turned to the assembled crowd. "Did anyone here see what happened?" he asked in a loud voice. "If you did, please line up." He turned to the other officer. "Chuck, get statements from those people."

Returning to Mario, the cop asked, "Do you have your driver's license? I'm going to have to ask you some questions. And we'll probably have to take you down to the station to get your full statement typed and signed. Any time there's a death, particularly a shooting death, we have a ton of paperwork to do. If nobody in line has anything useful to say, the whole thing might be completed quickly."

Mario dug his driver's license out of his wallet and handed it to the policeman. The policeman asked, "Is all this still the right information?"

Mario nodded. "I told you the truth, officer. It's his gun. I'm sure you can verify that. He intended to shoot me. I dove on him by instinct. I didn't want the gun pointed at me. I don't know how the gun went off. My finger wasn't on the trigger."

"Okay, Mr. Alvarez. It's the kind of detail we're going to need in your statement. It looks like self-defense to me, or an accidental death. I can't say for sure. There might be other witnesses in line. You probably won't be held."

"I didn't mean for him to die," Mario said. "I only wanted him to stop hassling my girl. I'm God-awful sorry."

"I'm sure you are," the police officer said. "This appears to be a tragedy. This kind of thing happens when you hand out concealed weapon permits to lots of people. Excuse me. I'm going to go find out what we learned from the other people. Don't leave."

After about ten minutes, the two cops came back to Mario. "None of them had anything. Lots of them heard the shot, and two of them saw you getting off the dead body. There's no actual eyewitnesses. We didn't learn anything from those people."

Another police car pulled in. "Oh good, it's the crime scene techs," the lead policeman said, as he turned to go to the newly arrived policemen.

The crowd thinned out as the police from the second car went to work. The police arranged for one of the officers to ride with Mario in his pickup when they went back to the station. It peeved Mario that they didn't trust him to go to the police station.

The second group of police were busy taking photos. When they finished, they gave Mario and the cop permission to take his pickup. Mario and the cop followed the first police car out of the parking lot.

Chapter Fifty-Seven

PHIL AND SHERRY WENT TO Ralph and Beth's apartment early Friday morning. Ralph had called in a panic late Thursday night. He wouldn't say why, but he wanted them for an early meeting.

"What's up?" Sherry said as she and Phil walked in.

"I think things went haywire in Dallas," Ralph said. "I set up queries with the names of people involved in our project. If their names show in the newspapers, we'll get a notice. Anyway, I put in Robert Sector and Darcy Nunez in the Dallas newspaper's site. Last night, Sector showed up in the online version of the *Dallas Morning News*. He's been killed."

"Oh my God... are there any details?" Phil asked.

"It looks bad. The man involved in the shooting is Mario Alvarez, who appears to be Darcy's boyfriend. He told the police he followed Sector home from his doctor's office. He wanted Sector to stop hassling his girlfriend."

"Mario shot Dr. Sector?" Phil asked.

"It's not simple," Ralph said. "According to the story, they got into a fight, and Sector pulled a gun. The shot occurred while the two of them were wrestling for control of the gun. At this point, Mario's been released. He hasn't been charged with anything."

Sherry broke her silence. "This is awful. We never wanted anyone to die. Sure, we wanted the harassers to be punished. Not this!"

"And it might be worse," Ralph said. "What if they ask Mario how he found out about Darcy being hassled? If they do, the Dallas cops will have a clear path to the email we sent Darcy and maybe the video, too."

"We were worried when Lucinda spilled the beans to her policeman boyfriend in Atlanta," Beth said. "Now it's very likely two big metropolitan police forces know about what we're doing. They both might have found out about In Hissa. It's time to shut down operations."

"I have to agree," said Sherry. "I'm still in shock. Our project lead to a death. A person got shot because of what we did."

"Let's erase all the computers we ever used in this project," Ralph said. "And Phil, destroy the credit card we used. We can pay off the bill and cancel the card. What other links are out there?"

"I'm not sure," Phil said. "Let's not panic. While we may have to do all the stuff Ralph's talking about, we don't have to do it yet. Our project with Darcy's finished. It means we don't have anything pending. Let's suspend operations and wait a bit."

"I'm not sure, Phil," Sherry said. "I didn't want anyone to die. This has thrown me."

Beth spoke up. "What worries me most is the likelihood In Hissa will be mentioned in crime reports or newspapers. If it is, the FBI might get involved. Remember, they were already alerted. And it started in connection with Sherry. It could lead back to us."

After a pause, Sherry said, "Beth's right. We're in real jeopardy. And I'm the cause."

"Don't be so hard on yourself, Honey," Phil said. "You had no way of knowing the FBI would be monitoring your internet clicks. And in the end, didn't Melissa drop the whole thing?"

"Yes, but I still led them to In Hissa, and they got interested."

"Our strategy is going to protect us," Ralph said. "There's no way the people who we were helping communicated with us directly. They only posted on the chat room, which is a public forum."

Beth jumped in. "Maybe the FBI could hack the chat room site like we did. They'd find out who the users are—everyone we worked with. Everything we did could be revealed."

"They still wouldn't discover who we are, right?" Phil interrupted. "It would require them finding out who sent the original emails, and they're not traceable, right?"

"Yes," Ralph answered. "To the best of my knowledge, they're not traceable. We did a good job of designing the communications strategy. It's going to protect us."

Phil continued, "Suppose the FBI does all the work to find the people we helped and figures out the whole scheme? What would they have? What's illegal about what we did? It's a series of break-ins. Breaking and entering isn't a federal crime. I guess they might alert the jurisdictions involved. Still, how much effort would those jurisdictions expend on unsolved breaking and entering cases? Breaking and entering where nothing got stolen."

"Oh Phil," Sherry put her arms around him. "It's why I love you. You're a glass half-full person all the way. Maybe you're right. Maybe we aren't in too much jeopardy. Still, we should cool it for now. I say we suspend operations."

"Yes," Beth said. "We're all agreed. We should suspend operations at this point."

Ralph added, "I'll monitor the newspaper sites to see if there are more stories about the people involved. I guess I'd better add Mario Alvarez to my list of queries in Dallas."

Chapter Fifty-Eight

TWO WEEKS WENT BY UNEVENTFULLY for the group. Ralph didn't detect any more alarming stories in the Dallas newspapers. He found a memorial service for Dr. Sector, but there were no more mentions of Mario.

Things got more exciting the next week when Sherry received a call from the local district attorney. The grand jury presentation for Bob McFall and Henry Marietta would occur in three days. They wanted to rehearse her testimony. The district attorney explained it should be straightforward. In order to enter her phone videos into evidence, they had to have her testify about her location when she took them. They had decided not to pursue the arson charges at this point. They said they might do so at a later date.

The day before the presentation to the grand jury, Melissa called and said she'd just come to town to observe for the FBI. Sherry and Phil invited her to go to Andy's for dinner.

Melissa hugged Sherry and Phil when they met at Andy's. "It's good to see you," she said after they got seated. "I've been wondering how it worked—you coming back from the dead and all."

"Oddly," Phil said. "Some people were peeved with me. They thought they should have been in the know. The head librarian at the college wanted to bite my head off."

"I tried to explain why he couldn't be told," Sherry said. "It's difficult to fake grief. And we didn't want too many play actors out there. I understand Phil did a good job, and I guess my brother did too. Phil just stayed home pretending to be all sad. He kept saying he didn't want to see anyone."

"Yeah, I got good at accepting phone calls and sounding upset. I guess I fooled everyone. No one has told me they suspected anything."

"Let's change the subject. How's your career going?" Sherry asked. "I've told Phil about your problems."

"I'm here partly because I babysat you and partly because I'm back as part of the team. I'm going to have to testify in the bigger trial, the human trafficking one. I did important early work there, and they need me. I haven't had to have any one-on-one dealings with Larry Clarkson yet. I think he's avoiding me, which is fine."

"I hope he doesn't take it out on you when it comes time to do personnel evaluations," Sherry said.

"You and me both."

During lunch the three talked about Sherry's testimony, and Melissa gave them more details about the larger case. Human trafficking was a big issue, which surprised Sherry and Phil. Women from many countries were smuggled into the U.S. and forced into prostitution. The gangs involved moved the women often. They used the barn on the McFall property, among others. The murder Sherry witnessed resulted from a rival gang trying to steal the women. The investigation had been long and involved. It had almost come apart because of the other gang's involvement.

After their meal, Melissa moved to another subject. "Sherry, you remember the chat room you visited and those crazy initials I asked you about?"

Phil began to sweat. He tried to stay calm.

"Vaguely," Sherry answered warily. "What about it?"

"We'd dropped it. Weird but not illegal. Then the initials came up two more times. First, in the crime report in Atlanta, a rape. And then in an accidental shooting in Dallas a couple of weeks ago."

"What's this all about?" Phil asked. "I don't know what you guys are talking about."

"I'm sorry. Let me fill you in. One of the techs monitoring Sherry's internet usage thought she spent an inordinate amount of time on chat room posts involving a mysterious group. It uses an acronym—I. N. something. There were a lot of S's in it. Anyway, Sherry didn't even remember it. We dropped it. Still, the tech stayed interested, so he tried to figure out what this group did. Then he got another more pressing assignment. Anyway, like I said, recently this acronym showed up in these two crime reports."

"Did you learn who they are, or what they're doing?" Sherry asked, trying to keep her voice calm.

"No, we haven't yet. The problem is jurisdictional. The FBI only has a limited scope. So far as we can tell, no federal laws have been violated."

"What laws are involved?" Phil asked. "I still don't think I understand what's going on."

"You need more detail," Melissa answered. "As best we can figure, this group finds a woman who is complaining about sexual harassment in the *Female Friends* chat room and puts video cameras in her workplace. When these videos show the woman is right, they send the video to the woman and ask her to file a sexual harassment complaint."

Sherry interrupted, "Does it work? Are the women's complaints upheld?"

"In the one case where we know all the details, yes. The woman in Atlanta lost her first try. Then on appeal she showed the videos. The company fired her boss, a real scumbag. The case involved a lot of inappropriate touching. In the Dallas case, the boyfriend intercepted the video. It led to the harasser getting shot."

"So, these people did the woman in Atlanta a big favor," Phil said. "I still don't see how they broke any laws."

"Yes, they helped the woman. The difficulty is it looks like they broke into her workplace when they installed the cameras."

"Didn't the women help put in the cameras?" Sherry asked.

"No, they heard about it in an email from the group. So, to get back to Phil's question, the illegal behavior is breaking and entering. Also, taking videos of people without permission isn't always legal."

"You said something about a rape," Sherry said. "What's going on there?"

"In the Atlanta case, the cameras they used to catch the man doing the inappropriate touching also got footage of a rape. The footage finally found its way to the Atlanta police department. It's how we learned about the whole procedure."

"A rape," Sherry said. "Wow, were they able to catch the guy?"

"I don't know. I think the case is still in the works. Anyway, I thought you might be interested. It's quirky. The FBI got interested because Sherry seemed to be looking at posts directed at this group. The one with the funny acronym."

"I didn't know anything about it," Sherry said.

"Yeah, I know, and when the tech got more data, he backed off his initial conclusion. We dropped the line of inquiry. When the acronym came up again in the crime reports, the tech remembered it and called me. It doesn't have anything to do with you, Sherry. It's interesting—one of those weird connections."

Sherry spoke up. "I remember. The acronym is mentioned fairly often in the chat room. Do you think these people helped lots of other people with sexual harassment problems?"

"I don't know," Melissa said. "They may well have." Then she paused. After a moment, she continued, "While I probably shouldn't tell you this, I have an idea about how to follow up on this."

"What is it?" Sherry responded.

"Sure, shoot," Phil added.

"This whole business is nothing the FBI is going to pursue. The only crimes involved are all matters for local authorities. The two situations we know about are in two different cities, Dallas and Atlanta. This group, the IN-whatever people, aren't local. They're national, heck, maybe international. Anyway, I have a friend who's an investigative reporter for the *Washington Post*. She focuses on crimes against women. What would you think about the idea of me feeding her all the information we have about this?"

"Why?" Phil asked a little nervously.

"She can do stuff we'd never do," Melissa responded. "She can go on *Female Friends* and post a chat to the people who've responded to this group. She can ask them to tell the details of their cases. The focus wouldn't be about illegal behavior like it would for us. For her, it would be about how the videos changed the outcome of the sexual harassment cases."

"Do you do that kind of thing often?" Sherry asked. "Refer cases to reporters?"

"Not often. It's not unheard of, though. I think Cynthia, her name's Cynthia Heard, would be interested in this. It should be right up her alley."

"It would be a real interesting story, a twist on the he-said-she-said problem," Sherry said.

"I suspect that's what this group wants," Melissa said. "They want the video to show who's telling the truth in one of these cases where there are two different stories."

"I understand," Phil said. "Innocent until proven guilty puts a big burden on the accuser in these cases. Suppose I made unwanted advances to Sherry. If no one else was around, I'd probably get away with it."

Melissa laughed. "My understanding is your advances wouldn't be so unwanted with Sherry."

Phil gave Sherry a hug. "It's only a hypothetical."

"I know, and actually it's a good one. It's the kind of issue Cynthia's interested in, so I bet she'll write a story."

Phil decided it wouldn't look bad if he changed the subject. "Do you have any idea how long Sherry will have to testify tomorrow?"

Sherry spoke up. "The district attorney said it wouldn't be more than fifteen minutes."

"Probably," Melissa said. "Your testimony shouldn't be controversial. My advice is to keep your answers simple and straight forward. This is the grand jury. I suspect you won't have to testify at the trial. I'd be surprised if there is a trial at all. These kinds of deals are usually plea bargained."

With that, they left the restaurant.

Chapter Fifty-Nine

A WEEK AND A HALF passed before Ralph's query on Cynthia Heard got a hit. The story in the *Washington Post* focused on Lucinda Wallace in Atlanta. Apparently, Lucinda had cooperated with Cynthia. None of the other women did. Lucinda had shown her emails, the original one and the one asking for the meeting. She also described Sherry and Phil from the meeting in the restaurant. Luckily, the descriptions didn't sound much like the two of them. All things considered, Sherry and Phil thought the story made the In Hissa Group sound like the good guys. They'd helped Lucinda, and they'd helped the police with the rape. They were on the side of right and justice.

Heard's conclusions were the interesting part. She said the insurance company's dismissal of Lucinda's original complaint followed from the notion the man is innocent until proven guilty. It implied the woman making the complaint had to be the reverse—guilty until proven innocent. The woman had to prove she wasn't lying about the behavior. The man didn't. The videos involved allowed the woman to prove her innocence at the same time they proved the man's guilt.

They met Ralph and Beth at the Mexican restaurant in Henderson. After they'd ordered, Ralph started the conversation. "I liked the *Washington Post* story. It painted us in a good light."

"We agree," Sherry said. "Phil and I liked the story too. We came out as a group on the side of what is just and right. I particularly liked the part about our getting the rape video to the police."

"And if they're like looking around for the fat lady with the frosted hair and her white-bearded friend with a limp, they aren't going to get very near you two," Beth said.

"It doesn't sound as if she's been able to find anything about any of the other cases. You two have seen where she's been posting on *Female Friends*. She's been asking for the others to contact her. Apparently, none of them have," Phil said.

"Yeah," Beth said. "Our original email made things clear. We didn't want them to tell anyone about our activities."

"I'd be surprised if more doesn't come out because of this story," Sherry said. "At least our acronym is likely to come out a couple of times. Suppose an employee comes up with a mystery video. Aren't you as an HR person or a boss going to ask what the hell she's doing videoing her workplace?"

"You sure are," Phil said.

"So, our women are going to say they didn't take the video, because they didn't. Then the boss or whoever asks who did. Maybe they'd say they didn't know. It's not going to be very satisfactory. I bet at least one or two mentioned the In Hissa group. Our name's probably out there more than we thought."

"So, when these people read the *Post* story, they're going to remember the acronym," Beth said.

"Bingo," Sherry said. "The details of the other women we helped are going to come out. I don't see how it can be avoided."

"I guess we all thought it might unravel eventually," Ralph lamented. "I didn't think it would happen this way."

"Is this the way we want it to end?" Phil asked.

"What do you mean?" Ralph sat back and folded his hands.

"Do we want other people to tell, or do we want the women to tell?"

"How can we help it if it's the other people?"

Phil replied, "Maybe we ought to send one more email to all the people we helped. We should tell we are suspending operations and they should email Cynthia and tell her they'll cooperate."

"Very clever, Phil," Sherry said. "If the story's likely to come out anyway, why not have it come from the sources who will put the right slant on it. Lucinda did it with this first story. Better to let the others do the same thing."

"This is good," Beth said. "And we can tell the women Cynthia might allow them to use a pseudonym or be an unnamed source. I don't know how this all works. Or maybe they'd be fine with their name out there. In most cases, the people they work with probably know about what's happened or have strong suspicions."

Ralph added, "Right, honey. Those who don't want their names in a national story will be the men, not the women."

"So, we're agreed," Sherry said. "We'll go back and compose the email. It will be the last act of the In Hissa group."

Chapter Sixty

A WEEK LATER, CYNTHIA HEARD'S story about the INHSSSA group ran on the front page. Except for Cindy Newsome, all the women cooperated. Again, the story turned out to be sympathetic to the work of the group. As with other big stories, the talking heads on TV and commentators on the internet grabbed on. There were those who loved the INHSSSA group, and there were privacy advocates who weren't as positive. Of course, some men thought they were horrible.

Those opposed to the group's work emphasized the illegal activity, the breaking and entering. They also made references to George Orwell's *1984* and ubiquitous video cameras. Also, a radical men's group—who seemed to believe women were made for men to molest—joined the opposition chorus.

Those who supported the work of the group were a mixed bag, too. Radical feminists said it was proof that men spent most of their time molesting women. Others pointed out the cases involved represented egregious situations, not the norm. The more reasonable supporters emphasized that initially the women weren't believed. In Cynthia Heard's words, they were "guilty until proven innocent." They needed the videos before they would be believed. According to these people, the whole sexual harassment complaint process tilted in favor of the men.

The group monitored all this without participating. On Wednesday, Phil's lunch group discussed it. When Phil got to Andy's, the rest of the group had already assembled in the back room.

"What's today's topic?" he asked as he sat down.

Bert responded, "The group—I can never remember their acronym."

"It's I. N. H. S. S. S. A.," Jeremy said. "It stands for it's not he said she said anymore. Their idea is to provide video cameras so a molester can't get off by saying he didn't do it."

"Do we want to live in a world where we're always on camera?" Bob asked. "I agree with the people who object to what this group's done because it's an invasion of privacy."

Bert put his wine glass down. "I agree with Bob. We don't want to live in a world with cameras everywhere. I know lots of stores have cameras, and London spooked me. There's a camera on every block in London. I don't like people looking at me all the time."

"The no-more-he-said-she-said people caught these men sexually harassing the women," Sally said. "And in every case, the men got off initially. No one believed the women until the videos were shown. This group demonstrated the current procedures make it easy for men to avoid punishment unless there's hard evidence."

George said, "Sally, it's because our justice system says you're innocent until proven guilty. The burden of proof is on the accuser. You don't want to do away with innocent until proven guilty, do you?"

"Yeah, I know," Sally responded. "But these people wanted to highlight the cost to women of having such a system. If the Me Too movement has shown us anything, it's the serial sexual harassers out there who've gotten away with it for a long time."

"I still don't like their solution," Bert said. "I don't want to live in a world with cameras recording my every movement."

William said, "Bert, I'm afraid it's too late for you. To name a few, we have red-light cameras, cops with dash cams, major buildings with security cameras, and like you said, most stores have cameras. Heck, my neighbor has a security system with cameras. That ship's already sailed. You are being surveilled whether you like it or not."

"And what about what Sherry did," Phil said. "She got the video of those two murders with the camera on her phone. Lots of people whip out their phone and start filming any time anything unusual happens. William's right. You're likely to be on camera lots of times."

"I can't believe those crazy people who take videos of an approaching tornado," George said. "They should be under a mattress in their bathtub or in their basement. Standing in front of a window filming an oncoming tornado or hurricane is stupid."

"Whoa," William said. "We've drifted from the topic we started with. The—what did Jeremy call them, the no-more-he-said-she-said people—did good work. We need to weed out sexual harassers. If they're worried about cameras everywhere, so much the better."

Sally slapped her hand on the table. "I agree one hundred percent. If you've got nothing to hide, you shouldn't be worried about cameras. The more of these guys who get caught the better. I want to hear more opinions about the *Post* reporter's notion. The system says the accused is innocent until proven guilty. This implies the accuser in a sexual harassment complaint is guilty until proven innocent. What do you say?"

Phil responded, "There's something there. Think about what the women have to endure in lots of cases. They have to prove they're not making it all up, or worse, they didn't encourage the guy. Rape trials have the worst examples. The *Post* reporter's right. The woman is often treated as if she's guilty."

"I agree with Phil," Jeremy said. "The woman is often treated very badly, as if she's the accused. It's one reason there aren't more sexual harassment cases than there are."

"We can't abandon innocent until proven guilty," Bert said.

"No Bert, we can't," said Sally. "Still, we have to think long and hard about the way women who bring these cases are treated. There's a balance, and we don't have it right yet."

After a pause, William piped up. "I have a prediction based on this."

"What?" echoed several others.

"I predict sales of small video cameras will go through the roof. And I predict lots of workplaces are going to have to establish rules governing where and when people can place those cameras."

"I don't have to like it. I'm going back to work, and I guess I'm keeping my head down," Bert said as he got up to leave.

****

When Sherry got home from work, Phil greeted her with a glass of wine. "My lunch group talked about In Hissa today."

"Did they like it?"

"Views were mixed. Sally's clearly a big fan. She liked the *Post* reporter's guilty until proven innocent bit. For the most part, the others were able to see both sides. While they recognized the problem, they didn't like the consequence they could predict."

"What, men not being able to get away with sexual harassment?"

"Sherry, you should know us better. No, they didn't want to live in a world where cameras were looking at them all the time. They fear we're headed there. While I know our group didn't start it, we probably gave a big boost to the trend toward cameras everywhere."

"I know, and I worried about cameras everywhere when I thought this whole thing up. I guess it's a lesser of two evils thing."

"I want to ask you a question I've asked a couple of times before. Are you happy with how this has turned out?"

"I was waiting for you to ask."

"I hate being so predictable."

"You are. Anyway, since I knew you'd ask, I've been working on an answer. On the main and on the whole, I'm happy. The doctor in Dallas getting killed crushed me. It made me wonder about our entire effort. Now this newspaper story brought me back. We accomplished a great deal. We made people see men who swear up and down they are innocent often aren't. We've shined a light on a big problem. And we got justice in quite a few cases, even a rape. So, I'm happy, real happy."

"Me too," Phil said. "We did a considerable service. The discussion started by the *Post* story is good."

Chapter Sixty-One

TWO WEEKS LATER, SHERRY RECEIVED an email from Melissa Jacobson. Melissa asked if she and Phil were available the following Saturday. She wanted to take them on a drive. Sherry emailed back saying they were free and asking Melissa to explain herself. Melissa gave a cryptic reply—just a short drive they'd find interesting.

When Melissa and a driver pulled up at the appointed time on Saturday morning, Phil and Sherry slid into the back seat of the big black van. "Here we are," Sherry said. "Now maybe you can tell me what this is all about."

"Sit back," Melissa said. "Joshua here is going to take us on a little drive."

"Why are you being so mysterious?" Phil asked. "When the FBI wants to take a person on a drive, it makes a person nervous."

"Only if they've got something to hide," Melissa responded.

"Fair enough," Phil said. "So, you want us to enjoy the scenery while we drive."

"Yes, right. Enjoy the scenery."

Sherry gave Phil gave a nervous look. He shrugged. She reached and held his hand. Silence ruled the rest of the drive. Phil and Sherry knew the roads, so they had a good idea where they were headed until they turned down a small farm road about thirty miles from Lackey. Finally, they pulled into the driveway at a large farmhouse with a car parked in its driveway. The car had a sticker from a rental car agency on the back bumper.

Melissa turned around in her seat. "We'll be getting out here."

Phil and Sherry got out, and the driver stayed in the car. They followed Melissa around to the front of the house. Inside, she turned left into the living room. A woman sat on the couch. She was young, blonde, and maybe quite tall, Sherry wasn't sure. She had on a dark blue business suit. The woman stood as Melissa, Sherry, and Phil entered. Sherry was right—very tall.

Melissa made introductions. "This is Cynthia Heard of the *Washington Post*," she said. "I'll let you introduce yourselves... if you want to."

Phil and Sherry were visibly shocked. Finally, Phil stepped forward and shook Cynthia's hand. "Let's keep this anonymous, at least for a while."

"Good idea," Sherry said as she shook Cynthia's outstretched hand.

Melissa pointed out where she wanted them to sit. She and Cynthia, who had a very amused look on her face, sat on the couch. As directed, Phil and Sherry sat in the chairs facing the couch.

An awkward silence followed as the two groups eyed each other. Finally, Melissa spoke. "Cynthia, this is the I. N. H. S. S. S. A. group." This pronouncement created more silence.

Sherry finally filled the silence. "I recognize Cynthia's name," she said to Melissa. Then turning to Cynthia, she continued, "You're the one who wrote the stories about the group Melissa referred to. What I can't understand is why anyone thinks we had anything to do with it."

"I guess you deserve an explanation," Melissa responded. "You remember when we were in South Carolina, and I talked to you about the tech finding you spent an unusual amount of time on the chat room posts to that group?"

"Yes, what of it?"

"You reacted nervously during the conversation. It made me suspicious."

"You said the tech dropped the line of inquiry after he got more data."

"It was a little fib on my part. Actually, you changed your clicking behavior after our conversation. It made us more suspicious."

Sherry and Phil exchanged a panicked look.

"You're more than suspicious. You seem to be sure. Why?" Sherry asked.

"Three more things." Melissa seemed to be enjoying herself immensely. "First, the last time I saw you two—right before the grand jury presentation—you both reacted strongly when the discussion turned to the I. N. H. S. S. S. A. group. Almost by definition, it's hard to stop involuntary reactions such as your pupils, respiration, and perspiration. FBI agents are trained to observe those things. Both of you lit up like Christmas trees."

"You don't have hard evidence," Phil said.

"No, let's move on to my number two. I took a picture of Sherry to Lucinda Wallace in Atlanta, the woman in Cynthia's first story. She said it matched the woman she met. While you disguised your body very well, Sherry, you weren't able to change your face. I actually drew glasses on the picture, and Lucinda became sure of the identification."

"So, let's hear number three?" Sherry sounded subdued.

"Our tech traced the most recent email you wrote to Rochelle Martin in Milwaukee. The one about contacting Cynthia. While he didn't get it back to a specific computer, he did get it back to this part of Pennsylvania."

Cynthia spoke for the first time. "Look, I don't need your names. And I don't even have many questions. Melissa's right, isn't she?"

Phil and Sherry looked at each other. Finally, Sherry shrugged. "Yes, Melissa's right."

"I don't want to press charges or anything. I won't ever speak of this again," Melissa said.

Phil spoke up. "What about the driver, and whoever owns this house? I can't say I like this one bit."

Melissa responded. "You guys thought you were so smart. And actually, you were. You had an ingenious communications scheme—no trail back from the people you were helping. You were incredibly unlucky Sherry got me for a babysitter in South Carolina."

"The driver and whoever owns this house?"

"They'll never have any idea about what happens in this room. And

Cynthia has agreed not to use names or anything else to identify you two in any way."

Phil and Sherry looked at each other again. Reluctantly, Sherry turned to the two on the couch. "Okay Cynthia. What can we tell you?"

Two hours later Melissa, Sherry, Phil, and the driver loaded into the car. Because of the driver, they were silent on the way back. At Phil's house, Melissa asked the driver to wait. She wanted to have a final word with her friends.

In the house, Melissa turned to Sherry and Phil. "This has to be the end of it. I can cover for what you've done up to this point, but no more. We're supposed to report any criminality we find out about. I haven't in your case, and I won't. Don't do anything else. Okay?"

"We're done," Sherry said, "The killing in Texas really shook us. We never meant for anything like that to happen. Now the *Washington Post* stories have exposed us. You don't have to worry. We're through."

"And what about you, Phil?" Melissa asked.

"I'm done."

Sherry spoke next. "Melissa, I have to be honest, I wanted to throttle you on the ride. Keeping us in suspense and springing Cynthia on us was cruel. I guess it turned out all right. I liked Cynthia, and I think she'll write a good story."

"Yeah," Phil said. "And it's really nice of her to be willing to let us see the story before it goes to press. She's going to email it to you, and you'll forward it to us, right?"

"Yep, it'll keep your anonymity."

"That's what we want," Phil and Sherry echoed simultaneously.

"Got it," Melissa said. "I've got to go now. I've got a ride waiting. And I guess you two will want to report to the other two in your group. You wouldn't want to tell me who they are, would you?"

Phil and Sherry shook their heads.

"Let us have some secrets," Phil said.

"Fair enough." Melissa hugged both Sherry and Phil.

About the Author

Robert Archibald was born in New Jersey and grew up in Oklahoma and Arizona. After receiving a BA from the University of Arizona, he was drafted and served in Viet Nam. He then earned an M.S. and Ph.D in economics from Purdue University. Bob had a 41-year career at the College of William and Mary. While he had several stints as an administrator, department chair, director of the public policy program, and interim dean of the faculty, Bob was always proud to be promoted back to the faculty. He lives with his wife of 47 years, Nancy, in Williamsburg, Virginia.

CPSIA information can be obtained
at www.ICGtesting.com
Printed in the USA
FSHW021506300720
71901FS